I0657609

Maria Vittoria Cavina Saporetti

AN ITALIAN SAGA

Youcanprint *Self-Publishing*

Title | An Italian saga
Author | Maria Vittoria Cavina Saporetti

Cover image by the author

ISBN | 978-88-27821-57-2

© All rights reserved by the author
No part of this book can be reproduced without the
prior consent of the author.

Youcanprint Self-Publishing
Via Roma, 73 - 73039 Tricase (LE) - Italy
www.youcanprint.it
info@youcanprint.it
Facebook: facebook.com/youcanprint.it
Twitter: twitter.com/youcanprintit

MMCCCXLX A.B.C.

SELF-PUBLISHED at BONONIA
ALMA MATER STUDIORUM STUDENTORUM

AUTHOR'S NOTE

This book is based on the accumulated experiences of twenty-six generations of the bloodline to which I belong, and the product of my own imagination.

Traditional systems of dating are used, which cannot be scientifically verified as accurate. References to Ab Urbe Condita (AUB - from the founding of the city [of Rome]) are understood as commencing from the year 753 Before Christ.

References to A Bibliotheca Condita (ABC) are understood as commencing from the year 333 BC, the established year of construction of the Library of Alexandria in Egypt.

This edition incorporates the trilogy *Nullo Nodo, Di Casa in Casa* and *Il Pacciaovo*, published in Italian and edited with the assistance of Katia Caddeo, with my sincere gratitude.

SEPARATION

"Are you coming to fight with me?" asked Martino.

"No, I'm staying at the base camp," answered Silvano.

"There is no base camp," Martino retorted.

Silvano contradicted him; "there's always a base camp. It's where the supplies are kept, and the cooks, and all the things you need when you're away from home. The surgeon stays at the base camp too, to treat the wounded."

"There is no base camp because there are no wounded. We're the good ones."

"Do you imagine you won't get hurt because you're good?"

"Yep."

"I see. And who wins?"

"We do."

"Why?"

"What do you mean, 'why'? Because we're good!"

"How will you win?"

"We're the strongest."

"Do you really think the good ones are always stronger than the other side?"

"…I don't know..."

"Listen, Martino," Silvano explained, "it's not always the good ones who win. People who go to fight know they have to set up base camps, where they can treat their wounded. A wounded soldier can't fight. The people who look after the wounded, and the people who treat them, never fight. They must swear to do no one any harm, because if they become fighters themselves they can no longer take care of the living. It's important to have base camps, and it's important to respect them."

"But that's no fun!" exclaimed the child, then caught sight of the cook chasing a cat with a broom and ran after them.

Martino's grandfather was sitting next to Silvano, the friend in whose care Martino's parents had left him the previous spring, about 2068 years after the founding of Rome.

The couple had then left for Hungary, where Martino's maternal grandparents were staying.

"I know the tutor will be coming from Gubbio," said the grandfather, watching his grandson playing happily in the courtyard of the urban domus. "When will they leave together?"

"The tutor's name is Aligerno," replied Silvano. "He's apparently from the Aristotelian school, and hopefully an expert in the art of rearing foals too; he should be here by the end of October, then he'll be leaving with Martino."

"Why do you speak of the child as if he were a foal?!"

That's not what I meant. You must excuse inaccuracies in my language. Your son Enrico bought a foal three years ago for Martino's fourth birthday, from the herd reared in the Cannobbio valley, below Monte Torriglia near Lake Maggiore. The foal is ready now, and I'm hoping Aligerno will be able to manage its separation from the herd, as well as Martino's separation from us - so the transition will be uneventful for both of them; that's all I meant."

"Won't you have Martino's milk brother to look after the foal? I've always had my attendant."

"Martino's wet nurse was widowed at the end of winter, so we let Martino's milk brother stay with her - her son Filippo. Apart from her brother-in-law, who's a little odd, Filippo is the only real help Giacomina has at the farmhouse."

"So, who has Martino been spending his time with these last few months, without his milk brother?"

"With me. Early in the spring he would often run away and hide so he could cry in secret, then he grew fond of our litter of sheep dogs and started sleeping with the bitch and her pups. I explained how they couldn't be taken away from their mother, so he pretended he was one of them and started acting like them, going around on all fours and yelping instead of talking."

"Astonishing behaviour. Bless him!"

"Yes, it was hard to keep from laughing when I saw the stableman, Giusto, handing him bowls of water and white polenta so he could eat without have to leave the pups."

"I can imagine how it looked, with the pups attached to the teats of big white bitch and the child curled up with all the dogs and sheep. When did he tire of that game?"

"In the summer. When the shepherd set off with the dog and sheep to work up on the mountain, Martino took his favourite pup and followed them, without any of us noticing. The bitch was distressed and started barking to raise the alarm. Giusto ran to fetch me. He stayed with the five pups, while I ran up the shepherd's path with Rea, the bitch, to look for the fugitives. Rea sniffed the air and followed their trail along the ground and round the back of the water trough; she found her pup with Martino, keeping quiet as usual, hiding in the broom on the slope near the oak woods."

"Did you scold him?"

"No."

"You're too lenient, Silvano. You must have been relived; I bet you even smiled!"

"You know me too well; I have a lot of sympathy for my pupil. Rea picked up the pup in her mouth by the scruff of its neck and set off resolutely back to the kennel. Martino came to me straight away to say he didn't mean any harm, and I know he was telling the truth. He held my hand on the way back and I explained to him that pups must be allowed to stay with their mother until she decides they're big enough, and pushes them out herself. He pondered it, and said that he was a big boy and wanted to go and see the summer pasture. From that moment on he lost interest in the pups and started helping Paolo prepare the cart. Organising the transhumance expedition was a learning experience for me too; I'd never taken part in it in all those years."

"How long did you stay in the mountains, and who went with you?"

Silvano poured Martino's grandfather a goblet of wine and started telling him about the summer transhumance.

"Our shepherd and the others had already started out with the male dogs the day before, leaving the female behind with the litter. We set off in the cart, drawn by the two cart horses from Casa Bellini and two donkeys that we got from Mezzomerico. Paolo, the carter, brought his eleven-year-old son, Lino. Martino was entranced watching the boy knotting horsehair to make fly swatters and harnesses. He became passionate about this new game over the fortnight, and I hope he'll continue with it when he's with Aligerno."

"It must be hard to weave and make secure knots, like sailors do," mused the grandfather, as Silvano showed him a rope that Martino had woven that summer with Lino, after the horses had been taken care of and the shepherds were making cheese in the mountain hut.

Silvano and Paolo had been very clear in their orders that no one was to go out of the meadow that lay between the hut and the beech and ash woods, where there were wild animals and poisonous snakes that might drop down out of the branches and inject them with venom for which there was no antidote.

Blueberry bushes and brambles heavy with ripe fruit grew in profusion at the edge of the woods, so the youngsters could pick them without breaking the rule and stay in sight of the adults.

A tiger-striped cat had given birth to three live kittens and two dead ones, which Silvano had buried under the woodshed behind the hut, in a hole deep enough to prevent wild beasts sniffing them out and coming to dig them up.

Martino loved watching the newborn kittens, all pink and with their eyes still closed, lying between their mother's paws. They were much smaller than the pups he'd played with at the farmhouse in spring, and he was disappointed he couldn't pick them up. He restrained himself though, because the mother cat hissed aggressively whenever he got too close.

"She allowed me to stroke her, possibly because I helped her before she gave birth, and afterwards," Silvano recalled, then went back to describing the child's behaviour to please the old man.

"Martino seemed to find it strange that the cat didn't eat much and was losing weight, but still produced a lot of milk. One evening he told me he was worried about the poor mother cat because she was being eaten alive by her newborn babies, so I gave him a bowl of water and a few morsels of raw meat to offer her. I was glad to see he could be gentle with small animals. The cat understood that he meant no harm, and from that moment on she allowed him to stroke her too. Another evening, before we went to bed, we were sitting around the embers of the fire under a starry sky, towards the end of August. Martino asked me 'where do the dead go?' I told him they continue to exist.

'But where are they?' the boy insisted.

So I told him what I know. 'The body undergoes changes. The flesh is eaten by particular types of animal, such as vultures and worms. Sometimes, if the corpse can't be left out in the open for carrion birds or buried for the worms, you have to throw it in a river or lake, or in the sea, to feed the fish. I've seen corpses being burned too, on top of bonfires; bodies of people who die from diseases. In the north they push the body out on a wooden boat, then an archer puts burning resin on the tip of an arrow and shoots it at the boat to set it on fire. Your father's brother was burned after he died. Do you remember him?'

'Yes,' Martino said, 'I liked him. When I was little we used to go to the kitchen garden in the courtyard behind the farmhouse in Mezzomerico. He showed me how good he was at archery; he used to aim at the fence in front of the heathland. He had a quiver with a peculiar decoration and three copper-tipped arrows with black and white feathers on the tails.

He used to sit me down on a hay bale next to the stable and listen to the wind - so he said - then take aim and shoot an arrow.

Is the carved emblem still there that he used as a target?

'I remember it, it was two years ago. I suppose it's still there.'

'Even though his body was burned, I believe your uncle has returned to Mezzomerico to stay there for good, in his favourite place. Where are his bow and his quiver with the arrows?

'He'd taken them out on a deer hunt when he fell ill and died, in the forest near Lake Maggiore, beyond the farmhouses in Pallanza. His companions brought back the head of the last deer he shot, an adult male with enormous antlers. They said it was shot because it was a notorious leader. It would come galloping out of the forest where it lived with the herd, and across the moor to the vineyards on the hillside to eat all the newly-ripened grapes at dawn. The farmers hated it.'

'You can hunt foxes too, can't you Uncle Silvano?'

'Foxes don't damage the grape harvest; they're hunted because they steal eggs and chickens. They sneak up the same as martens do, and there's nothing the rooster can do to save the chicken coop! I've never understood why those creatures kill all the chickens but don't eat them. Carnivorous animals usually just kill for food, for themselves and for their young too, during the weaning period when the mother stops producing milk. But martens, foxes and stray dogs often kill more than they need to feed the pack.'

The subject piqued Martino's interest, and he took the chance to broach a subject that was clearly very close to his heart, one that he'd never spoken about before. 'Why didn't Mamma nurse me? Why did Filippo's mother nurse me? And why can't my milk brother Filippo stay with me anymore, or I stay with him and Giacomina, my nurse? It's not fair! Why do you sigh, Uncle Silvano?

I took my time before answering, then replied carefully, 'I'm sighing because you ask me so many questions all at the same time, and it's late. I'll tell you, then we'll go to bed, alright?'

'Alright. Thank you uncle.'

'So, your mother didn't feed you because women who marry men like your father don't nurse. Women who marry men like Filippo's father, however, nurse their own children and the children of people like your parents. So the children become milk brothers and remain very close their whole lives. It's an alliance.'

'But why can't we stay with who we want? It's not fair. The bitch stays with her pups and the cat stays with her kittens. Why didn't I stay with my mother when I was little?'

'It seems complicated, and it really is very complicated, Martino. Women like your mother must travel with fathers like yours and go to places that are not suitable for babies and children. All animal species behave differently. It may seem that a cat behaves like a dog and that basically there's no big difference between a dog, a cat, a mare or a woman. Keep watching what animals do, but remember, we humans are able to handle situations differently from any other living thing. Sometimes we pretend to be like bears or wolves or wild boar or goats or fish. We even pretend to be half man and half horse, or half goat and half fish. But the hardest thing is to learn how to grow up as a human being. We can even paint our faces and put horns on our heads and pretend we're deer...'

Martino interrupted me in disbelief. 'Deer? I can understand someone wanting to be a bear or a wolf or a wild boar, but a deer is just absurd! It would be like wanting to be a fox or a marten - why would I pretend to be a pest to be shot at?!'

I went on: 'it can sometimes be useful to pretend to be a pest. We humans do some strange things, especially if the people watching us don't fully understand the rules, or our reasons for doing them. Some games are so old that no one can remember why they play them anymore, but it's important they're still played. But we do know why you were nursed with Filippo. It's called the *game of separation* and it's good training; it's about trusting people when you have to go away. Distance, you know, is like the wind: you have to know about the wind if you're a traveller. And now it's time to sleep.'

I feigned a yawn and covered my mouth with my hand to show good manners.

Martino yawned for real, but even though he was tired he still had one more question.

'How is distance like the wind?'

Helping the child into a comfortable position to sleep, I smiled at him and softly sang the old song that goes like this:

Distance, you know, is like the wind.
It puts out small fires but makes large ones grow.
Distance, you know, is like the wind, it makes you forget people you don't love.
But it's fire that makes your soul burn for those you love.

Lying among sheepskins in the drowsy warmth that comes before sleep and with his eyes half closed, Martino asked me what form the soul takes.

I didn't reply, I just stroked his hair and went to sleep myself too.

The next morning, the sun was shining high in the clearing when Martino awoke.

I had put the cat and her kittens in a basket next to him, so when he opened his eyes he met the curious gaze of a blue-eyed kitchen.

'Hello, Duse,' he said, but the kitten was too small to do anything but tilt its little head to see where the smell and the human voice were coming from.

'Get up, Martino,' Paolo shouted from the meadow in front of the hut, as Lino came in bringing dry bread and cheese.

'Come on, Fiflic is ready!'

Martino stuffed the food in his mouth whilst putting on his thick cotton shirt, suede trousers and leather boots to protect his feet and ankles, baffled by the newness of the situation.

I took him by the hand and we went over to the mare, who was grazing near the water trough.

'We will use neither bridle nor saddle, since the only harnesses we have here are for attaching the mares to the cart. Do as I tell you and you'll see how easy it is to ride bareback, balancing your body weight,' then I went up and stood by Fiflic's left flank; 'bravo, Fiflic,' I said, come on, Martino, stroke her neck from her head down to her shoulder, the same direction as the hair lies. That's it, gently.'

Fiflic sniffed, turned to look at Martino, then carried on grazing and didn't move. I told Martino to hoist himself up by putting his left foot in my right hand and grasping the bottom of the mane between the horse's neck and withers. The boy obeyed and climbed up excitedly onto her back. Fiflic raised her head and I took the opportunity to put on the headpiece from the right side and lead her into an enclosure that was empty for the moment.

Then I resumed the lesson. 'Martino, look straight ahead. Don't look down and don't look at Fiflic's ears, even if they move. Keep your back straight and flexible, and don't hunch your shoulders. Keep your neck loose, not rigid. Think of your spine as a bamboo cane that starts behind your eyes and goes down to join up with Fiflic's tail, without any sharp bends. Relax your grip. That's it, go on! Lift your hands up, then relax and repeat.

But the boy didn't feel steady enough to let go of the mane. Entering the enclosure set up for the horses, I took the headpiece off the mare and went to the centre, leaving Martino and Fiflic standing next to the entrance gate. Then I stood still and waited, watching what they would do.

Martino held onto the mane with his right hand and stroked the horse's neck with his left. The horse inclined its head slightly. The boy took the mane calmly in his left hand and stroked the horse's neck on the right side; the horse responded by taking the opportunity to sniff and observe her new rider.

'Good,' I said, 'you allowed time for you and Fiflic to get to know each other better. Now listen to me and do as I tell you. Keep your hands low on the withers and grip with your knees, keeping your legs close to Fiflic's belly. Bring your feet up and give her a tap with your heels. Try to keep your toes up and your heels down. WALK!'

Fiflic and Martino began to move obediently at a walking pace, tracing a circle around the inside of the enclosure. Whilst the new pair were familiarising themselves with the situation, I took the opportunity to throw in a little theory: 'every pace is important and is used for a particular purpose. Walking is good for exploring. You'll go far and you'll get there safely if you walk! This applies to everyone, especially if you're careful to observe the seemingly small things that are actually valuable sources of information. Think how important it is to pay attention to the nature of the place - the weather conditions and any wild animals that might be lurking: all this information is essential in order to stay safe! Trotting is useful to learn: it's the transition stage that allows sentinel horses to inspect the territory, ready to go into a gallop to escape danger if necessary. Galloping is the pace that wild herds use to escape. For this reason, a horse and rider team can only gallop after intense training and when a deep trust has developed between them, and only for attack - not escape. The rider must also be brave on behalf of his horse, who like all creatures is an empathetic creature capable of perceiving any signal - visible or invisible. At one time, instructor would put a bit in the horse's mouth to connect the animal to the rider's hands; the bit was attached to the reins made of leather or rope, or the plaited hair we use, as you've seen. We now prefer to establish familiarity by having direct contact with the horse's body, and using our balance.'

Martino thought for a moment, then asked me why the bit and the reins that the carter used were different from those used by horsemen like his father.

'Good question,' I assured him, and went on to explain the complexity of the problem. 'Different types of bit are designed for the different jobs a horse is required to do. When we get home, remind me to show you the family collection, which is kept in the coach house, behind Paolo's work bench. Relax your outer leg and bring your inner leg closer to Fiflic's belly. Lean forward slightly and touch the base of her neck with your inner hand; yes, the one towards me - I'm at the centre as if I'm the leader of the herd. Good, do you see how she turns to bring you gently to the centre of the circle? Excellent, that will do for your first lesson. Before you get down, stretch out and rest your back along Fiflic's back.'

'No, I'm tired.'"

"Martino's father was the same," observed his grandfather, "so what did you tell him, Silvano?"

"I allowed it, as I always try to do. I said, 'alright, we'll do it another time. It's an excellent way to build up trust between you and exchange energy. In nature, only those who trust each other go back-to-back with another living creature, to check what's going on around them without having to turn round. I know it seems strange to you to do it with a horse because you'll be looking up at the sky, but with practice you'll see how it helps to increase the trust you place in each other. Get down now; lean forward and let your right leg slide down, the same way you got up - on the horse's left side. Well done. Take these apples; one for Fiflic and one for you.'

'Was Fiflic a sentinel horse?' the boy asked me.

'Yes,' I replied, glad to see he'd been paying attention.

'How is a sentinel horse different from the rest of the herd?' he went on, inquisitively.

I explained that the leader of the herd is a dominant male; lower-ranking males stay around him with the mares and foals, but when he gets old or sick one of the lower-ranking males attacks him and replaces him as leader. Sentinels are usually the daughters of sentinel mothers; they are more accustomed to trotting than the rest of the herd and stay at the outer edges. They come and go between the boundaries of the grazing territory, and when the herd moves on they stay at the front and rear of the rest of the herd. They're different from lower-ranking males when it comes to taming them, and are often more defensive, which means they bite and kick more readily; but when they accept the relationship with humans they are the best of companions, for carters and riders alike!"

"Thank you for your account of the delightful summer you've had, Silvano. Times have changed a lot since I was a boy! In my day it would have been impossible to go with the shepherds for the transhumance: too many sudden attacks, too much danger. Did you know that the name Duse means soul, in Serbo-Croatian?"

"No, that's interesting. Thanks for telling me."

"Well, let's call Martino and sit down at the table; dinner should be ready by now," the grandfather concluded.

ALIGERNO and MARTINO

The old man was shut up in his study.

He was intending to call on the new arrivals, but didn't want to have dinner with them. In the absence of his son and daughter-in-law, the task of welcoming Aligerno was therefore left to Sara, the housekeeper, wife of Paolo the carter and mother of Lino.

In preparation for Aligerno's arrival, Sara had had the room cleaned that belonged to poor Nardo, Martino's uncle who had died the year before.

It was a large corner room with frescoes on the walls: tall ash and beech trees with red leaves provided the backdrop for clothes trunks and a large bed, as if the archer had chosen autumn as the season to take his rest.

A deer with large antlers appeared from among the trees of a forest, appearing to carefully observe anyone who sat at the table set in the middle of the room between the windows and the trunks, at the foot of the bed with its carved oak headboard. The carving on the headboard depicted a back view of a person standing naked on a beach, in the shallows of what could have been either lake or sea.

The archer was portrayed with an arrow in the string of his bow, as if shooting at the setting sun.

A Latin motto was engraved on a scroll on the headboard:

NUDO HOMINE VIRTUS CONTENTA EST

Sara checked there were no mends in the clean sheets, then drew the heavy Egyptian cotton curtains to prevent the room from becoming too chill and went down to the entrance hall, ready to welcome the unknown guest. She was preparing dinner in the kitchen with the cook when, to her surprise, she saw a whole family arrive around mid-afternoon.

Aligerno had given them no warning that he was bringing his wife and daughter, a little girl with long, red hair worn in a plait twisted around her head and fixed with pins. To Sara it seemed dangerous and intolerable for this house, which had been peaceful up until now.

Sara stood blocking the entry to the vestibule from the courtyard, and asked them to wait.

She tried control her voice and not betray any agitation, to which she was easy prey, and said, "please be kind enough to wait here. I'll go and inform Signor Bellini. I'll be back shortly."

Aligerno thanked her for her attention and waited, telling his wife and daughter to sit down on some stone benches against the walls. He himself went back to the gate that had been left ajar, and watched the merchants and farmers dismantling market stalls in the square.

Sara walked out of the vestibule and paused before knocking at the study door.

Her heart was pounding and her mouth was dry, but she dare not drink for fear that a little pee might escape when she adressed the old man.

Ever since he was widowed and his younger son had died, her master had retired to lead a solitary life, and had put his business in the hands of Martino's father to go off travelling more than he had ever done in the past.

In the spring he went to Liguria, where he said the flowering pittosporum gave off a delightful scent. In summer he went up to Folgaria in the mountains as the guest of an old friend who was an expert in taming foals. In autumn he returned for the harvest in Piedmont, then spent the winter in Bergamo to help the apostolic clerics of San Girolamo settle in at the church of Sant'Alessandro in Colonna. Sara had to prepare a case of wine every year for his trip to Bergamo, for the Ginami family at Gromo castle, which stood on a cliff overlooking the river Serio. Signor Bellini said he had an old debt of gratitude to repay.

Sara considered the old man an authoritative figure. She was afraid she would look silly for not knowing how to resolve the situation herself, but it was scandalous that a tutor should turn up for a job bringing his wife and daughter with him, assuming they were indeed related to him.

Determined to leave every decision to the superior judgment of the old man, she knocked on the walnut door and waited.

Signor Bellini often pretended to be deaf, so she knocked again, louder.

"Come in," came the deep voice of the old man.

Sara entered the room, determined to keep her voice low; she saw the thin profile of the man in the light from the oil lamp, sitting among some charcoal drawings.

Through the bars of the window she caught a glimpse of the last few merchants as they were leaving the square.

"Excuse me, Signor Bellini. The teacher has not come alone. There's a woman and a little girl with him."

"Thank you, Sara. You did well to inform me. Which room have you prepared?"

Sara twisted her apron nervously, and replied:

"Poor Signor Nardo's room."

She swallowed and waited, her eyes burning with emotion at the memory of the poor dead man.

"How old do you think the little girl is?"

"Seven, perhaps eight."

"Prepare the small room next to the library for her. Her parents can have Nardo's room."

"Yes, Signor Bellini."

"What instructions did Martino's parents give you? What are the plans?"

Reassured by the man's composure, the housekeeper explained that teacher and pupil were due to leave together after about a month; she knew nothing more.

"Good, continue. I will dine with Silvano and the guests."

"Thank you, Signor Bellini. Good evening."

Reassured, Sara concentrated on the preparations, then called the two children to have dinner in the kitchen with Paolo, Lino, the cook and herself.

Before dinner, the parents arranged their clothes in a large trunk of dark-coloured leather in Mr. Nardo's room, and their daughter's in a small green-painted trunk in the room next to the library.

Martino's grandfather was called to dine, and welcomed the teacher and his family without asking for any explanation of his extraordinary behaviour.

He did ask, however, how their journey had been, and the couple took the opportunity to tell him about the earthquake that had destroyed their house in Umbria, obliging them to deviate from customary practice. Tutors were usually single or travelled alone, leaving their wives and children at home.

Silvano lightened the conversation telling them about the summer he'd spent with Martino, and explained the schedule that his pupil's parents had planned for him.

The table had been laid with platters of sliced rye bread, a copper pot containing wild boar stew seasoned with juniper, water in black ceramic pitchers, two bottles of dark green glass containing red wine, and a white ceramic stand painted with ivy tendrils, bearing grapes, red and yellow apples, pomegranates, red dates and German medlars.

Cesarina the cook had prepared the same dinner for herself and the other people in the house, as she usually did, and they all ate together in the kitchen.

The fire in the main room also warmed the wall of the adjoining dining room, and a pleasant residual warmth even filtered up into Martino's room and that of his parents on the floor above.

The door between the kitchen and the dining room had been closed after the guests had entered, for privacy.

Cesarina decided at first glance that the little girl was undernourished, and handed her a piece of bread drizzled with rosemary-infused olive oil, asking what her name was and where she came from.

"My name is Meb," replied the girl, and after she'd eaten the slice of bread and took a sip of water, she went on, "I was living in the Apennines above Gubbio in Umbria, where I was born seven years ago."

At the memory of the house that had been destroyed, her voice broke and her eyes swam with tears, so she stopped talking and looked down, concentrating her attention on the plate that Sara was filling with stew for her.

Although her appetite had been stimulated by the bread and the delicious smell from the pot, Meb was brave enough to ask what animal the meat was from.

Hearing it was boar, she said it was not appropriate for her to eat it.

Cesarina was offended by the idea that anyone could refuse food she had cooked and became quite red in the face, but Sara intervened with an explanation that threw some light on it.

"Meb means she's not allowed to eat or drink certain types of food. Calm down Cesarina, she didn't mean to criticise your cooking!"

The cook sighed and asked her guest if she could eat cheese made from cow's or sheep's milk.

Meb was confused, so Sara helped her by telling Cesarina that anchovies from the pantry would be fine; it didn't matter if they were salted, preserved in oil, or crushed in a paste.

The cook sprang up and fetched the jar of anchovy paste from the pantry, spread two thick slices of bread with it and handed them to the girl on a plate. She looked at Sara like a castaway might look at a benevolent rescuer.

Martino listened and watched, struck by Meb's thin features and the copper-coloured glints reflected in her plaited hair by the lamp hanging over the table.

He had never heard of such a thing as a food shortage; he thought she was ill and hoped she was not going to die like his Uncle Nardo, because he liked her even better than him.

Meb said thank you and ate ravenously, and finished her meal with every kind of fruit from the stand, to the great relief of Martino, who realised that their guest was recovering quickly and was in good health and good humour.

After the meal, Sara showed Meb to her new room and left her there after helping her get ready for bed between the clean sheets warmed with a warming pan.

While she was having her plaits unravelled, Meb was amazed to see that the walls of her room were decorated with frescoed scenes in oval frames of white stucco, adorned with figures in high relief: garlands of roses and doves with open wings, which by the flickering candlelight seemed about to settle or take flight, in an endless aerial dance.

"What do all these decorations mean, Sara?" asked the little girl, curious in spite of her weariness.

"This is the signora's dressing room. A special place that Signora Bice retreated to when she wanted to be alone. The painted scenes depict events from the journey that the pious Aeneas made with his father Anchises and son Ascanius. They arrived in the Cave of Poetry after their own city of Troy was burned by the Achaeans of Mycenae, on the orders of Agamemnon and advised by Ulysses, lord of the island of Ithaca. Their adventures are told in books written in Latin by Virgil, which are stored with other manuscripts in the library, in the room next door. I'm taking the candle now. Close your eyes child, and sleep peacefully."

"Why did Signora Bice want the garlands of little white roses and all those doves flitting about?"

"Because she liked them. Go to sleep now, little darling."

"Thank you, Sara. Goodnight to you too."

The woman left the room and Meb opened her eyes to watch the shadows moving around her, illuminated by sudden flashes from the violent autumn storm that was raging outside.

In his own room, Martino's grandfather was dreaming.

He imagined himself, as he did many other nights, walking along a path that wound up a hill covered with bright green grass, like you sometimes see in spring after it's been raining. Or like travellers to Ireland often tell of as being common in that land.

Occasionally he came across groups of people gathered in a circle beside the path, celebrating.

He was invited to join them each time, and each time he thanked them and refused, continuing his solitary journey.

Now in view of the summit, he needed to quench his thirst but his gourd was empty and he was forced to accept an invitation from the last group he encountered.

The party were finishing their meal and offered him a cup of red wine and a slice of cake as well as the water he asked for. He accepted, not wishing to offend the people who had given him water to quench his thirst, but as soon as he drank the wine in his dream, his head began to swim and he lost his balance, and the slice of cake was too sweet and made him feel like he was suffocating, and he woke abruptly and sat up in bed to catch his breath.

It was a recurring dream that he'd had for many years, and was turning into a nightmare.

That night, however, he made a different decision.

He accepted the water but said he could not join in the eating and wine-drinking for health reasons. The group looked at him with suspicion, perhaps fearing he had some contagious disease, but their spokesman commented that he was wise to take care of his health and that he was free to leave whenever he wanted.

Thus left to his own devices on the side lines, he rested and observed the company, who resumed their merry-making activities.

For the first time since he was a child, he felt free.

The next morning Meb and Martino were eating in the kitchen with Cesarina, who had made them a hearty breakfast of milk and slices of bread left over from the day before, spread with wild honey.

This type of honey was collected by Paolo from the hollows of certain trees that only he knew, in the wood on the hill to the north-west of the house.

The little girl was amazed by its sweetness and aroma; it was richer in natural resins than the honey she was used to, which was produced by a beekeeper ten minutes' walk from where they lived, before the earthquakc. Shc wondered if the beekeeper had gone away too, and what had happened to the bees. Saddened by the thought, she asked if she could go to her mother, and Martino offered to go with her, holding out his hand for her to take.

The girl's parents had been summoned to the grandfather's office, where together with Silvano they were deciding what to do.

The grandfather didn't think it would be the right thing to do for the teacher to leave with his pupil, and told them a story:

"A pupil once told his teacher that he was not able to study, and asked his advice. The teacher gave him a cup full of wine, and advised him to revise what he remembered of the lesson he had just been given whilst walking with the cup in his hand. He should come back in three hours and bring the cup with him, as full as it had been when it was given to him. Three hours later the pupil returned and gave the cup back to his teacher. The teacher asked him what he remembered of the lesson. The student confessed that he'd been unable to revise and remembered nothing, because all his attention has been concentrated on not spilling the wine. The teacher then advised him to drink as much from the cup as he thought necessary to prevent it spilling, and remember that only those who consider study to be the more important activity manage to study. He told him to walk with the cup half full whilst revising, and come back in two hours. When he returned, the pupil smiled and repeated many of the ideas he'd been taught by the teacher, who poured a little wine into his own cup and toasted the joys of study with his pupil."

Silvano laughed and Rebecca looked at her husband Aligerno, who asked if they too could put study ahead of the planned journey.

The grandfather was very satisfied with the wisdom Aligerno displayed, and explained his plan of action:

"I advise you to stay here until Martino's parents return. It would be helpful if you could stay too, Silvano. You have been the most important go-between for Martino since his parents' departure, and Aligerno cannot replace you in this respect, because it would be too much for us to extend our family relationship to include his wife and daughter."

"I haven't made any plans yet. I could continue with the riding lessons, if you let me have Fiflic at least three hours a week. And I could go with Martino on any trips or excursions, and explain elements of a natural and artificial nature."

Aligerno approved the idea, saying he had more experience teaching reading and writing in various alphabets than horsemanship, which for him was restricted to caring for the animals and driving a cart when required.

"If we set out alone Martino and I would be walking, so we could only take a small gourd of drinking water and a bag of money. The plan was to go and study for a year at the Carthusian monastery of Pavia."

The grandfather was amazed, and interrupted, "Martino has never shown any religious vocation, and his mother is in excellent health, by the grace of God! Children become oblates if their mother dies and their widowed father wants to remarry, so where did you get such an idea?"

Aligerno explained that Martino would be considered a lay brother. He himself had been a lay brother at the Carthusian monastery of Galluzzo on Mount Acuto, at the confluence of the Ema and the Greve, in the Chianti region.

The grandfather conceded he was unaware that lay brothers could escape taking vows.

"Exactly, sir," continued Aligerno, "at the end of his formative journey, a lay brother can choose whether to follow a religious vocation and ask to receive the sacrament of the priestly order, or return to secular life to remain a lay celibate or marry and receive the sacrament of marriage with his bride. I lived for ten years in the Certosa del Galluzzo, then left to become a teacher with the Cadolingi. Two years later I was sent to teach the eldest son of Bosone di Casa Raffaelli, in Gubbio.

It was there that I saw Rebecca Fanti for the first time, standing by the fountain during the Festa dei Ceri on 15th May, nine years ago. We were married on 6th December that same year, and Meb was born two years later."

"By the way," he continued, reasoning with the grandfather, "I think it would be appropriate for Meb to take part in language lessons, as a pupil. The learning programme would be more formative if Martino were not on his own."

"Can Martino read and write in Italian?" Aligerno asked.

"No," replied Silvano.

"Well," Rebecca commented, "Meb can't read or write either, so there would be no initial disparity. Three pupils would perhaps be easier to manage, because Aligerno could adopt the dialectic method with them both in turn."

The three men look at her; they were puzzled at first but soon realised she was referring to Lino as the potential third pupil, and didn't know how to merit the possibility.

Silvano objected that Lino was eleven - four years older; too old to be in the same class with two seven-year-olds.

"Their accumulated life experiences are very different, and I think that's far more relevant than any difference in age or gender," said Rebecca.

The grandfather continued this line of reasoning. "In fact, if the teacher could focus the attention of all three students on the content, it could be beneficial for them to compare their performance. And it would be of great benefit if all three of them were to learn to read and write in different languages, and to count."

Aligerno made it a condition that the grandfather must decide on the reference texts, so that he could prepare a curriculum for each year of study.

The adults were talking this over when they heard a faint knock at the door.
"Who is it?" Signor Bellini asked gruffly.
"Martino."
"Come in."
"Excuse me, grandfather," Martino said as he entered; "Meb would like to see her mother. She's been alone for the first since yesterday evening, and she's already been very brave, for a girl."
His grandfather suppressed a smile and brought the meeting to a close so he could spend time with Martino until lunchtime.
"We saw very little of each other when you were small, you and I. You lived with your nurse Giacomina and Filippo, in the vineyard farmhouse in Mezzomerico. Then my Bice died. And Nardo too, shortly after. Your parents stepped in to take my place running the house, and I travelled a lot. This is my study, come and have a closer look."
Martino looked at the writing and the signs drawn on the parchment, but could only understand the meaning of one figure: "This is our bear's paw!"
"Bravo. It's our crest. Our ancestors from Oleggio were living in these hills before the imperial Roman army arrived. They were members of a Celtic tribe of hunter-gatherers on the moors. There were bears in the woods of Mezzomerico, to the north of Oleggio.
Each head of household presided over the rite of passage from childhood to adulthood for children of the tribe."

"Did every boy have to kill a bear, grandfather?"

"Oh, that story relates to a custom that was abandoned many centuries before the Roman army arrived. After agreeing a bloodless alliance with the Empire, the bear continued to be a special creature for us because it symbolised the fact we had learned to respect and be respected, without resorting to violence. Learning not to do to the bear, or any other living creature, what we would not wish to have done to ourselves, was an improvement at the time that has been worth remembering."

"Why is there just one paw on our crest, and not the whole bear?"

"It's not our crest, it's the crest of the House. We don't use it when we're travelling. Learn to think properly, Martino."

"Yes, grandfather. The crest of the Bellini House in Oleggio is a bear's paw. Right?"

"Yes, it's a bear's paw. The Roman army had arrived in the Ticino Valley and the Celtic tribes that inhabited the valley and all the way up to the mountains decided to negotiate agreements with them.

They offered to help the imperial army build the road, and supplied archers. The Romans also acquired the guarantee that one horseman from each family would serve in the Roman cavalry along with his horse, which had been trained by us and was of Celtic and north-eastern origin, because the Latins and Greeks were not horsemen by tradition.

They became Celtic men of the 'toga'; able to preserve their traditions since they had not suffered defeat, but worthy of negotiating honourable conditions without bloodshed: they were Roman citizens. They adopted the calendar that began with the founding of the Eternal City, the cradle of civilisation that allowed peaceful coexistence. Our ancestors learned the habit of shaving their hair and beards from the Roman soldiers, unlike the Celts from beyond the Alps who were still known as 'Celti Comati' - long-haired Celts - because of their thick manes of hair and long beards, in the custom all barbaric peoples who were ignorant of Greco-Roman customs. Our own ancestor was the first one in the tribe who decided to shave. He went to the army surgeon and demonstrated his confidence in him by sitting down and offering up his throat to have his beard cut off. The operation left his chin and neck completely hairless, and he thus started the tradition that we still preserve today as adults of the House."

"I've seen shepherds and cowherds with long hair and beards. I'll shave too, when my beard grows. When I was little, my nurse Giacomina used to cut my hair along with her children's; Uncle Silvano has been doing it this year."

"Good. The rite of passage from childhood to adulthood had long since changed and there was no hunting involved. It became a ritual of a personal nature. Every boy in the twelfth autumn after his birth had to spend three days alone in the woods. Before he returned he had to engrave the crest in the trunk of an oak tree, on the boundary with the northern heath."

"Why a paw, though? Is it because it's from a female bear and not a male bear?"

"Legend says that every boy from our tribe had to hunt down a male bear before he could come out of the woods again. The bear's flesh would be left for the wolves and other wild creatures of land and air, as an offering of gratitude for helping to keep our environment clean. After one night of the full moon in October, a boy who'd been sent out to hunt met with a she-bear and her cub, which had been born in the spring.

The boy carelessly approached the two bears as they reclined under a large oak tree."

"But everyone knows you shouldn't approach a bear with a cub!"

"That's right. But legend says that this boy was foolish enough to approach the bear, even though he knew it was forbidden to kill a mother and young of any species, and still is. He perhaps approached them to drive them away, but the story says nothing of this."

"It was foolish in any case, even if we don't know what his intention was. Did the bear kill him?"

"The she-bear got up and stood in front of her cub, to protect it. Then she growled at the reckless hunter and bared her fangs. The boy lowered his bow with the arrow already nocked, and stood there as if petrified with fear.

Perhaps he thought the bears would chase him if he started running; perhaps he was contemplating climbing the nearest oak tree; but then the bear sprang at him and pinned him to the ground, with her left paw on his heart. If she'd pressed hard she would have killed him, because bears are very, very heavy! The cub, meanwhile, had come up and was sniffing the air, to see if this was something to eat, but she bared her teeth at it, and it stopped and sat down to watch what would happen! The mother bear looked the boy straight in the eye, then removed her paw from his chest and sat down next to him. It was as if she understood he could have shot the arrow if he'd wanted to, but didn't."

"As if she wanted to show him it was in her power to kill him if she wanted to, but didn't," Martino went on, enthralled.

"The young man completed his mission without bloodshed," his grandfather went on. "He went and carved the trunk of the last oak tree on the edge of the moor. The bear and her cub accompanied him and growled at a pack of wolves to put them to flight. According to the legend, that evening Monte Rosa turned violet in the light of a splendid sunset. And when the last ray of sun fell on the water meadow, which is still there between the wood and the moor, the young man saw a green ray come up through the surface of the water. An ambiguous sign, don't you agree?"

"What does ambiguous mean, grandfather?"

"Tradition says that when the young man returned and told of the adventure he'd had, our ancestor interpreted the green ray as a warning.

The name Bellini comes from *belenus* you know, a Celtic word meaning splendour - that indescribable quality that our cousins from the northern isles call *glam*. Living beings change and we help them to understand the most harmonious way of doing so; in this case, our ancestor reckoned the green ray was a warning. Those who showed respect would be respected, but those who continued to perpetrate unwarranted acts of violence would be condemned to suffer as if under the effect of a slow and inexorable poison. According to the legend, the crest was originally the figure of a bear and was later transformed into a bear's paw, in memory of the prey that had become a teacher, and worthy of respect. Ever since then, we've had a reverential fear of all bears, which is why it is forbidden to hunt them in the territories of which we are the custodians."

"Why do you say custodians? Sara, the housekeeper, is a custodian... but I thought all this belonged to us. There was no one here before us, and it was we who built these houses and cultivated these lands, wasn't it, grandfather?"

"For the Empire and for the Roman Curia, we are custodians of the moorland and woods, and this territory is called the Bellini District by virtue of the presence of generations of our family over the centuries; millennia.

We are also custodians of the Terdoppio river and shored up its banks when they collapsed, but the Terdoppio is not ours. The open fields and pathways are ours to walk and ride and drive small, non-military carts. The vineyards and farms are ours, which supply us with food in exchange for aid, protection and advice. And anyone wishing to use our roads must pay us a toll in acknowledgement of the work we do to keep the paths open. But the House of Bellini and its crest do not belong to us. It's more accurate to say we belong to it. Each of us is like part of a single organism: some of us are like a foot, some like a hand and some like the stomach. There are some who have to think and make decisions for the others, as if they're at the top of a hill and must protect those who live in the valley. Whatever their individual function, everyone knows that the body is a single entity, just as life is. The hope of staying alive by acting for the common good is also unique."

"Grandfather, I'm tired. Shall we go and eat?"

"Yes, Martino. Go along to the kitchen, it's time for your lunch."

The boy left the room and encountered Meb near the wooden staircase leading to the upstairs bedrooms; she was helping Cesarina by carrying a bucket of water from the well.

It had been raining, and the scent of the mint that grew abundantly in the courtyard filled the air.

Meb helped Cesarina to clear the table after they'd eaten, then her mother called her to come and sew.

Lino and Martino played ball in the courtyard.

All three of them were called to eat polenta and milk and then it was bedtime.

The grandfather announced to the adults at dinner that he would take Martino and the tutors to Mezzomerico on the occasion of the full moon in October.

It would be kept as a surprise, so that Martino could sleep peacefully; he had not told Sara or Cesarina.

That night the grandfather dreamed about an Amazon riding a donkey. She was accompanied by a tall, broad-shouldered boy who walked beside her, followed by his horse, which was wearing no harness, but its mane and tail were finely plaited.

They came towards him, watching him with an intense, earnest and intelligent gaze. They kept their mouths covered and did not speak.

The boy wore a large, dark green woollen cloak with a hood, and a red scarf over his mouth.

The lower half of the girl's face and her neck were covered with a fine white veil, which also covered her hair, parted in the centre with two coiled plaits at her forehead, like the little girls who are dressed in green and decked with garlands for the festivals in May.

In the background, behind the boy's horse, stood an Austrian fir tree beside a white house with a pitched roof and a single square window below the roof, which was open.

A cobbled road stretched out white behind the Amazon, between meadows rising to a snow-covered pine forest and the snow-capped Alpine peaks.

The grandfather woke with the dream images in his thoughts, looking forward to the journey to the slopes of his beloved Monte Rosa.

After a few minutes, Silvano came out through the main door of the house and checked that the market square was clear and quiet, as it usually was at dawn on non-working days. The grandfather followed him out with Martino and the teacher.

They were acknowledged by the guards standing by the portal in the perimeter wall, and after passing through the eastern gate they had a view of the wide Ticino valley.

The farms, cultivated fields and streets melted into forest, where the river disappeared into the Milanese landscape with its perennial disturbances linked to absurd conflicts over non-existent problems, at least according to Signor Bellini.

Martino's grandfather warned him to distance himself from that chaotic way of life, and asked Aligerno how he planned to tell the story of Ulysses.

Whilst the teacher was talking, they made their way around the walls built of bricks fired in the nearby kilns, and set off from the other side.

As the mist cleared, they climbed into the north-western hills, which had been controlled for millennia by the people the Romans referred to as the Gens Beleni.

The noble name had changed to Bellini since the emperor Lothario had granted the privilege of managing activities on the hills around Oleggio and Mezzomerico to the head of the family, classifying the territories and urban district between the market square and the ancient Celtic road to the west of the praetorian walls as the Bellini District.

Occasionally, the grandfather interrupted the master to describe the herbal properties of plants growing wild beside the dirt road.

The tall yellow daisies with dark centres (which we call "rudbeckia" from the surname of the person who first classified them centuries ago) were still blooming, and there were patches of purple heather growing in the meadows of the particular bright green that is rich in the vital sap so beneficial to life.

"Ulysses had to leave because he was an islander, and all islands limit the freedom of those who belong to it," his grandfather said suddenly.

Martino had never been on an island and didn't understand, but Aligerno and Silvano listened attentively.

"Those who are born and brought up on islands learn to fish and understand how important navigation is to their continued survival. But islanders struggle to manage the drama of relationships which we on the mainland experience through managing the resources available to us here, a land that is ours by virtue of our understanding how to be its faithful servants."

Silvano asked if he was referring to them being Celts of the toga.

"Not just that. Interpreting the past in respect of current legislation, for the common good - present and future; this task is more difficult than the one Agamemnon had to deal with. They called him king but he was just an ordinary man who made scorched earth of a heritage he did not understand. He didn't understand what it meant to be a member of a single humanity in a single situation, which you can only improve by giving thanks, honourably. Ulysses was guilty of some terrible frauds at the expense of gullible people, nothing more. The Greeks won without honour, and honour is everything for a man. The only lesson we can draw from their history is that it serves as a reminder not to use it as an example!"

Aligerno helped Martino to put his boot on, which had slipped off as he was climbing and collected a small stone that was bothering him, then bade him walk faster to catch up with the others, who were still discussing old stories hand-written in volumes in the library.

"So, Signor Bellini, do you think that we tutors of the new generation should be critical of the received tradition?" the teacher asked the grandfather.

"Preserving memories is a precious commodity, Silvano. It's like preserving the snow-capped peaks, the pristine springs and the forests inhabited by bears and wolves; the white heath and the purple heather, with hares and wild boars and deer, which gallop as fast as our thoughts.

But preserving the memories of the living means interpreting signs of the times, every night and every day. Keeping memories alive over time means learning to exist in constant vigilance and with the peace of knowing that there are changes to be managed. Opinions may change, just like the traveller's point of view changes.

Only reality is a single entity; we belong to it and we cannot know it, we can only interpret it in our own individual way."

Martino was distracted by the beauty of the landscape; he skipped rather than walked, until he was distracted when he heard Aligerno ask,

"Signor Bellini, do you believe in the freedom of humans?"

His grandfather did not answer but kept on walking, his gaze fixed on the sunlit mountains.

The mist had disappeared and the air was warm.

Martino walked beside him, holding his hand.

Arriving at a crossroads, they halted.

"Let's have a drink," said his grandfather.

They took the gourds from inside their woollen cloaks and drank. Martino sat down on a large grey stone veined with white quartz; he was tired, and wondered why his grandfather didn't answer the teacher's question.

The grandfather continued to ignore Aligerno's question and began to describe the features of the crossroads.

"If we entered the woods to the west we would be walk along the Terdoppio river and through the vineyards on the Roccolo hill, below the farmhouse where Giacomina lives and where you grew up, Martino. In the other direction, the road leads to the church dedicated to the Archangel Michael in the village of Oleggio, and further on we would come to Novara, a trading centre between the cities of Turin, Milan and Genoa, and some Alpine passes into other parts of Europe."

"Grandfather, are there cities beyond the Alps too?"

"There are, because the Roman army has been building roads and expanding villages for more than fifteen hundred years, advancing in its course. Travellers can walk along comfortable roads as far as Spain, the African cities, the eastern steppes and Hadrian's wall in the northern islands, and bathe at Roman baths, all because of the *Pax Romana*."

"*Pax Romana*?" Martino repeated.

"The peace guaranteed by the Law of the Eternal City. The ability to legislate gave rise to the Res Publica and is still its most valuable legacy," explained Aligerno.

Silvano was bored with all the learned discussions and had gone to pick wild rosehips, which he encouraged Martino to eat.

The grandfather went on describing the attributes of the crossroads.

"To the east we would come to a hamlet where some Jewish Christian families live, and if we continued across the plain, we would come to a wide bend in the river Ticino where the river transport boats come in."

Silvano remarked how good the ripe pulp of the rosehips was, and urged Martino to eat plenty.

Aligerno explained to the student that they were also very good for the health because they strengthened the body, and unconsciously dampened his enthusiasm.

"We shall continue towards the north-west and keep the domus viscontea of the Massari family to our right, then we'll come to a path leading to a small farm where we shall stop and eat," concluded the grandfather.

It was a sunny day. Children chased each other around the tenements of Mezzomerico, between the houses surrounded by high walls.

The women sat chattering on stools around the water fountain; the men smoked pipes or played dice in the doorways of their houses, sitting on wooden stools outside kitchens.

When they saw the party approaching, some of the farmers got up and went up to greet them.

They lived in a large building in Mezzomerico owned by the Bellinis. Surrounded by high walls, it was built on the corner where the main streets crossed, and consisted of apartments to accommodate fifty people, three animal enclosures and a crop field with good exposure to the sun.

"Good morning, Signor Bellini. Will you come in?"

"No, thank you Nella. I hope the family is all well?"

"Yes, by the grace of God. My youngest grandson is walking now, and he's as strong as an ox. Is this young man our Martinetto?! A couple of years ago he was just a babe in arms, and now he's almost a man?!"

Without waiting for a reply, the farmer lifted the boy up to show him the world from up above, even higher than when he sat on Silvano's shoulders.

Martino laughed and greeted him with a warm handshake, like he'd seen grown-ups do; then he ran to greet the other children, friends from his early childhood.

Once the social pleasantries were over, they went on to the little house where Giacomina had just finished preparing the food. Filippo and Martino sat next to each other and chattered as if the rest of the world didn't exist.

Giacomina gave them each a large helping of chestnuts boiled with bay leaves, then served the adults.

"These chestnuts are from Momo, who lives on the high plain, Monte Giudeo. He's lived alone since he was widowed; he didn't want to live with his married daughter. The only thing he can do is look after his three goats and pick chestnuts in the woods, but he's a good man. Whenever he comes here, he brings us a kid or some chestnuts, depending on the season, in exchange for a few bottles of wine. Look over there, in the donkey enclosure. That goat that has become inseparable from our donkey - Momo brought it."

"I don't see Juanìn, Giacomina. Where is he?" asked the grandfather.

"He's in the vineyard, Signor Bellini."

Turning to Aligerno, Silvano remarked,

"he's so diligent in his work, everyone calls him Juanìn of the vines..."

Aligerno went on jokingly "...if he ever goes on a long journey, he could use the high-sounding name Juanìn De Vine."

Then Martino joined in with the joke, chanting

"Juanìn De Vine who cries and whines!" This became a popular way to poke fun at the winemaker. Before going to look for him and take him some food, they drank to his health and the health of Giacomina, who had continued to live with her brother-in-law after her husband died.

From the vineyard they were able to take in the view of the Alps in the autumn sunshine, without having to go through the woods and across the moors.

Dog roses were left to grow at the end of each row, as a charm to bring happiness and a reminder of the fact that a few tears must be shed for every happy event.

Before returning to the house, the grandfather inquired if it would be helpful to organise a wild boar or deer hunt. Juanìn confirmed that the boars were churning up the land too much, perhaps in search of truffles, and mainly under the nut trees that separated the vegetable garden from the vineyard. The grandfather assured Juanìn that he would send the gamekeeper to rout the wild boars out of Oleggio, then they set off home to arrive before dusk.

It was hard for Martino to take leave of the people and places that were so dear to him, but the adults dismissed his tears and Silvano told him to wipe his nose, saying the boy was getting a cold.

Giacomina shed a few tears too, but nobody noticed because she was alone in the kitchen at the time, peeling a pile of onions.

Martino was very tired by the time they were half way there, and Silvano lifted him onto his shoulders, pretending to be his horse.

"Do you remember when you rode Fiflic? Now listen carefully, because we're going to continue with your riding lesson.

Keep still, little horse
let me climb up on your back!

On the road we'll trot, trot, trot.

Trot trot trot to Gran Bretagna
to buy some Pan di Spagna!

Then gallop to Delfinato
to buy some Pan Pepato!

Then walk straight ahead
for our everyday bread!

Do you feel how the difference between the paces?"

Martino was having a good time; he wanted to play the game again and again until his grandfather told him to stop it and get down and walk again.
"Martino, you're growing up now. There's always time for playing, whatever age you are, but you won't be able to play when you're in an imperial city.

OLIVIUM CIVITAS FUIT ET MAGNA CIVITAS ERIT

Learn this motto and commit it to your memory and your heart, then set it aside. It will be useful to you."

Aligerno repeated the motto aloud and Martino followed his example, convinced that it would be useful to him if even his teacher wanted to learn it, foreigner though he was.

Still excited by the trip, the boy chanted a nursery rhyme out loud that was useful for remembering numbers.

One horse was playing
on a spider's web
Enjoying the pretty dance
So he went to call another horse

and then there were two horses playing
on a spider's web
Enjoying the pretty dance
so they went to call another horse

and then there were three horses playing
on a spider's web
…

When they were home and the door was finally closed behind him, the boy took his teacher's hand and said in a low voice,
"my name is Martino and your's is Aligerno, but what's my grandfather's name? It feels like I don't know him if I don't know what his name is."
"I don't know," replied the teacher, puzzled.
The conversation was interrupted by Meb, who was in the courtyard collecting some mint leaves for Cesarina to make a digestive infusion.
The girl greeted them cheerfully and ran to the kitchen, followed by Martino, to prevent Lino from eating all the food.
Rebecca told Aligerno that she preferred to eat in the kitchen with Meb, and leave Signor Bellini and Silvano to enjoy their meals alone together. Aligerno agreed reluctantly that this was a wise decision and kissed her right hand in gratitude.
Paolo was sitting at the table beside the fireplace drinking a goblet of wine, while Sara ladled out risotto cooked with milk and pumpkin.
Lino was eating bread spread with anchovy paste. Cesarina quickly handed slices to Martino and Meb too,

so the hungry mites wouldn't have to fight over it or burn their mouths on the hot risotto.

"Here you go. Whilst you're eating it, stir the risotto with your fork and when you eat it, start from around the edges. Martino, did you see your nurse, Giacomina?"

The boy told them about his trip and asked the others how they had spent the day.

Lino said he'd given Aura and Fiflic a wash, then went to the saddlery to grease the harnesses while Paolo was repairing the cart.

Meb had been sewing with Rebecca and had helped Cesarina prepare the risotto.

After dinner Sara helped clear the table and wash the dishes, and the others went off to their rooms.

In the dining room the grandfather showed Silvano and Aligerno the curriculum he'd prepared, to agree any changes they thought necessary.

"I think a weekly lesson plan is in order, until his parents return. The first, third and fifth days of each week, you Silvano could have Martino clean out Fiflic and the stable, before and after his riding lesson."

"Three mornings, on alternate days. Good," said Silvano.

"Exactly," the grandfather agreed.

He went on, addressing the teacher. "Aligerno, on the afternoons of those days, I suggest you teach him drawing and geometry. On the second and fourth days, writing in the vernacular in the morning, and reading in Latin and Greek in the afternoon, with your comments in the vernacular."

"Where will the lesson be held?" asked the teacher.

"On the first floor, in the library. Go up the stairs, the first door leads to Martino and his parents' quarters. The second door is your bedroom. The third is Meb's. The library is the fourth door. In addition to the scrolls and parchments on the shelves, there are also some papal bulls and an archive of patent letters with the imperial seal. There are desks for study in front of the four windows. On the table at the back of the room you'll find some slates and chalk."

"Good. Could I ask you a personal question now?"

Silvano glared at the teacher Aligerno, but the grandfather nodded his head and went on eating his risotto with gusto.

"Martino asked me what your name is, Signor Bellini."

The grandfather didn't answer; he just poured himself a goblet of wine, took a sip, and said,

"it's getting quite late for me. Stay and finish your dinner, take your time. Good night."

He disappeared to his room, next to the hall.

Aligerno looked quizzically at Silvano, who told him how the grandfather had given up using his name when his wife died.

"I've never heard of such a tradition before," remarked the teacher, "what's the explanation?"

"When the Bellinis marry, their wives continue to use their noble maiden names, according to Roman tradition. They often ask to be buried with their own ancestors, rather than their husband's."

"Yes, it's the same in many regions, not official regions of course, I mean within traditional boundaries..."

"Martino's grandparents loved each other and used both names, complete with their noble surnames. When she died, he decided to give up his own name. In mourning, I imagine."

"How poetic," remarked Aligerno, pensively.

"Yes," Silvano agreed, "it's as if the man died along with his bride, so the element of transition between living generations could be kept alive. The noble name connects him with his children, his grandchildren and the territory he's responsible for."

"Martino's grandfather is a special man. He uses total logic, doesn't he?"

He does. He loves logic. He tries to communicate every change in a simple way. But he doesn't reduce logic to simple rationality. It's no coincidence that his favourite classical author is Publius Ovidius Naso."

"You've enlightened me, Silvano. Gratias tibi ago. I'd like to join your riding lesson tomorrow morning; where will it be?"

"You'll find us in the stable at nine o'clock, getting Fiflic ready. Good night, Aligerno. See you tomorrow."

"Good night to you too, Silvano. Until tomorrow."

When Aligerno retired to his room, he found Rebecca already asleep.

He was thinking about how he could explain the grandfather's decision to Martino when he slipped into a dream full of fearless knights and magnificent horses.

The coming together of so many different personalities under the same roof made for a happy cohabitation.

Studying the works of Ovid, the boys laughed when they read the idea of the ancient Roman that said conflict is a wife's dowry.

Martino noticed that Meb was learning how to be a good wife; she asked questions constantly and insisted on having explanations that were acceptable, at least in her estimation.

The girl pointed out that it was not about eulogising a woman's argumentative nature, but recognising the value of discussing things within a relationship.

Lino interrupted her saying that, actually, love is not beautiful if it is not argumentative, and his parents were living proof of this.

Meb was irritated and was about to lash out at Lino to punish him for his superficial comment, when Aligerno stopped her and summarised the discussion, ruling that the classical tradition provided an understanding of how to handle all conflicts, even those that were irreconcilable.

The teacher steered the lesson to an analysis of the content of some classical texts, and his students were soon distracted by the snow that had started to drift down outside the window, in the square.

Five months had passed since lessons began, and the children were confident they'd learned to write quite well in the vernacular.

After a few unsuccessful attempts, they had won their greatest battle: obtaining permission from the grandfather to be excused from studying Greek and Latin rules. It would be enough if they recognised the Greek alphabet and memorised some fragments of poetry and mottos attributed to classical authors.

When the two hours of afternoon lessons were over, Aligerno joined Rebecca in the kitchen for some hot herbal tea.

The boys put on waxed hemp cloaks over their boiled wool coats and went out into the courtyard as the last light snowfall of spring was falling in soft flakes.

The grandfather heard their squawking laughter and stood at his study door to watch them play.

Sara was setting the table in the hall. She was worried he might be cold, and looked out to ask if he wanted to sit in the kitchen with a cup of hot herbal tea.

Without taking his eyes off the children in the snowy courtyard, the grandfather replied in a tone somewhere between serious and facetious,

"The hills are warm while the sun's still on them. This is the time for silence, Sara; and drenched is the earth where evening leads. Like the sleeping bear, stop snarling and leave me alone to watch our cubs at play."

The woman made no comment and carried on with her work, grumbling quietly that it was no laughing matter. If he made himself ill, it would be up to her and Cesarina to get the old man back on his feet; his head was as hard as Istrian marble!

At dinner the grandfather announced the curriculum for summer and autumn to Silvano and Aligerno, to give them time to prepare their pupils.

"We will leave with Martino and Lino in May. We will stop at the Ginamis' house in Val Seriana to see how they work metal, forging it in the fire and the icy waters of the river Serio. Then we'll cross the open spaces above Gromo castle, towards La Presolana. I want to show the children the rock carvings in Valcamonica, made thousands of years ago by the Camunni; Celts of the toga from the Republican Age, like us, whose distinguishing trait was that they loved horses and archery more than the Latins and Greeks."

Silvano and Aligerno smiled at the wordplay, and the grandfather raised his goblet of wine to toast the nectar that could put all the citizens of the old republican faith in agreement. The tribal kings actually preferred ale or mead to wine.

Although he was clearly tired, the grandfather went on to explain that they would be back by September, because Lino would be commencing the twelfth year of his life in the autumn.

"How long does he have to stay alone in the woods?" Aligerno asked.

"Three days and three nights," replied Silvano.

"We will continue tomorrow. Good night." The grandfather rose abruptly from his chair to bring the conversation to a close, but lost his balance and fell down, banging his head on the edge of the table and kicking his chair against the wall.

Paolo and Sara heard the sudden commotion and came running from the kitchen, where they sat talking.

Paolo lifted the unconscious Signor Bellini up off the floor and took him to bed, where Sara was removing the warming pan containing the still hot embers.

Silvano said he would stay awake and call Paolo only if necessary.

They all tried to sleep, in spite of their anxiety at the thought of their master being close to death.

Meb was still awake, watching the nocturnal shadows playing on the garlands and doves in relief on her bedroom walls, unaware of what had happened.

Outside, the snow continued to fall lightly.

When Martino got up the next morning, he found Silvano waiting for him in the kitchen, on the pretext of eating bread and honey and drinking a cup of hot milk.

The boy knew his instructor's habits well enough to know that something was wrong, and asked him what had happened.

"Your grandfather is staying in bed. After breakfast I'll take you to his room," said the instructor, placing his hands on Martino's shoulder and giving him a serious look.

"Uncle Silvano," Martino asked quietly, "if grandfather dies... if mother and father don't come back...what will happen to us all?"

"If is not good company for a knight," the instructor murmured; "now finish your milk then come and see your grandfather."

"Yes, uncle. But where have the others gone? Everything's covered in snow outside; I can't hear any voices and I don't see anyone around. I don't like it. It seems like everyone has gone and left us on our own."

"Sometimes it's good when there are just two people left alone to talk; go to your grandfather's room alone. I'll wait for you in his study. Do you remember how to conjugate the verb to be in Latin?"

Martino looked at him questioningly, but got no other answer than Silvano's left hand, pointing at the door to his grandfather's room.

Sara waited three hours, then knocked on the study door and asked Silvano if there was anything she could do.

Silvano told her to bring baked apples and chamomile.

The diligent housekeeper obeyed, and also brought tea made from mallow, echinacea and mint.

After eating the light meal with Martino in his grandfather's room and sharing some happy memories with him, Silvano sent the boy to Aligerno and went back to studying the sheets that Signor Bellini had left on the table. They were charcoal drawings of the house, with notes on how to improve the water supply and a plan to rebuild the portico.

After the work was done, the sheets of hemp paper would be recycled; they were drawn in charcoal so that the marks would last a long time, until the work was complete.

On the calendar sheets, however, Signor Bellini would write with a temporary ink, so they could be re-used shortly afterwards.

The riding instructor felt a sense of well-being similar to when he went to swim in Lake Orta, and promised to go on serving the household to his last breath.

PROGRESS

The period that followed was intense and full of formative experiences for all three children.

Lino came through his initiation, leaving a deep carving of a bear's paw on the trunk of the last old oak tree on the northern border between Mezzomerico and the moorland.

Whilst carving it with his hunting knife, he gave thanks to the tree and asked forgiveness for the wound he was causing.

"Trials often cause pain to the trunk or branches," Lino explained with a steady voice, "dear old oak, remember that it's the head that continues with the greatest effort and dedication, even if it doesn't appear to be wounded. Deciding what to do and how to act - that's the hardest thing!"

The impression that Lino left on the trunk was quite different from the reference model he'd been taught.

The boy didn't just carve a right paw in memory of the one the mother bear laid gently on the chest of his forefather; giving full flow to his creative inspiration, he carved a bear's face with long, curled eyelashes like those of a girl he saw at the market every week.

The bear that Lino engraved also had its head resting on its left front paw, as if it were half asleep during hibernation.

The artist stopped to looked at his work and announced to the arboreal being that this would perhaps be the last carving, and could perhaps be considered the conclusion to a tradition that had been preserved up until then; a tradition in which the existence of the clan seemed to have lost any reason to go on.

"Tree of our tradition, natural oak, may your existence continue at length. Friend: *Ave atque vale,*" he said, gently caressing the bark as if asking for forgiveness for the brutality he had used in his carving.

His mother Sara had filled a bag with ready-prepared food for him, so he wouldn't have to cook meat for his evening meal, which might attract wild animals.

He lit a small fire to keep warm, and ate the last of his bread and cheese, drinking sparingly from his gourd.

He meditated on the deep meanings of the myths of Narcissus and the *sol invictus* when the first snows on Monte Rosa turned red in the sunset.

After the fire went out, he left the embers to warm the air and warn any wild animals around to the presence of danger.

Wrapped up in his woollen cloak under a waxed canvas cape to keep out the damp at night, he fell asleep.

A curious owl settled on a branch above his head, and flew off to its nest at first light.

Lino ran cheerfully to the farm vineyard when he woke up. Juanìn was busy clearing the ground beneath the vines and pulling off leaves gnawed by insects. He called out,

"Don't touch the vines! And don't pick the rosehips!"

A robin hopped onto the path and cocked its head when the young man greeted it, reminding him of the words of a poet whose name he couldn't remember:

I will sing for you too

because the secret of eternal life lies in song.
I would like to be like you
with strong wings so I could fly
a spirit that's free
drinking the light
from some ineffable cup.

Innocently and happily would I pay
with wings impervious to dew.
I would like to ride the wind
and defend my territory
as you do.

But now I would rather
accept the life and love I know.

I would rather sing as I walk
than keep quiet as I bend
like a straw
in the wind.

Farewell, redbreast.

I will sing for you too.

Filippo saw him. He rested his axe against a branch he was chopping and greeted his friend warmly, inviting him to step into Giacomina's house for hot refreshments. He was about to take a sip from his mug of warm barley milk when he noticed a long, fair hair that had settled on the surface. He pulled it out and held it up to the light, pensively.

Giacomina saw what he was doing and remarked that women's hair is like snakes.

"What do you mean, nurse?" the boy asked, puzzled.

"It's a saying," replied the woman, putting a plate of millet bread and cheeses made from sheep's milk, goat's milk and cow's milk down on the table.

Philip commented that you have to learn the difference between venomous snakes like vipers, and those that are beneficial for crops.

"Not just that," his mother went on; "apparently, there are some vipers that when you cut their heads off they grow back and multiply. If you cut one head off, three grow back; if you cut three off, nine grow back."

"Interesting," said Lino. "So tradition teaches us that one head grows into two, and if you cut off three heads, they multiply by themselves to become nine..."

"What it means, I think, is that it's pointless cutting off a snake's head. It's better if you breed turkeys," said Filippo.

"Why would breeding turkeys be useful? To protect yourself from vipers?" Lino asked, intrigued.

"Yes. For example, we keep our rooster and hens in the chicken coop," Giacomina explained, "but the turkey is free to roam wherever it wants, and it comes into the kitchen to sleep."

"... you let it come into the house like a servant, and then wring its neck when you want to eat it, nurse?" Lino was astounded.

"Of course not, what are you saying?" Filippo intervened. "Mother would never do such a thing!"

"The flight of the chicken, the stride of the turkey and the carcass of the duck..." Lino insisted, reciting the ancient adage, useful for selecting the best part of each bird.

"Excellent rule," said the nurse, "and correct, in general.

But Meleagro will die of old age, as long as I'm living under this roof. He chased a viper out yesterday, and nobody's going to wring his neck, he's done well!"

They all looked at Meleagro the turkey, who sensing he was being observed looked back at them, scrutinising them from the doorway with just pride.

Feeling refreshed, Lino said goodbye and bade them call in and say hello if they should be in Oleggio.

On his way back he saw the girl he liked, at the market. He told himself he would to approach her the following week, when he was clean.

He knocked at the main door of the house and was welcomed by his family, who were celebrating his coming of age.

A banquet had been prepared in the hall and the doors were held open with bricks, indicating that anyone could come and go as they pleased that evening.

It was the 19th of October. In a steady voice, Lino thanked everyone and also the bear, which had protected their great family continuously for many generations.

He didn't mention grandfather Bellini. He went to see him in his room, where he spent most of his time now.

After dinner, Lino and Nonno Bellini stayed alone together until late into the night.

On the morning of 20th October, Aligerno told the children that classes would continue as normal, and Lino said he was going to live in the house next door as an assistant breeder with the Visconti hunting pack, which Nonno Bellini had arranged for him.

Meb and Martino were happy because they would still see their friend, and it would provide an excellent opportunity to visit the hunting dog pups.

The tutor waited for his pupils to calm down, then began the lesson for the day.
"The village of Oleggio was constructed as an encampment for the Roman army after an alliance was formed between the Government of the Roman municipality and the Transpadane tribes, represented by the Senate and the People of the City, which was Eternal by virtue of His Law.
The walls around the village were rebuilt a few years ago, after centuries during which the moat full of water surrounding the village was considered sufficient.
Neither raids nor wars were feared for a long time because of the agreements they had made with the various armies that passed through, who would not plunder the territory in return for victuals and lodging.
But fifteen years ago Oleggio was occupied by soldiers in the service of Galeazzo Visconti, who felt compelled to protect the village with high walls, before continuing his run to power.
The captain, who was twenty-four years old at the time, had married Beatrice from the House of d'Este a year earlier. She was eleven years his senior and recently widowed, having been married previously to an esteemed judge.
It seems that the sobriquet given to the mature bride was Noble Viper, and the influence of Casa d'Este was from that time considered by many to be dangerous.
But we consider it pointless to judge people; we stick to the facts, which we discern by looking at the inexorable

flow of time. Oleggio was occupied in the year MMLIV after the founding of Rome; a year that can be dated according to various methods, but which in common use is defined as MCCCI ANNO DOMINI. Are you following me?

"Yes," said Martino, and specified, "we are now in the year 1317, the one thousand three hundred and seventeenth year of the Christian era, in other words, the common era. Oleggio was occupied by the Viscontis in 1301, sixteen years ago."

"Why do you use the adjectives 'common' and 'Christian' as synonyms?" Meb enquired.

"Because anyone can receive the anointing and fulfil the mission specific to his individual divine grace," Lino explained patiently.

"What Lino means is that anyone can attain the right social standing if he accepts the appropriate training and fulfils the duties relating to his rank," Aligerno added.

Lino thought he had been clearer than the tutor; he kept quiet out of respect, but farted silently.

Martino took the smell let off by his neighbour as a personal offence and delivered him a kick, which sparked off a violent scuffle on the dusty floor of the library.

Meb took advantage of the situation to go and stand by the window that looked out over the yard where Lino would be moving; she had never looked closely at that part of the urban island in which they lived before.

She'd always considered it more instructive to look down on what was happening in the square and at the large house on the other side, which had a long portico facing their own, identical to it and running parallel, but at that moment she was more interested to find out where her friend who had attained social majority would be.

The tutor allowed the children to take a break and joined his daughter looking out of the window.

"Look Father," Meb pointed out, "from here you can see the tower near Gaggiolo and the road that goes down to the Cameri rice fields. Will Lino live in that little hut at the back of the yard, between the back of the shops that open on the portico in the square, and the end of the block?"

"As far as I understand, yes."

"Can he come and eat with us? Or will he have to stay with the Visconti's dogs all the time and not leave them?"

"I don't know," said Aligerno, turning to the boys who had settled their differences, as they always did after these innocent Greco-Roman fights.

Sara and Cesarina grieved for the poor mothers who must always bid farewell to their grown sons and conspire with the other women of Oleggio to weave a dense network of information to gain insights on what their children were doing; children who seemed so brave in facing the trials of adult life.

A week later, a messenger appeared at the door of Casa Bellini with a missive to be delivered into the hands of the head of the family.

After having washed and changed his travelling clothes for clean indoor clothes, the messenger was received by the grandfather, who was helped by Silvano into a chair in the study to hear the news from his son Enrico.

Enrico had written and sent the letter while staying as a guest at Casa Hunyadi, and sealed it with the Bellini bear's paw alongside the raven of the Hungarian dynasty. The diplomatic mission had been fruitful.

On 9th April 1256, Pope Alexander IV had issued the Augustinian Order by writing the Bolla Ecclesiae Catholicae and affixing his papal seal to it.

The Bellini couple had stayed a week in Verona as guests of the new Order of Eremitical Friars at the construction site for the church of Sant'Eufemia.

Brother Federico Cruciani had shown them sketches for the Tomb of Truth, which would be located outside, on the perimeter wall to the right.

Other interesting projects concerned the archangel Michael, to whom the Bellini were also devoted, and the story of Tobias. As soon as they arrived they had attended the funeral of one pious Enrico, whose life had been exemplary for all contemplative hermits. Ugolino de Liaziario, defender of the people, had arrived from Bologna on 28th November 1315 and invited the Defenders of Trivigi to attend a congress in Ferrara to agree a common approach in respect of the Republic of Venice. It was impossible to understand how far the Venetians would take their ambitions, and Bellini had concentrated on international issues, hoping that the patricians of the Serenissima Republic would respect local autonomies. They had continued their journey without incident until they reached the Angevin court in ancient Pannonia, which had been devastated by barbarian invasions that had spared not even Sabarìa, the birthplace of St. Martino, protector of travellers.

On 8th September 1316 twin girls were born, to the joy of the Bellini dynasty. They were born without complications at the nomads' camp on the banks of the River Tisza, where the Cumans had been welcomed after their defeats by other nomadic tribes, further north. With the blessing of the tribe's shaman and the priest of the Hungarian garrison, the parents had baptised the twins Margherita Clemenza and Clemenza Margherita.

The grandfather interrupted Silvano's reading to recall Clementia, daughter of the Roman emperor Rudolph the First of the House of Hapsburg and Gertrude of Hohenberg.

Clementia of Hapsburg died on 8th February 1293 as she was giving birth to a daughter. The daughter was given her name and remained with her father, Charles Martell of Anjou, who was granted the government of Naples which was engaged on the Hungarian front as well as in Mediterranean mercantile politics.

Orphaned on her father's death when she was just two years old, Clementia of Anjou had been crowned queen in Reims cathedral on 24th August 1315 and offered as a sacrificial lamb to Louis X of the Capetian dynasty, son of Philip IV and Joan I of Navarre.

Louis, a known troublemaker, had committed uxoricide by strangling his first wife, Margherita of Burgundy, on 15th August 1315.

The choice of names was therefore a delightful opportunity to pay tribute to these noblewomen.

The Bellini couple believed in a supreme justice that would protect at least the right to memory of the innocent.

The grandfather perfectly understood the decision to use these names, and commented that the choice was a wise practical demonstration of the one faith that unites humanity and inspires hope in the exercise of virtues.

Enrico reported that they would stop at Aquileia on their return, and that they planned to return before winter.

The rest of the letter, written in fading ink, convinced Signor Bellini that everything would be fine, God willing.

The couple had also sent a tile and a letter to their son, written in indelible ink.

The grandfather dismissed the messenger, entrusting him to Sara's care. Then he drank a bowl of hot broth and was helped back to bed.

He instructed Silvano to give Martino the terracotta tile and the letter addressed to him, then fell asleep, exhausted.

Silvano waited until he was alone with Martino to show him the gifts from his parents.

The round terracotta tile bore the following inscription in bas relief:

LEGUM BONONIA MATER PETRUS UBIQUE PATER

In the centre was a tutor sitting under a trilobed arch, looked ahead and pointing to an open book on the desk; at the sides, further down, two students sat reading at university desks.

"What does the writing mean, master?" Martino asked, "and why did my father and mother send me this message?"

"Because it's important that you too, like them, learn to ask the right questions at the right time."

"But didn't grandfather go to study in Paris? He told me that Paris is the Alma Mater Docentorum; how can there be so many university mothers?"

"I didn't know your grandfather had already spoken to you about university learning. Bologna uses a bottom-up approach to teaching, with dialogue between students and their representatives, who become the spokespersons for teachers and receive direct payment; they are therefore bound to the will of student nations - real corporations, such as the ones for arts and crafts. Paris, on the other hand, uses the top-down approach of "sentimental education", through the example of teachers like Abelard and Eloise, who were scholars, yet human beings and victims of their passions."

"I don't understand, master."

"I'm sorry, I haven't made it clear. Do you remember the celebration we organised for Epiphany on 6th January?"

"Yes. When Paolo replaced Aura with an ox in the stable, and Fiflic with a donkey. A couple brought a small child and put it in the manger, then stood beside it in silence. Everyone brought a gift and even the shepherds came from Mezzomerico; the mayor, the parish priest and the surgeon pretended to be the Magi, wearing crowns on their heads."

"Exactly. In Bologna they set great store by the shepherds and other people who come bearing gifts for the child, loaded on pack saddles on donkeys or mules. In Paris though, bakers prepare sweetmeats and housewives buy them for the family. At every dinner table on 5th January, one of the diners finds a model of a Magus in his slice of cake, and is crowned king with a cardboard crown, a gift from the baker. The moral of the story is this: in Paris everyone can be treated like a king, while in Bologna everyone can feel like a donkey."

"So what shall I do? I would like to study in both Bologna and Paris!"

"In just five years' time you can choose where to start, if you want to; when you study it's good to travel. Like when we read; do you remember what I always tell you?"

"Don't read from a single author."

"Bravo, you're a diligent scholar!"

Along with the tile there was a letter written by his mother in Hungarian.

Susanna had studied Latin, Greek and French with a tutor.

Her paternal grandmother was Croatian, with a Serbian father and a Hungarian mother, and her father was a descendant of the House of Spinola, who for centuries had been keeping the waterways open via diplomatic means.

Enrico, on the other hand, had studied Greek and Latin but loved Bavarian, the mother tongue of his former university student Johann Windmanstetter, who was born in Munich.

The two had become friends whilst studying at the University of Bologna and the letters they exchanged were a source of joy for them both; they managed to meet up on rare occasions at Lake Garda or at Pallanza on Lake Maggiore.

Johann's wife, Aglaja, who had a Siberian father and a Serbian mother, exchanged interesting letters with Susanna in turn; they challenged each other in what little they knew of the Glagolitic alphabet.

Martino stared at the parchment as if he could engrave it on his heart, then looked at Silvano, his eyes shining with tears, and confessed that he didn't understand the writing.

The tutor said that he too was not able to read it, but that his father had written a letter to his grandfather with a translation of the letter in the vernacular, which he had learned by heart. Martino wanted the instructor to go over his message thirty times, holding his hand. When he was too tired to go on, he closed his eyes but squeezed the man's hand and said "again." Silvano recited it again, then tried to let go of his pupil's hand and stand up. Martino squeezed his hand again and said "again."

The adult whispered "once more and that's all.

We
a couple in the open fields

a uniform alliance by sea, land and firmament
custodians of the night and custodians of the day
dark creatures versus iridescent ones
will continue to oppose the pull of gravity.

In the brief dance of generations
in this story of humanity.

Sleep now, and dream."
He turned back the blankets and took his leave.

The following day was a Wednesday and the riding lesson was enjoyable.

Lino had brought Jole, a black bitch with light patches on her breast and eyebrows.

Fiflic paid no attention to her but Meb bombarded her friend with questions and the bitch with caresses, which both endured without too much effort.

Meb was fascinated with Jole's leash, which Lino had made from knotted hemp thread given to him by a girl who worked at the market.

While Fiflic and Martino were trotting around the meadow of Gaggiolo under the watchful eye of Silvano, Lino and Meb decided to make some leashes to sell on one of the weekly stalls.

They worked on their project in the kitchen before the afternoon lesson, and Paolo was enthusiastic about it as they would be able to use offcuts from other work without having to pay any duty to the Viscontis, who profited from all the goods that entered or left via the walls.

When Rebecca told Aligerno about the project, the tutor was concerned but said nothing, to avoid tiring Signor Bellini or cooling Meb's enthusiasm. In any case, he thought it would be good for his daughter to learn the art of knotting that neither he nor his wife knew anything of.

*

Sitting by the mill on the River Tisza, Susanna nursed her twins, alternating them on her breasts swollen with milk. She had never considered breastfeeding like a nurse and she was happy in the knowledge that she was capable of feeding her own daughters.

Iana the miller's wife lived among her extended family, where there were always a few newborns, and was happy to wash the small items of laundry. Susanna happily entrusted the girls to her because it was in her nature to trust people and receive help. In return, she gave her small items of jewellery she'd bought during the trip, though Iana insisted it was not necessary because she loved Margherita and Clemenza, who had the same fine features as her granddaughter who lived in Zara, near the herb and grain market.

The two women had become friends because they both knew a little of the Latin vernacular used on the Italian peninsula and the Adriatic coast, as well as the Hungarian and Serbo-Croat that was spoken in that part of Dalmatia.

When Enrico decided it was time to leave, Iana asked Susanna to call in on the priest who had recently arrived at the parish church of San Michele, on the road between Mezzomerico and Oleggio. The good man was a friend of her father; they were both on the island of Rab.

Susanna assured her that she would remember the message because Rab was also the birthplace of Marino, founder of the Res Publica from which it took its name: San Marino on Mount Titano, an isolated position but accessible from both via Emilia and the port of Rimini.

Marino's final words were: "Relinos vos liberos ab utroque homine," the value of which was such that they continued to be taught by the free and the powerful.

Beyond the borders of the small republic in the land of Romagna, this intention showed the power of human will, capable of inspiring great deeds every time someone threatened the freedom that humans enjoyed to live in dignity.

After spending a night at the home of the miller's daughter and son-in-law, the Bellinis decided not to sail because they were not accustomed to the water, and instead went north along the consular road to Aquileia, where they spent a few months.

The vast Friuli territory had not belonged to the March of Verona since 1076.

Henry IV had descended on the Italian peninsula to obtain a revocation of his excommunication by Pope Gregory VII, with the intention of humiliating him and causing the decline of his authority.

The nobles who controlled the Alpine passes had taken advantage of the conflict and allied themselves with the Austrian nobles.

Only Sigeardo of Beilstein, a Bavarian like Henry IV, had granted him the right of passage.

When Henry IV succeeded in re-establishing his imperial authority, he wished to give credit to the loyalty shown by Sigeardo and granted him the feudal investiture of Duke of Friuli, Marquis of Istria and Ecclesiastical Prince of Aquileia, a direct fiefdom of the Holy Roman Empire.

The territory of the ecclesiastical Principality known as Patriae Foriiulii was bordered to the north by the Alps, to the east by the river Timavo, to the south by the Adriatic Sea and to the west by the Livenza river.

Over time, Sigeardo's successors, elected by imperial appointment, had consolidated their power by including within their borders the Istrian peninsula, Carinthia, Styria and Cadore.

Armed skirmishes continued for thirty years between the feudal lords and the Republic of Venice to establish who would exercise control of the coast and navigation in the Adriatic Sea.

Henry studied what was happening in order to report to his own people and to the bishop of Novara, to whom he had sworn loyalty in the name of Gaudenzio, the pupil of Eusebio who was faithful to the salvific value of pledges against Aryan heresy.

Far away from home, the spouses dreamed nostalgically of the celebration that had taken place in Novara on 22nd January, when the *dies natalis* was celebrated for Gaudenzio, bishop and saint; in other words the moment of bodily death as it passes to the dignity of memory.

Every year on 22nd January, representatives of the municipalities and patrician houses of the diocese handed over an annual dowry of wax and branches of blooming calicanto to the Basilica of San Gaudenzio in Novara, to perfume the air with a delicate, memorable aroma.

Enrico and Susanna had joined in the procession in San Gaudenzio several times, where they'd had Martino baptised.

The name they chose for their child was also a tribute to the tradition that had given rise to cultural meeting points like their little village of Oleggio and great cities such as Sabarìa on the Amber Road.

Nostalgia increased the weariness of breastfeeding, and Susanna found comfort in Ilka and Silvia, daughters of the householders Greta and Paolo della Torre, a cousin of the Pagano della Torre who aspired to be elected leader in the land of Friuli.

Greta and Paolo had offered to accommodate the Bellinis in their home since they shared some political leanings, and Silvia was engaged to their cousin Bernardo, eldest son of the House of Negri.

They were all in agreement about Marian devotion too, which consisted of venerating the conception of Mary by her parents Anna and Joachim as sinless, and reciting litanies to the Virgin during daily prayers.

They were opposed to theocracy and kept as a precious reminder of this the memory of the meeting between the emperor Octavianus Augustus and the sybil Albunea, who protected the mountains and kept the book of the Senate of Rome in the Campidoglio.

The army, the people and some of the senators wanted to deify Octavian Augustus to increase the symbolic value of imperial dignity, but the general preferred to call the Sibyl Albunea to a consultation, saying that if she had indicated someone more powerful than him, he would not have agreed to be deified.

At noon, the sibyl pointed to a golden almond in the sky, at the centre of which was the baby Jesus at his mother's breast. The emperor burned aromatic incense and forbade anyone to refer to him as Divus Augustus.

Dante Alighieri was one of the poets loyal to the Golden Legend, and had recently published verses 64, 65 and 66 of Paradise in his *Divine Comedy*:

> thus the snow comes unsealed from the ground
> thus in the wind or the light leaves
> the Sibylean sentence is lost

That day, a messenger from Cangrande della Scala had arrived from Verona and recited these verses to the Della Torre family gathered around the table, in the presence of the women and Paolo's parents.

After the meal, Susanna noticed a coin minted a few years earlier by the patriarch of Aquileia, Raimondo della Torre. On one side Raimondo was depicted sitting on a throne, with a staff surmounted by the cross in his right hand, and the tower on the other side.

She shuddered at the thought of ever having to live shut up in such a building rather than in a domus, and hoped that the towers would continue to be used as spaces for storing provisions or for guarding the passes, and not becoming places to live in.

She did not like the singing of the bards, who sang about people locked in or out of towers and castles in France and Spain, where violence had been rife for centuries. It seemed to her that both the inmates and the excluded were prisoners, all victims of low intelligence and too much wickedness.

A tear trickled down her cheek as she watched Clemenza lying on her stomach on the wool carpet, her arms outstretched and her head up, looking at her mother; her movements were like a funny little bird trying to fly.

Margherita was sleeping peacefully in her crib, an embroidered cap framing her little face.

Ilka saw that Susanna was crying and embraced her, thinking how lonely she must be feeling, so far from home. Paolo and Enrico had gone to collect signatures and seals on documents to be sent to Rome.

There had been no news for three weeks and there was the possibility that they had been attacked by a gang of thieves, or worse, by political enemies. But it was better to keep quiet about this possibility.

"Ilka," said Susanna, "I feel the distance between Cavalier Bellini and myself more than usual today.

Could we leave the girls with Greta and go to the basilica together?"

"I will stay with the little ones," replied Ilka "go with Silvia, she likes going out more than I do."

So Silvia accompanied Susanna that afternoon, and showed her the symbolic world illustrated in the basilica, which was built following the promulgation of the Edict of Milan a thousand years before, when the persecutions had ended and the Christian Jews had begun to practice their religion openly.

The floor of one of the rooms built at the time of the Emperor Constantine was covered with mosaics.

In one fishing scene they read an epigraph that recalled how Teodoro had bought an area where some warehouses stood and replaced them with two halls and a baptistery, intended for the rite of baptism. One of the halls was used for celebrating mass, a memorial to Christ's last supper with his disciples. The other hall was used for anointing with olive oil the baptised who had been summoned to state their personal testimony of the Christian faith.

Susanna struggled to focus on the story; she was too preoccupied. She asked what the figures depicted in beautiful mosaic tiles of delicate colours and finely-constructed design represented.

"The great fishing scene is the work of the master of the sea, an interpretation of the words of Matthew: follow me, I will make you fishers of men," Silvia explained. "Jonah threw himself into the sea and was swallowed by the whale. Then he agreed to fulfil his mission, became a witness and could rest in the shade of a pumpkin plant."

Susanna was hungry. She offered her friend some of the biscuits she'd brought in her bag, and a drink from the gourd.

Silvia was amazed at this pilgrim habit and declined the offer as she was not used to eating outside mealtimes, and especially not outside the house.

With the snack over, they continued to admire the mosaics, in particular the birds and the hippogriff.

"The hippogriff is a strange beast; it's a hybrid like the mule, but it's an omnivore rather than a herbivore - it eats everything, like bears do. A griffin is a raptor with the ears of a horse, the head, neck, chest, wings and front legs of an eagle, and the belly, hind legs and tail of a male lion.

If a griffin mates with a mare, the mare gives birth to a foal with a beak, head, chest, front legs, feathers and eagle's wings like its father. The ears are equine, inherited from both the mother and the father, so they remain as such in the offspring. The withers and tail of the foal are like the mother's," explained Silvia enthusiastically, and went on:

"A hippogriff can be ridden with a normal saddle and bridle, provided it's suitable for an eagle's beak.

It's as fast as lightning and is the perfect mount according to the poet Virgil, because it combines the courage of a lion with the vigilant attention of an eagle and a horse. Horses, however, do not let griffins approach the herd without fighting them."

These fantasies were not pleasing to Susanna.

She was alarmed when she saw a horned goat pictured with a staff, and said she sensed heresy in it. She did admire a mosaic depicting a hare, however; a merry little creature known to all lovers of the moor.

She enquired about an image of a turtle and a cock facing each other beneath a shelf holding an amphora.

"Some say they're fighting," explained Silvia, "like night and day."

"Day and night are not in conflict. On the contrary, together they form the time of day. They are like the two sides of the same coin," Susanna observed, and then remarked "it seems like the turtle and the cock are conversing. Perhaps they each know something that the other doesn't."

"I agree with your theory," said Silvia. After a moment of reflection she added "perhaps the amphora contains their wisdom."

They greeted the canon in charge of the consecrated place and Susanna gave him an offering of some local coins in a bag, sealed with her birth seal bearing a peacock with its tail feathers spread, a symbol of energy used with honour.

When they returned to the house Ilka was feeding Margherita assisted by her mother Greta, who was feeding Clemenza. The mush was everywhere; on their hands, on the table and all over the kitchen floor, where a cat and a dog were licking up the mess.

Ilka stroked Margherita and exclaimed: "This Verde will forever preserve the grace of childhood, look at the light in her eyes!"

Greta said that Clemenza was like a Balsamina plant and blessed her, predicting that her bloodline would be trustworthy.

Then she stood up to fetch raisins, pine nuts and an apple tart that was filling the room with its aroma.

Susanna sat down at the table in the large kitchen and entertained them with the story of Ambra and Alba.

"There was once a cat that did not get along with her sister," she began in a low voice. She took a sip of cool water, and then went on.

"Ambra hated her sister Rachele because she was always leaving her alone. Hate does not arise from indifference, but from the disappointment of expectations. When they were very young and had not yet started walking, Ambra thought she would always stay with her sister and her mother, so the separation that came with growing up caused her great suffering. Rachele would go off on her own and disappear for weeks. As if this were not enough, she hissed to warn other cats to keep away, even her sister, showing them no respect whatsoever. This independent cat would climb trees looking for eggs, and throw them on the ground so that she could to lap up the yolk and albumen. If she found chicks in the nest she would gobble them up too, and never shared anything! She was a wild cat with a long, soft, silky coat; her eyes were big and as bright as stars shining on a moonless night.

Ambra, on the other hand, had a poor sense of balance. If she tried to climb she would feel her head spinning. If she tried to jump onto the table from a chair she would fall on the floor, and no one was afraid when she hissed because her teeth were so small. Her claws were sharp but she couldn't retract them very well, so they often got entangled up in cloth; she was afraid when this happened because it hurt her paws."

Ilka laughed and said that Ambra was a real disaster.

"But fate was kind to her in the end," Susanna continued. "Sadly, Rachele died under the wheels of a cart while she was crossing the consular road after a nocturnal hunt. The cat's body was found by the gardener, who buried it at the bottom of the garden under the watchful gaze of Ambra, who felt even more alone now. So she went to see some orphaned kittens in the woodshed. She took care of them and taught them how to hunt lizards and mice. When they grew up though, the kittens turned into big, unruly males, independent and aggressive. Ambra used to get very angry with them and drove them out of her territory. For the first time, she discovered she could hiss and growl and scratch as much as Rachel, perhaps more. Ambra didn't know it, but she was now behaving like other cats, intolerant of male cats except when they're in heat and nature urges them to accept a father for their kittens."

Greta sighed and muttered that solitude was sometimes preferable to having to endure the company of certain males, then she put the dirty dishes in the sink and brought two bowls containing baked apples for the little ones who were weaning.

"It seemed that nature had condemned Ambra to a life of silence and solitude, when the woman who lived in the house adopted a puppy and they became inseparable. It was a white female with black tail and ears. One eye was brown and the other blue; the brown eye was good but the blue eye was blind. She was delicate and fragile and so spoiled and mollycoddled, she thought she was the most important creature in the house. She became very bossy. She would bark furiously if she didn't get her way, so the woman gave her everything she wanted.

Ambra watched and kept quiet.

Alba continued to lord it over the household and started sleeping on the bed by the lady's feet.

When the lady went to visit a neighbour who didn't allow animals in the house, she was locked in the kitchen with the cat. The cat went up to her. Alba was shocked; she'd never noticed the cat before and was intrigued.

She'd been adopted at a young age and didn't even remember her mother; she thought she was one of the humans, only smaller in size and greater in intelligence, since she was able to dominate them so easily and they pandered to her every need.

The cat sat down in front of the dog and kept as still as a statue.

Alba approached her and sniffed, then lay down next to her.

The cat sat still and began to purr.

Dogs usually growl when they hear a cat purring, but Alba knew the language of neither cats nor dogs, so she felt only Ambra's warmth and it made her happy. When they were thirsty they drank from the same bowl, and when they were sleepy they rested, lying down back to back for safety, because they trusted each other.

They were not separated when the humans returned, and they all lived a long and happy life together."

"Thank you for the beautiful and not too long fairy tale!" exclaimed Silvia, who was famous for her often thorny sincerity.

Dinnertime was over for Margherita and Clemenza too, so Susanna and Ilka took the twins to the bedroom, while the other women in the house cleaned up the kitchen and prepared dinner for everyone.

They spent the evening singing well-known songs together.

Ilka and Greta intoned the refrain, which went something like this:

"That bouquet of flowers
that came from the mountain"
then Silvia sang the verse:
"And make sure he doesn't bathe
the one to whom I give it.
I shall give it to him
as it's a lovely bouquet
I shall give it to my lover
this evening when he comes."
Ilka and Greta: "This evening when he comes
will not be a good time."
Silvia: "And because on Saturday night
He did not come to me.
He did not come to me
he went to see Rosina.
It's because I am poor
It makes me sigh and weep."
The others repeated the refrain, then Silvia sang the ending, in a tragicomic tone:
"It makes me sigh and weep
on my bed of tears.
Whatever will people say,
what will they say about me?!
They will say I've been betrayed,
betrayed by love
That's why my heart weeps
and forever will it weep."
They all laughed at her interpretation, which was worthy of a jester, and then sang *Look at the old man under the ladder* and *The song about the chimney sweep*:

"Up and down the Valcamonica I hear it, I hear it
And up and down the Valcamonica I can hear it coming
Lovely lady of the mountain looking through the portico
The chimney sweep is calling you, he's calling you
First let him in and then sit him down
Give him food to eat, the good chimney sweep!
And nine months later if a darling child is born
He will certainly resemble the good chimney sweep."

They enjoyed the singing, and before bidding each other good night they sang the song most beloved at crossing places all over Europe.

From the highlands of the eastern steppes to the Alps, across the Apennines to the Murge plateau in Puglia and up to Lyon, the Pyrenees and the lands of Ireland, England and Scotland, cheerful souls like Susanna and Silvia loved to sing *The song of the flower*:
"When I woke up this morning
I got up before the sun
When I woke up this morning
I discovered the invader
Oh partisan! Take me away
I feel like I'm dying."

It had grown too late for the horsemen to return, so Greta bade her guest goodnight and refrained from scolding her daughters.

When she retired to her room, Susanna wrote a letter to the abbot of Sveta Lucija Ajurandvor on the island of Krk. It was written in the same alphabet that Demetrius Zvonimir used for a donation to the Benedictine abbot Drzhiha, and expressed the lady's state of mind:

MEN OF GREAT TALENT
TELL US THEY WANT TO BE LOVED
FOR WHAT THEY ARE.
BUT WHATEVER OUR VIRTUE,
WE ARE ALL PERISHABLE AT THE END OF THE DAY.
WE LABOUR WITHOUT CEASE, WATCHING LIFE
THROUGH A DISTORTED LENS,
NOT CARING IF OUR HEARTS BLEED.
THE RULE SAYS THAT COUPLES MUST BE ALLOWED
TO ENTER THE ORATORY,
BUT SEPARATE FROM EACH OTHER, OR AT THE BACK,
NOT TAKING PART
IN THE CHORAL SINGING OF THEIR BROTHERS IN
FAITH.
WE HEAR THE WORDS OF SALVATION,
HOPING TO ONE DAY SEE
IN THE EYES OF OUR BROTHERS AND SISTERS A
REJOICING FOR OUR DEEDS. IN FAITH.
SUSANNA

She sealed the rolled-up parchment with a few drops of red sealing wax melted with the candle. She stamped it with the peacock seal engraved on a ring that she wore around her neck.

Then she looked out of the window and gazed at the full moon shining on the sea, imagining herself swimming like a mermaid, half woman and half fish, up to the Gulf that Dante described in his Inferno as "Kvarner Gulf, enclosed by Italy and bathed in its words."

She would have liked to study Glagolitic again, the alphabet that was a mixture of Hebrew and Greek, and runes, but she knew her martial status imposed other duties on her.

She sighed and looked up at the sky, whispering the words of Sappho:

"Asterès mèn anfì kàlan selannàn aps apucruptoisi faennòn eidos gàn epì paisan argurìan."

"Even the stars hide their bright faces when the beautiful moon shines on the silvery earth," Enrico translated. He had entered without making a sound.

Embracing his wife, he told her the mission had been successful and that Silvia would be leaving with them, to marry Bernardo Negri in Oleggio.

Susanna was delighted with the news; it was proof that alliances between ancient peoples continued to produce positive results. They checked the little girls were well, and went to sleep full of hope.

Before dawn, Susanna dreamed she and Silvia were weaving glorious perfumed garlands of violets and roses.

PLAY

"The master is arrogant," said Lino, with his chest puffed out and stomach held in.

"My father's not arrogant. And he's not fat," Meb retorted. She always became a little touchy when Lino questioned Aligerno's authority.

Here we go again thought Martino, trying to concentrate on the manuscript containing aphorisms by Ovidius that he had to memorise. "Dum loquor hora fugit" the boy read to himself. He was almost twelve years old and wanted to demonstrate that he was ready to go and study outside the family circle.

The library in the house was well lit. It was the end of October in Oleggio, a warm day approximately 2075 years after the founding of Rome; 1654 years (approximately) since the Library of Alexandria was built. "Approximately" in both cases because all human calculations seem to be open to opinion.

"I heard that," said Aligerno, approaching his students.

Lino looked the tutor in the eye, defiantly. Meb smiled, waiting for her father to teach the troubled teenager a lesson; he was becoming increasing disrespectful.

"Excellent neologism Lino," the tutor went on. "I shall be more careful how much I eat, since our cook Cesarina pays great attention to the quality of our food. At least judging by the result it's had on your growth. In what way, however, would I be arrogant?"

"Master, I meant magnificent in terms of the extent of...your knowledge," explained the teenager, clutching at straws to demonstrate how persuasive he could be.

"Thank you Lino," the tutor conceded, and continued without further ado. "Today's lesson is about the stamina needed to become a student at the Universitas Studiorum."

Three pairs of eyes focused on him.

"But first I have to check if you understood yesterday's lesson properly. Martino, take an aphorism of your choice and explain the context."

"Dum loquor hora fugit" the boy articulated, explaining in a steady voice "while I speak, time flies. The author was Publius Ovidius Naso, born free thirteen centuries ago to a family of equestrian rank. At the age of twelve he went to study in Rome, where he attended the Domus of Messalla Corvino, a republican by tradition, and the Domus of Mecenate, where he discovered his vocation as a poet. At the age of fifty he was exiled at Tomi on the Ponte Eusino - the Black Sea - by the Emperor Caesar Augustus, because of a work he wrote and a political error. He died there ten years later. He used writing as the ideal means to free himself from irrational passions and as an aid to calm reasoning. His works are useful to us all in meditation, which is why we study them and consider them worthy of remembering. During his exile, Ovidius continued writing in the hope of obtaining an imperial pardon and being allowed to return to Rome. I don't understand why, since he was in a town on the coast of the Pleasant Sea, if my translation from Greek is correct..."

"Thank you, Martino. You have studied and translated well," said Aligerno. "Before it was conquered by the armies of the Macedonian and Roman emperors, the sea was called Axeinos, which in Greek means inhospitable. The change of name is apotropaic, from the Greek verb *apotrépein*, which means to distance, to demonstrate the will to eliminate all negative prejudices and make it possible to introduce improvements. Unfortunately, even though many centuries have passed since the time of Ovidius, it seems that the region is still inhospitable. Nonetheless we still call it the Mare Ponto Eusino."

"Did Ovidius live his last ten years alone?" asked Meb, anxiously.

"For people like us who belong to the classical world, those who study are never alone," her father replied. "In the classical world, *auctor* is a noun derived from the Latin verb *augeo*, which means 'I allow to grow'. Public opinion still defines any person who knows how to prove him or herself responsible as an author. *Auctor* is any person who promotes ideas, studies, works useful for improving the quality of human existence. For example, the author you studied was an expert and critic of the concept of *mos maiorum*, the written and oral tradition passed on by ancestors and teachers. Conservation in change - that's the challenge for classicists. And Ovidius was and will remain a great classical author. But let's get back to the point. Which of you will remain in Oleggio and which will be going to Bologna?"

"I'm staying," said Lino. "I have to help my father repair the cart, and Lilla in the kennel is about to have a litter."

"I don't know," said Martino, who at twelve years old felt neither child nor adult. "Since my grandfather died, there have been no initiation rites. I don't know if I'm ready to leave. If I say yes, will you come with me, Aligerno? What about you, Meb, what will you do?"

"I can't, even if I wanted to. Girls can't be roaming clerics," said Meb. "I'm learning to weave with my mother and Cesarina is teaching me how to cook. Not to mention helping Susanna to care for Clemenza and Margherita, whom I love as if they were my own sisters."

"If we can settle what everyone really wants to do, we can talk about it with the women at lunchtime," the tutor reasoned. "We'll negotiate a proposal with them, and in the afternoon I'll put it to Enrico for his scrutiny. Martino, what can you do, and what do you want to do?"

"I can ride a horse, but it's hard to take care of my horse and grease the harnesses without Filippo. I don't like dog breeding or agriculture, but I know how important it is. I don't even like hunting on the moors, and game has a savage smell and taste that upsets my stomach. I like keeping good vines healthy, but to eat the grapes rather than make wine out of them. I like walking and studying. I know how to tie knots that can be untied. I would never do what Alexander the Great did with the Gordian knot. Actually, I think all clean cuts just multiply the problems, like cutting the head off a dragon or a demon and it grows back a hundredfold."

"Gratias tibi ago, Martino," Aligerno interrupted him. He knew how long-winded Martino could sometimes be.

"The*Anabasis Alexandri* by Arrian, le *Historiae Alexandri Magni Macedonis* by Quintus Curtius Rufus, Justin's epitome to the *Philippic Histories* of Pompeo Trogo and the text *On the nature of the animals* by Claudius Aelianus tell us how Alexander fulfilled an ancient prophecy by cutting through an inextricable knot with his sword," the tutor reminded his pupils; "and this ability to make decisions is still exemplary. Also, in our case we are at a turning point between tradition and will.

Can you imagine the path of tradition and the path of will as parallel, divergent or convergent?"

"No," replied the students in chorus.

"I want to follow tradition and stay here," said Lino.

"Tradition would counsel you to leave, Lino," Aligerno contradicted him, "because you were born free but not an heir."

"I don't understand, master." How can tradition not recognise the fact that I spent three days and three nights alone in the woods, where I carved a bear in the trunk of the old oak tree? How can tradition send me away from here, where I've been working in dog breeding for five years for the Casa Visconti? I'm almost engaged; how can tradition deny me the right to marry the girl I love and who loves me?!" Lino expostulated.

"Tradition is like a tower: it's used for guarding something precious and marking the presence of people who guard the treasure," the tutor pointed out to him. "If you want to stay, you can stay. But as far as the how is concerned, you have to negotiate, because your will must be useful to everyone, not just you and the girl you love. Martino, what do you want to do? Do you prefer to stay or leave for the university tower?"

Martino replied "I would like to leave but I have to stay, because I'm the heir of the Casa Bellini."

"Does your heart want the opposite of what your mind dictates?" the tutor asked him earnestly.

"Yes, master."

"Are you afraid your parents will suffer if you leave?"

"Yes. I want to honour them and my grandfather; I want to be faithful to my Gens and our traditions."

"That's honourable," the tutor conceded, then asked him an unexpected question: "Do you think of Lino as a brother?"

The two pupils looked at each other. Five years was a big age difference and they had never played together as infants. They had never even fought each other, as Lino often did to assert himself with his peers.

"I don't know, master," said Martino. "It's like I'm an only child; my sisters are small and when they grow up they'll leave with their husbands, like doves that fly away. My grandfather told me the burdens and honours of the Casa Bellini would be in my hands, and I want to be live up to it."

"Grandfather always taught us it's important to preserve freedom," Lino intervened, "so we are all free to choose."

"Nonsense," Meb pronounced; "freedom is participation - you must do your duty according to traditional teaching."

Aligerno massaged his temples, closing his eyes to rest them for a moment and concentrate, before proceeding with his reasoning.

"Imagine that tradition is this library and that I have the ability to light sparks, in the words of the various texts, to illuminate your intelligence," he explained. "You must interpret the signs of whatever light reaches you individually. It is a mistake to follow a tradition without assuming the responsibility of putting your own interpretation on it; those who do so renounce the freedom to make choices based on their own judgement. A turtle cannot fly and an eagle cannot pretend to be a crow without paying the consequences."

"I would like to go and study, but how can I do it and still keep the house safe?" asked Martino, perplexed.

"Safety is not a problem that can be solved, Martino," observed the tutor. "Houses are like organisms that are born, live and change. They are not constant, but they exist. In our case, I cannot see any logical impediment to your going to university, since Lino will be here to conduct the House alongside the noble Enrico until you return after your graduation as a notary."

Meb listened. Lino and Martino looked at each other, seeing an opportunity they had not considered before. The elder boy kept quiet as the younger one said in a steady voice, "I shall say what I want to do. If Lino agrees, I shall leave." The elder boy confirmed his willingness; he understood he was being offered the opportunity to do what he wanted.

"Will we have to go with Martino?" asked Meb, and went on, "do you and I and Mother have to leave everything and follow where Martino goes: but to do what?"

"To continue living," her father replied. "For the moment, we'll go to inform the women; it's lunch time now."

They went downstairs to the kitchen where Susanna was just finishing her meal with Verde and Balsamina.

Martino told his mother immediately that he intended to leave for Bologna with Aligerno, Rebecca and Meb. He would study the *Liber Paradisus*, the *De Officio Tabellionatus in Villis et Castris* and the *Flos Ultimarum Voluntatum* on the compilation of testaments, for use by notaries. Susanna approved and said that becoming a notary in the Visconti tradition was an excellent choice for the eldest son of the Casa Bellini in Oleggio. After they'd eaten she left the twins with Sara and Meb; they no longer took an afternoon nap. They were similar in vivacity but different in their personal tastes, each preferring different games, and only came together to do embroidery with their mother Susanna, or knead the bread with Cesarina the cook.

Margherita, whom they called Verde, was curious to find out how things worked, and went around discovering things; she would even go to the saddlery when Paolo was greasing the harnesses to keep the leather supple. She also enjoyed watching the blacksmith at work, who occasionally came to nail iron horseshoes on the hooves of Aura and Fiflic, the two horses used to draw the cart. Verde would pretend she was a blue horse without a tail or a mane, and when she tried on her mother's shoes she said they were her horseshoes for travelling the world.

Clemenza, on the other hand, whom they called Balsamina, was an active thinker; when left to her own devices she would listen. When adults were talking she would spin around with her arms above her head, and in open spaces like the courtyard or countryside she would leap around, trailing behind her a long, blue silk ribbon that she'd been given for her fourth birthday.

When they went out walking on the hills of Mezzomerico they played ring o' roses with the daughters of the Visconti farmers, and wove garlands of wildflowers to wear in their hair.

That afternoon, Meb entertained them by pretending to be a cat, and Verde imitated her, going down on all fours. Sitting with their hands and knees on the ground, they first looked at each other, stretched out their necks and sat with their backs straight, then stretched their arms out in front so their foreheads were touching the portico paving. Meb and Verde were playing under the staircase, while Balsamina leaped around the courtyard, twirling her blue ribbon. After greeting each other, Meb and Verde imitated the typical movements of cats: they arched their backs and took in deep breaths, then hissed and exchanged looks of defiance, walking along beside each other on all fours. Finally they rolled on the ground with their legs in the air.

Sara sat sewing at the kitchen threshold. She watched them, happy to see them growing well.

The cook Cesarina called them in for a snack, and they went into the kitchen where baked apples and mint tea were waiting for them. As they drank, Meb told them a lovely old story. "About 1891 years ago, Pharaoh Uahabré was the ruler of Egypt. When the pharaoh went off to war with Nebuchadnezzar's Babylonians an internal revolt broke out which Uahabré had instructed his general Amasi to quell. But Amasi took advantage of the situation to kill Uahabré, who was given an honourable burial, and Amasi assumed leadership under the name of Ahmose II. This choice of name was an homage to the founder of a ruling dynasty from a thousand years earlier. It turned out to be a wise choice and won him the good will of his subjects, who obeyed him for over forty years until he died and Egypt was invaded by the Persian army led by Cambyses II. At that time, the slave Aesop surpassed all others in his talent for telling stories, like the one I shall tell you now: *'Antropos katazraùsas àgalma.* "

Balsamina exclaimed "...but what you're saying doesn't make sense!"

98

"If you don't understand the words it's only because you don't know the language I'm speaking in. The words are not meaningless," said Meb.

Verde said, "if a cat sees a dog wagging its tail, the cat thinks it's going to hiss at it. I don't know if it's worse having different body language, like some animals do, or not understanding what people are saying, like we humans do when we speak different languages."

"I don't understand things like this. Animals and humans will both continue to use different languages, won't they?" said Balsamina, exasperated.

"I suppose so," said Meb, smiling, and went on, glad that she had the little ones' attention. "That's why it's useful to learn to understand the language of animals and the different languages that people use. We never know who we're going to meet, but it's good to learn the art of relationships so you can be sure you won't misinterpret any signs.

So, *'Antropos katazraùsas àgalma.*"

That's not fair! exclaimed Verde. "First you have to teach us the language you're going to use! *'Antropos kata ... àgalma* what language is that?"

"Greek. Now listen and don't interrupt, because I'm going to recite from memory. I promise I'll translate it afterwards. *'Antropos katazraùsas àgalma. 'Antropòs tis xùlinon zeòn iskon pènes on kazikéteue tù agazopoiésai. Os a taut'épratte kai mallon en penìa diéghe, zumozèis, ek tu skélus àras autòn tò toìko prosékuse. Tès de kefalès autù parakrezéma klaszeìses, èrreuse krusòs ex autés, òn sunagagòn ò antropos edda.*

A simpleton kept asking a wooden statue for help. When he got no help he lost his temper, grabbed the statue by the legs and threw it at the wall. The statue broke and

99

gold coins poured out. When the man saw this, he exclaimed, 'you are really strange and very different from me: when I was being polite you gave me nothing, and when I destroyed you, you overwhelmed me with gifts!'

Verde commented that the fable seemed to advocate disobedience, which didn't seem a good thing to teach.

"Beware, Verde!" said Meb. "An object cannot teach us anything we don't already know. A statue, a mosaic or a painting can only be useful to those who endow them with a particular meaning. Objects certainly don't satisfy those who delude themselves that they can do something, if the person does nothing!"

"Aide toi, le ciel t'aiderà" recited Cesarina, who had a good understanding of French as her brother had married a beautiful girl from Lyon.

"Ah, of course! Balsamina exclaimed "Help yourself and heaven will help you!"

"Speaking of heaven," Meb resumed her thread, "another of Aesop's fable is dedicated to the astrologer. Every night an astrologer would go out to admire the firmament, walking along the street, looking upwards. He was so absorbed in it on one occasion that he fell into a hole. A passer-by heard his cries and came up, but before helping him out, he advised him to observe the ground on which he walked as well as the heavens!"

The twins laughed and Sara commented that she knew a lot of people like the astrologer.

"Papa is not an astrologer. Isn't that right, Meb?" asked Balsamina after a moment of reflection, looking worried.

"No, noble Enrico studies astronomy," explained Meb, "which is important for both travel and agriculture." Sara noticed it was getting cooler and intervened. "Girls, let's go to the bedroom and get our woollen shawls and play with the dolls. They'll be feeling lonely, won't they?" The girls went upstairs with her, talking about dressing the dolls and combing their hair.

Susanna and Rebecca, meanwhile, were sitting in the upstairs room with its frescoes of ash and beech trees in autumn. The image of the deer between the tree trunks seemed to observe anyone seated at the study table, as they were, in front of the window that looked out over the square dedicated to the martyrs of freedom.

"Martino will be leaving with Aligerno. I don't know what Meb and I will do," Rebecca confided. "Stay with us!" replied Susanna. Aligerno and Martino will return for the holidays, and they'll be back here for good when his studies are over, within two years I hope. Your being here has given this place a new lease of life; it had become sad after being so much lived in by those who are no longer with us, and we miss them! Apart from that, Verde and Balsamina love Meb like a sister."

"Thank you, Susanna," replied Rebecca, heartened "it gives me joy to hear you say that. But Aligerno and I have been inseparable since we first met. I might ask Meb if she wants to stay here, but I shall go to Bologna."

"I understand," said the lady of the house, and put no pressure on her that would have invaded the freedom of her welcome guests. "I'll go and tell Cesarina you're having dinner with us in the hall. That way we can have an adult conversation without having to repeat it later. Good afternoon, Rebecca."

"Good afternoon to you too, Susanna," said Meb's mother, happy that she could now have a discussion with her daughter as to the best thing to do.

The atmosphere at dinner was peaceful. Enrico was elated at the idea of his son becoming a university student.

He recalled the intellectual discussions, the fights, the amorous encounters and the charismatic tutors, almost all of whom were modest enough to consider themselves eternal students themselves, willing to engage in debates with those who were less experienced, but likewise willing to learn from those who proved to be wiser. He wondered if he should advise Martino to avoid favouring the Guelphs, whether black or white, or the Ghibellines. He knew that those from a dominant culture can decide what to teach and those who rule by force may change the rules, but no one can change the rules of logic; the discipline that requires the utmost respect. In the end he decided to silence his personal convictions and leave Martin free from paternal prejudices. Late that afternoon, Enrico gave his son a small manuscript, telling him he was happy with his decision to become a Visconti notary and would like to celebrate the next new moon with a nocturnal outing. Without adding anything else that might spoil the surprise, he wished him a peaceful night and joined the other adults for dinner.

The hall was lit with many candles and the table had been decorated with squash, apples and bunches of black and white grapes.

Cesarina had placed a platter of yellow polenta flavoured with melted cheese in each place, and there was water and red wine to drink. The gentlemen of the house sat at the ends of the long table, which was like a refectory table in a monastery. Susanna raised her goblet for a toast: "to us, faithful to the spiritual love that benefits life, in this story of mankind!"

Enrico raised his goblet, looking at his wife and added: "may those who remain keep the spark alive. And may those who leave return, content to serve those who serve!" The other guests exclaimed in chorus "to serve those who serve!" Then Enrico announced he was taking everyone, including the twins, to Mezzomerico on the occasion of the black autumn moon, and to take advantage of the mild temperature he and his son would admire the Great Bear in the sky.

Aligerno made a joke, saying that Martino should definitely remember to observe the ground as well as the sky in Mezzomerico, in view of the considerable number of potholes and excrement around the place.

Silvano was pleased at the thought of accompanying Martino to take his leave of Filippo, Giacomina and Juanìn before his departure.

"After the visit, we could travel to Bologna together," the instructor suggested, returning to the discussion about university, "where I can take lodgings with the monks of Santo Stefano. I don't know who the prior is now; but there will certainly still be people there I know from when I attended the study following the Rule of Benedict." "When you were a student," Susanna asked, "did you by chance encounter Master Arnolfo, son of the notary Messer Lapo and Donna Perfetta?"

"I would have liked to meet that builder of bridges!" Silvano answered. "I know that Arnolfo went to Bologna a few years before me; unfortunately I never met him in person. In Rome I admired the crib he carved for the Basilica of Santa Maria Maggiore. I remember the child sitting at the mother's left foot under the protection of Joseph, with an ox and a donkey nearby, while the astronomer kings offered gifts."

"Arnolfo was a pupil of the Cosmati masters, famous for their pavings and epigraphic inscriptions," interjected Enrico, who loved writing, even when it was engraved in stone. The conversation continued on art and culture topics, in accordance with the rules of good manners, which forbids any discussion of food and drink around the table. After the feast, Susanna went to tell Sara and Cesarina about their plans for the next few days, then joined Enrico on the upper floor, in the main room of their quarters, where the heat from the chimney breast in the kitchen below rose up to warm the air.

FAREWELL

It was like a procession.

Enrico and Martino walked in front with Susanna, followed by Meb holding hands with Margherita and Clemenza, a little ahead of Aligerno and Rebecca. Silvano brought up the rear, riding Pegaso. The riding instructor was armed with a long sword which he carried prominently at his side, unlike Enrico who always carried a hunting knife hidden in his boot and a stiletto inside his leather jerkin.

The morning was mild and the fog was lifting to reveal the harrows in the well-ploughed fields, ready for sowing. The landscape towards the hills was enchanting, with autumn hues ranging from golden yellow to sepia, orange and purple shrubs with small, fiery-red leaves, red and dusky green oaks and pale green grass; rising up to the indigo of the mountains, their summits vanishing in the pure azure sky.

Susanna recalling the white hills of the Karst region and the harsh Apennines of Liguria as she walked along; the spaces of her childhood she conjured up in her mind in colours more vibrant and uncompromising than any she could observe. The melancholy brought on by memories of the past accompanied her more closely than the voices of her companions. How many times had she travelled the Via Postumia to visit her paternal grandparents in Liguria or her maternal grandparents in Pannonia! How many times had she got to thinking how blissful is the life of a traveller who can follow the rhythm of the seasons!

"Papa, did you live at the farmhouse, too, as a child?" Martino asked his father.

"I, like you, was not nursed by my mother," Enrico replied. "It was a tradition that the mothers belonging to the Civitas, that is descendants of or married to members of the community's Societas, gave their newborn infants to nurses. I lived in Mezzomerico with Nella and his family for three years, before coming to live in Oleggio. You grew up at the vineyard farmhouse for seven years. Newborns have always lived with the nurse and her child, who becomes a milk brother to the future nobleman or lady. It was like cutting the genetic umbilical cord to establish a strong and lasting social relationship with the territory. In the times of clans, our male lineage was the Celts who chose to become men of the toga, in other words they wore the gown of the Res Publica Romans following a bloodless alliance. I was enrolled in the register of citizens, like you. At the Basilica of San Michele, where we are now going together, is the baptismal font of holy water with which we natives of Oleggio are all baptised. From an administrative point of view, the Basilica of San Michele is at the centre of a circular area, which together with other similar areas forms the diocese, which is essential to the imperial organisation."

"But the Roman Empire you speak of has not existed for a thousand years!" said Martino, astonished.

"A thousand years may seem a lot, but it's like a mere breath of air. It can displace a seed of humanity, nothing more," replied his father.

Susanna refocused her attention on the present and turned to tell her daughters to hold her hand as they entered the basilica, as there was often work going on and holes in the paving. Everyone was intrigued by the frescoes, and the baptismal font prompted many questions from the children, who were curious to know what it was for.

They continued their walk across the moors, where a stag and its herd of does and fawns were drinking from the Terdoppio river.

The ferns growing in front of the Roman bridge were luxuriant, and Susanna asked them to remind her to gather some on their return.

"What are you going to do with them?" asked Meb.

"I'll plant the ferns from the undergrowth with the maidenhair that grows in the courtyard, and make a paste from it with olive oil to soothe skin irritations."

Juanìn della Vigna was hoeing between the rows of vines on the slope between the small farmhouse and the Terdoppio river. Hearing their voices he looked up, and seeing some sparrows on the vines, started yelling at them to drive them away.

Martino noticed the years had not changed the old winemaker's habits, and remarked that if he got tired of that work he would make a good scarecrow!

Filippo was in the donkey enclosure and called to his friend to show him the latest foal, which was white as milk. Meb and the little girls went to look at it with Martino and were delighted with the charming creature. Only Giacomina could convince them not to take the white donkey away, saying it was like a grandchild to her, something that Filippo had yet to give her. Martino linked arms with his milk brother, and leading him aside asked him in a whisper if Giacomina had not gone crazy, talking about children with people who were only twelve years old, even though they would soon be turning thirteen. Filippo told him that Lucilla, the shepherd's daughter, had given birth to a handsome boy at the age of eleven, fathered their mutual friend Antonio, who had become a father at the age of fourteen.

Martino made no comment about the news, which seemed completely absurd. He ran over to the table laid in their honour with yellow polenta and wild boar stew seasoned with wild fennel seeds in a contemplative frame of mind. Susanna had told Giacomina that Rebecca and Meb would be coming, so she had prepared polenta and goat's cheese for them. Filippo sat next to the Meb and entertained her with a tale about how he saved a leveret from the clutches of a cat, and if she liked he could take her to the barn after they'd eaten, to show her. Martino blushed, but refrained from punching his friend and instead pretended that he too was curious to see the young hare.

It was cooler in the afternoon. The men lit a few bonfires around the farmyard. Giacomina kept the fire burning in the kitchen and the women and girls prepared lots of pumpkins, cutting out the flesh to save for dinner, and making nocturnal decorations. Susanna and Rebecca cut the tops off the pumpkins so they could be replaced like lids, then peeled the skin off the flesh and left the children to amuse themselves scraping it with wooden spoons.

Martino and Filippo went off with Silvano to ride the horse.

"When I came to Oleggio I didn't see the horse with Aura and Fiflic. Where you keep him?" Filippo asked.

"Pegaso is an intact male so he's kept in the stable with the Casa Negri males, when they're in Oleggio," replied Silvano, stroking the neck of the gray stallion fondly;

"we've been together since he was a three-year-old, and he's almost twenty-two now."

"Nineteen years! Did you tame him yourself?" Filippo asked.

"Yes, in Folgarìa. I have friends there who are experts in taming horses. We don't use coercion to get them accustomed to the saddle and the bit, just the logic of the herd. They taught me how to ride a horse by just shifting my balance. Mount like this, Martino - bareback."

Martino mounted the horse and took the reins, keeping them loose; he settled himself and sensed that Pegaso was calm and attentive. With his legs close to the horse's belly, he leaned forward slightly and stroked the base of its neck, then set off walking through the meadow towards the roccolo, a small two-storey building used as a resting place for hunters when out hunting wild boars on the nearby moors. When they came to the path they had recently come by amongst the bushes, Pegaso began to trot to warm up, then went into a short well-paced gallop that allowed Martino to remain seated and the horse to take the bit.

Filippo admired his friend's ability to control the mount at different paces, very different from the donkeys they used in the country. When he returned from the heath, Silvano told Martino to lie down on the horse's back, and for the first time in five years of lessons, his pupil obeyed. Without commenting on this novelty, the instructor asked the boy to get down and invited Filippo to mount, which the boy did gladly, showing no fear. Martino was a little put out to see Pegaso obeying Filippo the same as himself, and after a few minutes asked if he could remount himself, saying he wanted to take care of the horse before its evening rest. Filippo obliged willingly, and Silvano considered his self-denial highly commendable.

In the farmhouse, meanwhile, Giacomina had laid some blankets on the kitchen floor that she'd borrowed from the big farm, so that anyone who was tired could lie down.

Susanna and Rebecca could sleep in the double bed in her own room behind the kitchen fireplace; she would lie with Meb, Margherita and Clemenza on the floor, wrapped up in tanned sheepskins perfumed with lavender flowers and bay leaves. In the kitchen, the twins sat on the floor eating pumpkin flesh and the women finished carving the shells for outdoor lanterns, to prevent the candle flames setting fire to anything.

Meb went outside to Juanìn, who was picking red dates from small trees in the garden, between the chicken house and the vineyard.

"Red dates and apples, pomegranates and grapes - that's heaven, little lady!" said the farmer, handing his guest the basket to take to the kitchen.

The girl put the basket on the ground and sat down on a large stone. "Were you born and brought up here?"

"No," Juanìn replied. "I was born in the hills above Barcelona; my mother was Iasmina, a traveller. I grew up with Mamma in the fishing village called Lei Santei Marias de la Mar. I remember well the smell and colour of the sea. And how strong the wind blew! So strong that the trees all grew crooked. In the year of the Lord 1290 we moved to Montpellier, where I heard Raimondo Lullo and discovered it was important to learn to read and write. But when I met Maestro Lullo again in Genoa, on his way back from a visit to Tunis, I was disappointed to hear how bad men could be, even if they could read and write. So I left Genoa and went to work on the land with the farmers of Rapallo in the Gulf of the Griffins. I was employed on the farmland belonging to Donna Susanna's grandfather, whom I followed here when she came to marry the noble Enrico. I saw Martino grow up from when he was born until he moved to Oleggio, at the age of seven. I love him like a son, as I do Filippo, even though I am father to neither of them."

"In Oleggio," said Meb, "they say that when Giacomina was widowed, she continued to live here because you are her brother-in-law. Her husband was one the brothers of the Mezzomerico farmer, so I thought you were too."

"That was the easiest thing to tell them in Oleggio, don't you think, little lady?" said Juanìn, and without waiting for an answer he handed her a few yellow, green and white squashes. "These squashes are good for decorating the kitchen. Don't get cold tonight."

"Thank you, Juanìn de la Vigna!" said Meb, getting up.

As she was returning, holding the basket on her head, she saw Martino galloping back from the moor on Pagaso's back, and stopped.

Silvano and Filippo were on foot, so they were a long way behind; they didn't see Martino slow down and take the basket from Meb, nor did they see her mount up behind her friend and cling to him with her arms around his waist.

Martino lengthened the reins and sat loosely in the saddle to prolong the pleasant ride, but the horse knew it was near the stable and arrived in the farmyard a little too soon to suit the riders. As Martino was removing Pegaso's harness to allow the horse to drink, Meb took the basket back to the kitchen and went inside, smiling.

When Filippo and Silvano arrived they found Martino taking care of Pegaso, with an attention his instructor found touching.

Enrico returned at sunset and announced that the next day they would all go to the village of Mezzomerico to celebrate.

Everyone was animated at dinner, and afterwards the twins went into the large, darkened room with Giacomina, where they romped and played amongst the sheepskins until all three fell asleep.

The others put on their cloaks of boiled wool and went out into the dark night with the new autumn moon.

They made their way carefully in the eerie light of candles shining through slits in the hollow pumpkins resembling eyes. The large pumpkins had been left uncovered, so the light from the candles inside them shone out like thoughts flowing from the heads up to the starry sky.

Arriving in the vegetable garden enclosed by stone walls, the cheerful company closed the wooden gate behind them and sat down on stone benches among the rows of fruit trees, in the silent company of the apples, pears, red dates and medlars.

"Lift your eyes and see that long ribbon across the sky, so vast we cannot know where it ends," said Enrico, transfixed.

"Those stars are like eyes watching us," said Meb.

"Your eyes are like stars to me," whispered Martino, who was sitting very close beside her.

"One of the two eyes seems to be opening and closing," the girl went on, speaking aloud and pretending she hadn't heard her friend.

"Some people are afraid of that winking," said Rebecca.

"But others interpret it as the ardour of someone who's in love," Susanna added, "and have dedicated that constellation to Perseus, who freed Andromeda from the sea monster to which she was destined."

"Where's the Great Bear?" Meb asked.

"Over there - those four stars form the Ursa Major, and together with those three brighter stars they form the Plough. The Romans called them the Septem Triones, which means seven oxen, from where we get our word 'settentrionale' meaning north. The Plough rotates slowly around the Pole Star, the fundamental reference point for all travellers.

There's something that looks like the eyes of an owl near the last star of the Bear, looking at us as if it wants us to help Athena against her father's incontestable judgement. But that's just one of many myths to discuss with educated people, not something conjure up any superstitious stories about."

Meb was shivering in the cold, damp air and the candles in the pumpkins were dying, so they all went back inside as the first night of the Celtic new year proceeded, bestowing on them dreams profoundly linked to the land and rocks.

The next morning Fiamma and her five daughters welcomed Enrico and his family to Mismaricch, as they called it in the local Mezzomerico dialect. There was bread for everyone and Fiamma showed them how to cook millet in chicken broth with beans, cabbage, carrots, onions and celery, adding a little red wine at the end. Enrico and Martino loved this traditional dish from their early childhood and had their bowls filled three times before they were satisfied!

Meb noticed a few bags lined up outside the stable, and Cristiana, one of the five sisters, explained that she had planted some red dates in the ground with some manure, in the *hortus conclusus* behind the big house.

"What's manure?" Meb enquired.

"Cow dung," said Cristiana, "we mix it with the earth but keep it away from berries and seeds, and from any roots they've started to put out."

"Oh!" Meb exclaimed, a little embarrassed at Cristiana's language; "but why?"

"Because cow and horse dung enriches the earth but destroys roots. Pee kills roots as well. When I sweep the litter out of the barn I put it at the bottom of the farmyard. And when I'm making manure I'm always careful to mix it in with the earth, making sure it doesn't come into direct contact with the cuttings I want to grow."

Another sister, Benedetta, realised that some of the people listening to her were struggling to understand, so she and her friend Aquila entertained everyone by improvising a cheerful dance to the beat of a tambourine decorated with the Milanese serpent emblem.

The family into which Fiamma was born had operated the mill in Oleggio for centuries; her husband, however, farmed the land that the Visconti family owned in Mezzomerico. He had died three winters ago when his cart and mule fell into Lake Maggiore, since which time she and her daughters had been responsible for the farm and its coat of arms.

Seeing the beloved serpent emblem painted on Aquila's tambourine, Cristiana took the opportunity to show it to

Meb and explain it to her, even though she hadn't asked for it. "The blue serpent on a white background has been the *vexillum civitas mediolani* for centuries."

"... isn't that the emblem of the Casa Visconti?" asked Meb, who was discovering there was a different point of view from her own on every subject she touched upon with Cristiana.

"The Viscontis took their coat of arms from that of the Milanese municipality," Susanna interjected; "or to be more precise, the serpent is the emblem of the alliance between the bloodlines that represented the City of Milan in the Senate" she said, putting an end to a discourse she realised might have been uncomfortable for her husband Enrico, who was intolerant of the highhandedness of anyone who used force rather than reasoning.

After lunch, Enrico and Susanna thanked their hosts and Nella gave them a cart and two mules so they could return to Oleggio ready for their upcoming journey to Bologna for study.

They left three days later; Silvano riding Pegaso and Aligerno driving the cart carrying Rebecca, Meb, Martino and their trunks.

They took a route that avoided the turbulent territory of Milan, going across the Pavia countryside as far as the westernmost church of the diocese of Piacenza. In Casteggio they stayed as guests in a villa belonging to the House of Del Carretto, a family to which the Bellini family were bound by mutual assistance agreements. The farm was surrounded by a high wall in the Roman tradition, within which stood a two-storey square building. The style of the building helped to make guests feel at home, accustomed as they were to this way of living in an enclosed village, but with the addition of a portico leading to the market square and lacking a vegetable garden, to save space. In the hills, the vineyards with their orderly rows vines added to the sense of peace infused with the colours of autumn and silence of the countryside. Flocks of migratory flew across the sky.

They were welcomed by Valentina Leonora, who had married Giorgio del Carretto after being widowed by Bernabé D'Oria. The daughter of Federico Fieschi of Chiavari and Teodora Spinola of Genoa, Leonora had brought the strategic lands controlling the transit between the Genoa and the Po Valley as a gift to Giorgio, who was already the Marquis of Finale and Noli. With her at the villa were her children Lazzarino, Carlo, Enrichetto, Giovanni and little Maria, who wanted to play ball with Meb in the inner courtyard, the one attached to the quarters for her mother and ladies in waiting.

Traditional dishes were offered at dinner: slices of cured pork, beans with pork rind, stuffed chicken, miccone bread and omelette without any hop shoots. When Rebecca and Meb found out what ingredients went into the various dishes, they ate only the bread and omelette. It was a good, simple omelette made with salt and cheese, but unfortunately without the hop shoots that grew wild all over that region, but only in springtime.

The next morning they continued their journey along the busy Via Emilia, taking a diversion to pay a three-day visit to the castle of Montefiorino at Casa Montecuccoli; Silvano was to deliver some documents from Enrico and receive information for Gregorio, a professor at the

Studio of Bologna and son of a sister of the Abbot of Vallombrosa.

When they finally reached Bologna, they took lodgings at a farmhouse owned by the House of Azzoguidi, notary friends of the Bellinis for generations.

Silvano left Pegaso in Martino's care, assuring him that he would come and see him every Sunday afternoon, and went to the Santo Stefano monastery complex on foot.

Aligerno chose Convenevole da Prato as his first professor in the disciplines of Trivium (grammar, rhetoric and logic), not knowing that several of his students had been disappointed by his chaotic methods as a result of which he had lost precious texts such as a *De Gloria* by Cicero! Convenevole was conscientious in explaining things, but often digressed, getting lost in chivalrous references or puns. Faithful in an almost mystical way to Roberto D'Angiò, this somewhat distracted professor was a close friend of the noble Gaudentis, devoted to Maria Gloriosa. In respect of this Marian militia, Aligerno told Martino they had created a fascinating riddle that was worth remembering:

DIS MANIBUS
AELIA LAELIA CRISPIS
NEC VIR NEC MULIER NEC ANDROGYNA
NEC PUELLA NEC IUVENIS NEC ANUS
NEC CASTA NEC MERETRIX NEC PUDICA
SED OMNIA
SUBLATA
NEQUE FAME NEQUE FERRO NEQUE VELENO
SED OMNIBUS

117

NEC COELO NEC AQUIS NEC TERRIS
SED UBIQUE IACET
LUCIUS AGATHO PRISCUS
NEC MARITUS NEC AMATOR NEC NECESSARIUS
NEQUE MOERENS NEQUE GAUDIENS NEQUE
FLENS
HANC
NEC MOLEM NEC PYRAMIDEM NEC
SEPULCHRUM
SED OMNIA
SCIT ET NESCIT CUI POSUERIT
HAC EST SEPULCHRUM INTUS CADAVER NON
HABENS
HOC EST CADAVER SEPULCHRUM EXTRA NON
HABENS
SED CADAVER IDEM EST SEPULCHRUM SIBI

Martino translated:

To the Mani
Elia Lelia Crispi
neither man nor woman nor androgynous
neither child nor young woman nor old woman
neither untouched nor public nor reserved
but all
subject
not to hunger nor to the sword nor to poison
but to all
not in the sky nor in the waters nor on the lands
but everywhere she rests
Lucio Amato Antico
neither husband nor lover nor relative
neither sad nor happy nor crying

this composition
neither mountain nor pyramid nor tomb
but all
knows and knows not to whom it is dedicated.
This is a tomb that contains no corpse.
This is a corpse not contained in a tomb
but the very corpse is a tomb for itself.

When Martino repeated the riddle, the tutor explained that, as far as he knew, it was very old and had appeared in the writings of the poet Agazia di Mirino, who lived during the Byzantine Empire 954 years after the Library of Alexandria was built. The style reminded him of some epigrams worth hearing in the vernacular, since they would not appear in any exam to become a notary, but were still useful for anyone who wished to become a gentleman or lady.

"If you love do not beg, be reserved and raise your eyebrows with a benevolent look," recited Aligerno. "Those who are haughty are unworthy of esteem, as are those who complain. The best lover can move you with no loss of honour and convince you with no lack of respect." Glad to see that his student was attentive, the tutor continued: "The lover says: I do not like drinking wine; but when you want, taste it first then pass your cup to me and I will accept it. If you touch it with your lips I will not remain sober and I will not flee the delicate cup-bearer, nor will I avoid taking the cup that your kiss and the grace of your hands transmit to me."

Martino made no comment, but he was clearly interested in the topic of romance, for which reason Aligerno added "The slender Melita, though old, is as fascinating as in youth. Her cheeks still blush, her gaze is intense;

even though her years count above thirty, she has yet the grace of a child. From her I learned that time does not win the personality - "

"Who are the Mani?" Martino asked, after some deep reflection.

"Manes in Latin means benevolent; it refers to people who in harmony and unity wish to do good works beyond the limits imposed by bodily death. Agostino cites Apuleius when he writes in his work *The city of God* that the Mani are the souls of the dead who have acted for both good and bad. The Lari, on the other hand, are the souls of deceased family members, of whom only good deeds are remembered; ghosts though are the souls of the dead who have done much damage to themselves and others.

(Apuleius) dicit quidem et animas hominum daemones esse et ex hominibus fieri lares, si boni meriti sunt. Lemures si mali seu larvas. Manes autem deos dicit, si incertum est bonorum eos seu malorum esse meritorum. Agostino di Ippona scripsit. *De Civitate Dei*. IX,11."

Martino thought the inscription didn't concern him much since he could only remember good deeds that his predecessors had done, so it would mean doing extra studies just in gratitude and in honour of his family Lari. He still didn't understand how important it was to honour and respect even the Mani of every Genius Loci where you lived!

During that first winter in Bologna, Rebecca and Meb made friends with the washerwoman Sara, who introduced them to Aronne, a teacher of Hebrew. In return for three hours of lessons on Thursday afternoons, the mother and daughter would prepare two plaited loaves, to be delivered every Friday to Ruth, Aronne's wife. Ruth was busy looking after her husband, who was always absent-minded (or concentrating on his studies, as he said), their nine children and their youngest daughter, Tina.

For the first few weeks, Rebecca prepared two plaits, about a hand's breath and a half long, but as time went on and out of respect for the large family they were intended for, she lengthened them to amuse Meb, mindful of a fairy tale she'd heard as a child and which she told Tina one Friday noon.

"There was once a young woman who lived in a tall ivory tower built by her father," Meb told the little girl. "The girl could not play or study because she had to knead white flour and pure water to make bread, night and day. To avoid going crazy, the young soul learned to embrace her heart and live on the crest of the universe, writing what she saw while the dough was proving or while the loaves were baking in the oven. The universe was pleased with the service that the delicate girl rendered him, and replied by shining a ray of hope on her plaited hair one cold winter morning. The girl then kneaded three long, narrow loaves and plaited them, like she did every morning with her long hair. Without thinking any thoughts attributable to words, she threw the braid that she had kneaded but not baked out of the tower window, and looked down, curious to see what would happen. The dough was very elastic and stretched down to the grass, where a knight errant had stopped to rest his horse, which was grazing. The knight followed the strange elastic plait with his eyes, and looked up to see the young woman. He asked her to come down, and looking him straight in the eye, she told him to knock at the door and introduce himself to her father, if he wanted to. He did as she bade him. The father thought the arrival of the knight was a blessing, and suggested he marry his only daughter and become the heir to his vast estate. The knight agreed and the young woman proved to be compliant, and lived more hours of love than there were stones in the river Po, with the husband her father thought he had forced upon her."

Ruth was pleased with Meb's efforts because Tina had eaten up her food without making a fuss, and she'd enjoyed the fairytale herself too, relaxing a little as she listened to the story.

Meb came again the Friday after, as Ruth was feeding Tina, and offered to feed the infant for her. The offer was readily accepted by both mother and child, who found the baker's smiling face and fairy tales amusing.

With a wooden spoon and a bowl of chestnut polenta in her hand, Meb began her story: "There was once a little girl who lived next door to a large house. One day, finding the door open, she went inside."

Tina tried to grab the spoon, but Meb was quicker and handed her a bell instead that she always kept with her, and told her to tinkle the bell at every break in the story. Then she resumed:

"The girl's name was Bice. As she entered the house she asked permission to cross the threshold, calling out her name. There was no reply, and following the rule that says silence can be taken as assent, she entered. She closed the door behind her walked across the damp hallway and looked around the square courtyard. There was a smell of damp in the old courtyard where some maidenhair was growing. She saw chamomile and mint sprouting between some round cobbles that someone had brought from a nearby riverbed and arranged carefully on the ground in a white circle around the well. At the bottom of the courtyard was a staircase rising up to a wooden gallery, but Bice was attracted by the smell of porridge from an open door on the ground floor. The tempting smell reminded her it was time to eat, and she realised she was very hungry. She crossed the threshold into a large kitchen. The embers were still glowing in the fireplace and there were three steaming bowls of different sizes, set on the square table of heavy walnut. The biggest bowl was enormous and very hot; the second bowl was of medium size and seasoned with too much bay; the third was just the right size, the porridge was still warm and it had no peculiar seasoning.

She picked up a spoon - just like yours - and ate until her stomach was full. She took a long drink of water from the smallest cup and stood up, yawning. In the room next to the kitchen she found a bed that was too big and high for her, but at the back of the room, behind a beautiful embroidered curtain, there was a lovely wooden bed with a carved headboard and high sides. She lay down gladly and closed her eyes. She was dreaming about picking mint and chamomile when she heard a voice that was not part of the dream, and opened her eyes." Meb had finished feeding the little girl. She wiped the child's mouth as the child tinkled the bell and thought about the story, then helped her to drink and climb down from the high chair. When the child was on her feet, she allowed Meb to lead her by the hand into the next room, where there were cloths for nappy changes and a bed made up for her mid-day nap. She continued with the story.

"Bice opened her eyes and saw a strange cub looking down at her in amazement, with mama and papa bear

behind. She was afraid when she saw these enormous animals and didn't know what to do, so she just lay still."
Sitting on the carpet where she had just been changed, Tina noticed how Meb's eyes had widened when she saw a small statue of a bear on the floor, standing up on its hind legs as if to say hello. She picked it up and asked, "So mama papa baby? ...me baby."
"That's what mama, papa and little bear did. You're a baby; Bice thought the little bear was a bear cub, not a baby."
"Like baby - din-din, bye-bye" Tina insisted.
"Yes - din-din, bye-bye, mama, papa for the bears in the wood too," Meb continued, folding the cloths. "Bears in the woods are wild beasts, but these bears were special because they lived like people. In fact, even though Bice was frightened, they didn't do her any harm because they weren't wild, they were tame. They lived with the family that had built the big house; mama bear did the cooking, papa bear was the carter and the little bear played with the children to amuse them, and had good manners just like they did."
Wearing a clean nappy, Tina climbed into the cot, clutching the wooden bear in her little hands, and said, "Bice baby like me, here. Bear?"
"Mama bear put her paw on the cub's shoulder and pulled him back to show Bice there was nothing to be frightened of, so Bice got up and left, mumbling an apology and trying to get away as quickly as possible. Mama bear tried to make her understand that they could be friends; she held up her paw, just like your wooden bear. Bice understood the sign meant she should wait, so she stood still, her heart beating fast. Papa bear had gone out to the courtyard. The little bear sat and watched her

while mama bear went to the kitchen and came back with a shopping bag full of fruit, which she gave to her son, pointing at the little girl. The little bear took a fig and popped it in his mouth because he was a greedy bear; then he held the bag out to Bice, who took it and thanked him politely. Mama bear pulled the little bear towards her to leave the way open. Bice could go home with the shopping bag full of fruit. Better than going to the market! The moral of the story is: bears that behave like humans are better than humans who behave like bears!"

Tina was sleepy and had lain down on her side, but before closing her eyes she asked "what then?"

"Then they met again in the square and became good friends," whispered Meb, "now go bye-bye."

Ruth was in the kitchen, preparing food for the evening meal and the day after, so they parted without further ado.

The master was studying and didn't want to be disturbed. His sons were out working and would be back just before sunset. Martino was attending a lecture on jurisprudence. Rebecca and Aligerno had gone to a tailor to order new hoods and special wool for a riding cloak ordered by the noble Enrico, who had given Rebecca a design he had done for it in pen and elder ink on parchment.

Meb walked back slowly, passing between the outer walls of the dwellings that seemed like country farmhouses, although they were built within the ramparts, with no porticoes or shops on the street side. She admired the leafy branches of trees hanging over the garden walls and said hello a cynical black cat sitting on a doorstep.

She stopped to pick up a ripe pomegranate that had fallen from an overhanging branch. She tasted the sour seeds, trying not to stain the dress and cape of woven wool with threads of periwinkle blue that Susanna had given her the year before. An old fig tree still bore a few leaves that autumn had turned to gold.

The house of the Hebrew master stood between the ramparts and the Aposa river, near the tower of Via di Porta Nova.

The house where Martino was living with Aligerno's family was further to the south, leaning against the ramparts on the banks of the river that flowed down from the hill through the malpertuso, a small gap in the walls left open to allow passage from the village to the oak woods.

Meb would be back within a few minutes if she went straight there, but that day she decided to make a detour to the west and pay a visit to the church that the Franciscan friars were building next to the monastery, in a run-down area called "civitas antiqua rupta" in memory of the ancient muicipality that was broken up by clashes between the Byzantines and the Lombards about six hundred years before.

The church seemed immense to the little girl. She knelt reverently in a small chapel dedicated to Mary and her son Jesus, behind the high altar. Then she left by the same door near the apse where she had entered. She stopped beside some noblemen's graves to listen to a Dominican friar who was leading the prayers for a group of worshippers near the tower of Porta Nova. The air was growing cooler, so Meb decided to return by the road that passed through what was perhaps the most extensive walnut forest in Bologna. Some street vendors had been given permission to sell walnuts they gathered there beside the dirt road, but she had no money and so she continued on her way, lost in thought. On the border between the municipal walnut forest and the stables attached to their house, she encountered Martino, working with his tutors.

Convenevole said: "Hic oriendo fides surgit, quam sive relides aut ipsam rides, operum non robore fides. Martino, translate."

Martino: "Here faith rises, and whether you refuse it or deride it, you cannot count on the strength of the works alone."

Convenevole: "Spes hic sure boni firmatur quae rationi heret, dum fatur quod vera lege probatur."

Martino: "Here the sure hope of the good attached to reason is confirmed, affirming what is proven by the true law. Hi, Meb!"

Aligerno raised his right forefinger and placed it against his lips as a sign to his daughter not to answer. Meb raised her hand in greeting and sat with them, wrapping her woollen cloak more tightly around her and lowering her hood over her forehead against the damp chill of the afternoon.

Convenevole continued, undeterred: "Nascitur hinc carus qui fervet amor nec amarus est cuiquam certe, quia cunctos zelat aperte."

Martino: "Here are born charitable deeds, certainly not bitter for anyone, because it is intended to benefit all."

"What does the word cunctos remind you of?" Aligerno asked.

"The Edict of Thessalonica of 1133 Ab Urbe Condita. The emperors Gratian, Theodosius I and Valentinian II (who was nine years old) decreed that the Creed of the

Council of Nicea was normative. It was sanctioned that Rome and Alexandria in Egypt would be the two episcopal seats, with theology taking first place. Christianity was the official religion of the imperial territories; it prohibited pagan rituals and heresies such as that professed by Arius. 'Cunctos populos' means 'all peoples within the borders of the empire'."

"Good. I'm going now; until next Friday!" Convenevole bade them goodbye and set off toward to his lodgings with a chair-mender on a street lined with tall, shady ash trees that ran between the south-west walls and Porta Sant'Isaia.

"Aligerno, I'm confused," said Martino, walking along between Meb and his tutor; "it seems to me that the municipalities of Bologna, Prato and Florence are becoming firmer on corporate positions. They do not consider all the freemen with votes as being part of the people, and only select members of certain corporations as their representatives. Landowners and noblemen have no right to be elected and cannot propose laws. The serfs liberated by the Liber Paradisus seem to enjoy greater opportunities than those who are born free, at least in terms of being elected to public office."

"Political marginalisation is often caused by reinforcement of the strong powers that support those who desire better control," said the tutor. "Don't worry; it's better to serve in the shadows than to be sacrificed in the light of the sun. The important thing is to cultivate the spirit of service and the intent to benefit by personal deeds. If you are subjected to false accusations, know that it is useless to react; it is better to be silent and decline to respond to the offences, rather than utter words that may be easily misunderstood."

"Better to keep quiet and look stupid than remove any doubt by speaking!" Meb joked, to lighten the sombre mood a little. Martino gave her a shove and the two friends started running towards the house, where a cloud of smoke was issuing from the chimney on the red-tiled roofs to mingle with the purple and orange clouds of the cold winter sunset.

The following few months passed quietly in spite of the snow that fell, since there were lots of porticoes to shelter under when out walking.

Aligerno often said that Bologna was the ideal city for teachers of classics like himself, who preferred to walk as they reflected, rather than shut themselves inside a classroom where the smell of people grew nauseating.

In January Martino welcomed Marcolino, the son of a sister of the great traveller Marco Polo, into his quarters. The boy had come to Bologna to study to become a notary and assist with his family's mercantile business. The two students had met on a visit to the Order of Notaries building and had formed a friendship. Martino was happy to share his room with this extraordinary teller of stories about a world so far away that it seemed like a fantasy. One evening they were all in the kitchen with a fire in the grate, eating minestrone with cabbage, chard, boiled chestnuts, polenta and cheese. Aligerno drank red wine, Susanna and Meb an infusion of mallow or chamomile, and the boys hot milk with honey. Marcolino said, "my uncle wrote to my mother from Cathay, and told her the story that I'm about to tell you. In Chin Sai, which means 'city of heaven', there is much trade in spices like ginger, and grains such as rice. Silk is another common commodity there, but cotton, linen and hemp are rare. The fruit of the peach tree is fleshy, soft, sweet, delicate, very juicy and thirst-quenching; sometimes it's yellow and sometimes pinkish white. But the biggest difference between us and them is apparently their use of paper money."

"How can paper be used in place of forged precious metals?" asked Rebecca, whose family numbered many counters and lenders of money.

"We are accustomed to thinking that the purchasing power of coins should vary in proportion to the amount of precious metal they contain," explained Marcolino, "but the Great Khan, who rules over those lands, has established a fixed value for sheets of paper, which serve as money to facilitate trade, without fear of inflation."

"Didn't your uncle describe anything particularly weird and wonderful?" asked Meb, who was getting bored and wanted to change the subject.

"The mountains of Tibet are at war and the inhabitants insist on speaking only their language of origin, refusing to learn the language of the Tartar invaders," said Marcolino. "They make clothing out of tanned leather, and coarse carpets in highly odorous wool. Musk is considered very precious; they obtain it from the glands of animals that they call 'gudderi', which I cannot describe to you." Meb's imagination was appeased, and the young man resumed his narrative on the subject that Rebecca found interesting. "They accept neither paper money nor coins made of metal or glass, and only exchange their merchandise for salt, perhaps because they live a long way from the sea, and salt is needed for health, so it's precious.

My uncle wrote that these are bad people since they don't consider stealing and killing as crimes punishable by law, if the person who commits them is strong enough to be a threat to the judges," he concluded.

"So they fear neither the judgment of man nor the first judgment that every immortal soul must face when it takes its last breath?" asked Martino in amazement.

"No. It seems they don't even know that all souls rise again in the Final Judgment," replied the young man, adding that in the last letters that his Uncle Marco had sent, the Great Khan seemed intent on inviting Western tutors to teach them oriental astronomy and to learn about our moral philosophy.

AVE ATQUE VALE

Silvano stepped up his lessons in the spring, and Martino improved his relationship with Pegaso, who proved to be as sensitive as he was generous. At the end of May, Rebecca asked if she could move to Porretta, where there were said to be waters good for the health. Since the days of the Roman Empire, only those who had to work stayed in the heat of the city; women and children especially went to the hills to escape the epidemics that were more frequent between May and October. So Rebecca and Meb set off in mid June on a goods cart laden with trunks of clothes and manuscripts for study, and were welcomed by the Costas in Porretta, an arrangement that had been agreed in Bologna. On Friday 22nd July Rebecca and Meb took part in the feast of Mary Magdalene in the village, where Aligerno joined them in the early afternoon, riding a new bay horse that he'd bought, and Martino on Pegaso, a gift from Silvano to mark the end of the exams that he'd passed with flying colours.

The two riders were very hot when they arrived, and didn't want to join in the celebrations. Aligerno lifted Rebecca up into the saddle in front of him, and Martino did the same with Meb, obliging him to hold her close in order to reach the reins. On their way out of the village, they took the narrow Sassocardo gorge and stopped at the thermal springs to shake off the dust and sweat of travel on that sultry day.

Rebecca hung their cloaks on branches that dipped down to the stream, to shield herself and her daughter from the view of the men. Although she had been told not to do so, Meb took off her clothes and dived in, without checking if anyone was watching her. Martino was actually quite curious, but Aligerno commanded all his attention by talking, until the women reappeared dressed and with their wet hair piled up on their heads. The tutor and his pupil then left their own clothes and the stilettos and hunting knives they carried for defence with the women, and bathed in the thermal waters of the spring.

It was a splendid evening. Their host family had laid a table on the lawn between the house and the vegetable garden, protected by a stone wall, and invited the two visitors who were staying in the vicinity to join them too; an agreement had been struck between the various families that belonged to the same guest house. It was the custom of the guest house, and it established the convention of mutual assistance between the houses that were allied to it; visitors were thus not obliged to take lodgings and pay for their services, which might be problematic for horse riders since they did not habitually carry much money with them. Martino spent that night between 22nd and 23rd July of the year of the Lord 1323 under a bright starry sky, lying on the path inside the *hortus conclusus* of Fiorenzo Costa, a friend of Enrico Bellini's from his university days.

The student dreamed of becoming a notary in his second year of study, and of being betrothed to Meb by the end of August and celebrating their marriage in Oleggio, where he intended to build a new wing to the urban insula of Casa Bellini. There was already a portico on the square, and shops too; a two-storey residence and a stable on the free sides of the courtyard was all that had to be built, and they too would have a marital home!

A nightingale sang and he thought how similar these birds were to man. Like nightingales, we too can speak and change our language into thousands of idioms, perhaps to make the mothers of future generation fall in love. He pictured the nest the female nightingale had built among the bushes, and the young ones being fed by both parents, who were now preparing for a second brood.

It occurred to him that he should write to his father concerning his idea of building a new wing, or perhaps he should talk to Aligerno first, or to Meb the next morning? How, what, when and to whom? Only the why was clear. He closed his eyes and let himself drift off to sleep, lulled by the song of the nightingale.

Looking out of her window, Meb too was listening to the nightingale, and thinking how much she would like to be beside Martino, who was growing stronger and more eloquent every day!

Enrico and Susanna arrived in Porretta on the new moon of Tuesday 2nd August with the twins; Susanna and Rebecca had kept up a frequent correspondence during the months they had been apart, weaving maternal plots. Ulisse, one of Ginevra and Fiorenzo Costa's eight children, was almost nine years old, and his even-tempered nature found in Margherita an alter ego that was perfect for playing ball games in the garden. Clemenza chose Rebecca as her female companion because she preferred the company of adults, asking questions and questioning answers. Ginevra gave each of the children a piece of amber, telling them it was good for the health to hold the resin in your hand and smooth it around your neck to help energy to circulate. Clemenza thanked her for the gift and put it inside the velvet bag where she kept her other strange and precious items, confiding to Rebecca that she wanted to see what happened to the others before doing as she was told. Martino and Meb celebrated the arrival of the family from Oleggio by holding hands and looking up at the stars in the night sky. On Wednesday 10th August, the first quarter of the crescent moon did not disturb a spectacle of shooting stars, and they both entrusted them with their hopes in the form of vague desires and dreams. "Malum est imperitia rerum," whispered Meb, gazing into deep space, "but inexperienced in life as we are, how can we avoid making mistakes?"

"Errare humanum est," Martino reassured her, in a low voice "persevere no: I suppose the secret is to learn by experience."

"...in conjunction with tradition? ...or one-to-one, deciding just between ourselves?" said Meb, shifting her gaze from the sky to look into her friend's eyes, who felt butterflies fluttering in his stomach and his knees turn to jelly, as well as a sudden urge to sneeze that dissipated much of the tension of the moment that was in other respects romantic.

"At...choo! Sorry, Meb, I'm not cold. You have this effect on me."

"What - I make you sneeze?!"

"Yes. I don't know why, but sometimes you make me sneeze; it's as if you infuse the air with some indefinable aroma that makes my nose itch and my eyes water."

"I'm sorry," said Meb, irritated, thinking that Martino's aroma by contrast made her feel secure and euphoric; "maybe it's better if you move away from me."

"No. I'm fine next to you. In fact, I think if we were to move even closer, I would stop sneezing. It never

happens when we're riding together, but if I hold you in my arms...have you noticed?"
"You're a good knight."
"You're my lady."
It's not a game.
I'm not joking.

On Wednesday 17th August, the moon was shining at the height of its splendour and the two youngsters embraced, their lips brushing each other's lightly, before a joyful band of friends broke them up to join them in a country dance around an old oak tree on the crest of the hill.

On Wednesday 24th August their betrothal was announced, and on Thursday 8th September the families of the betrothed organised a feast on the meadow near the springs. There was spelt bread, hard-boiled eggs and slices of roast turkey; sheep's and goat's cheese, cherries, plums, white grapes and apricots from the Romagna valley afterwards, and water and wine to drink. The children chewed clover stems and chased each other around, rolling down the slope under the watchful eyes of mothers and nurses. Some fawns gambolling in the meadow stopping to watch the scene, then disappeared into the unspoilt woods that stretched towards the Apennines, colder and more inhospitable than the beautiful Alps and the enchanting Dolomites, where Susanna dreamed of returning along the Amber Road.
Following tradition, Martino had gathered daisies and chamomile flowers at dawn, and Verde and Balsamina had woven them into a garland that now adorned the

long plait that Meb wore wound around her head, radiant with joy.

At the moment they signed the engagement contract, Susanna gave her son an amber ring, which the young man slipped onto the middle of the right hand of his betrothed.

The two youngsters were then subjected to various jokes, and above all kept apart. The oldest of their friends took Martino prisoner. They confiscated his weapons, and thus disarmed had to defend himself with his fists against Giovan Battista Costa, the son of Ginevra and Fiorenzo, a boy the same age as himself. When he was knocked down for the third time and declared himself defeated, Martino was forced to walk under some brooms, which were called with great ceremony "caudine forks". Margherita watched this ill-treatment of her elder brother attentively, and tried to make out the sense of what was happening and why nobody was putting a stop to such barbarity. She asked everyone around her what passing under the "caudine forks" meant.

"400 years after Rome was founded," replied Ulisse Costa, "the Romans waged a war against the Samnites who lived in the mountains of Hirpinia. The Samnites won, and took the Roman army prisoner. After long negotiations, the Roman government gave back the Samnites hostages that they'd taken in battle, and received their own soldiers in exchange, who before returning had to walk under a beam, half naked and without their weapons. Those who showed themselves to be arrogant were killed. On their return to Rome, each defeated soldier was locked in his house and all the citizens mourned; the shops remained closed and activities at the forum were suspended. In the government, Marcus Valerius Corvus proclaimed Quintus Publilius Philo and Lucius Papirius Cursor as consuls, both of them military commanders."

"So Martino is treated like a defeated soldier because your brother Gio Batta beat him in a fight? But it's all a joke. If someone wanted to hurt him you would step in to defend him, wouldn't you?" the little girl asked her new friend. "Yes," said Ulisse, twirling the piece of amber his mother had given him between his fingers. "I too will soon be ready to fight; for my family and for our allies." His elder sister Elisabetta was standing next to them; she interrupted their conversation to invite them to take part in the sack race that was about to start in the main street.

The party ended in the middle of the afternoon and the carts carrying the women, children and trunks departed, accompanied by the riders equally divided between the front and the rear, all armed. At nightfall, the sight of will-o-the-wisps in the undergrowth of the chestnut woods provoked tales of horror from the cart drivers.

One said will-o-the-wisps were the condemned souls of black Guelphs and white Guelphs, another that they were the souls of children who had died before they were baptised. Both produced the effect of terrorising Margherita and Clemenza, who didn't stop crying until they were at Luisa Rava's house with bowls of warm milk in front them, sweetened with honey from the family hives. When Luisa found out it was the twins' birthday as well as the engagement, she gave them two little dolls wearing dresses embroidered with blue and purple thread. The carts and the men on horseback were staying at Vergato's inn, so the next morning Meb had time to play with the girls before they set off for Bologna again. She was terribly disappointed to discover she wouldn't see Martino again until the following autumn. But both sets of the parents were in agreement: she should return to Oleggio to make the necessary preparations, while the student would finish his studies and become a notary as soon as possible. Before he would allow his son to leave, Enrico explained to him how important it was that he learn to translate documents written in the Latin into the vernacular, because the Guild of Notaries required this skill in order to confer the degree and consequently the authority to practise the profession of notary.

"Convenevole will be replaced by Pietro Boattieri, the professor of Rhetoric, from November," explained his father. "Pietro contributed to compiling the Statutes of the Profession of Notaries, in MCCCIV Anno Domini. He will prepare you for the exam you will take in front of Giovanni di Bonandrea, who represents the committee that selects those who will accede to the Chancellery of Bologna, and he also awards degrees to external professionals like you, who will take the exam to become a Visconti notary so that you can practise in the territories controlled by our ruling family. Remember to practise writing from dictation; it's essential."

During the course of the academic year, Martino often went to the square in front of the church of San Francesco to hear Giovanni del Virgilio and Bartolino Benincasa, who ran a study group that would become well-known for attempting to modernise whilst retaining tradition values. At these meetings he met brothers Francesco and Gherardo Petrarca and a friend of theirs who was inseparable from them, Guido Sette, who wrote poems in the new style known as "dolce".

A meeting with Hebrew professor Aronne Nahmiel was also instructive for Martino. He introduced himself as Meb's fiancé and Ruth welcomed him in, offering him a cup of water and inviting him to sit at the kitchen table where she was working. Hearing mention of Meb's name, Tina insisted on sitting next to the young man to eat, bombarding him with questions as well as with her mush made with chicken and vegetables. After feeding the child, Ruth brought Martino a basin of water to wash his hands and a towel made of hemp cloth that Meb had given her before she left. She then told him he to go and knock on the door at the bottom of the courtyard, where the professor was studying.

Martin knocked but got no answer, and tried three more times without success. At his fourth knock the door opened and the professor appeared, looked him up and down and asked him if it was Stefanòs Beleni's "nèched". The student's heart skipped a beat when he heard his grandfather's name, which he had never known, and replied that he was his grandson, son of Enrico, son of Signor Bellini. "Good," said the professor "Martino, son of Enrico, son of Stefanòs of the House of Bellini of Oleggio. Enter."

Over the following months Martino learned to ask many questions about how consonants were written and how they should be pronounced. It amused him to hear that the teacher considered vowels sometimes as young, sometimes adolescent and therefore selfish, and sometimes old or veteran, when they didn't change their behaviour whatever happened around them. He learned to meditate on the visible and invisible components of dynamic bodies in time and space. He was fascinated by the origin of words, as if they were dragon's eggs or hazelnuts, full of mysterious plant essences. Martino would bring a basket of fruit for Ruth by noon every Friday and after three months he was invited to stay for dinner with the family.

The table was laid with a hemp tablecloth decorated with rust designs made with wooden stamps, in the tradition of some hill towns in Romagna. There were two white ceramic jugs of water and two pewter jugs of red wine; two plaited loaves covered with a clean napkin, and in each place two cups, a flat plate for vegetables, a deep plate for soup and cutlery like the ones they used for stately banquets. The father's place at the head of the table was distinguished by a wine goblet, engraved around its circular edge. Observing it, Martino recalled the relationship between a circumference of 22 units and the diameter, which is 7 units. With regard to various units of measurement, Martino reflected how every place used its own systems: in Oleggio they used the merico; in Val Seriana the gromo; in Florence the arm in architecture and thumbs, feet and palms for smaller things. The young man thought that studying the Hebrew alphabet was an opportunity to contemplate how many norms were in accordance, and it pleased him as a notary, who appreciated order and the keeping of valuable memories.

Before sitting down at the table, everyone washed their hands in a terracotta basin on the kitchen worktop. There were clean hemp rags on the selenite top beside the fireplace in which the embers were still glowing. Ruth lit two beeswax candles before the sun went down, and the scent from them added a sweet note to the appetising aroma of the food. Aronne recited the evening blessing, and when the diners made the toast, the nobleman dedicated the dinner to Meb. He raised his own goblet and joined in the toast, without speaking.

The next day was Saturday, and Martino went on a visit to Padua with some friends. The young Bellini rode on Pegaso, while the Petrarca brothers and Sette travelled on a goods cart, with their trunks containing clothes and study texts and a few barrels of wine belonging to the carter. On the way the students discussed the fate of Ezzelino, who committed suicide after suffering a military defeat on the banks of the river Adda. There was one school that argued every sinner could avoid going to Hell if he repented, according to the doctrine of indulgences. Was it therefore possible that a tyrannical monster like Ezzelino could end up in Purgatory?

If this were the case then the living would be able to shorten their suffering through prayer, pilgrimages and pious offerings permitted by the Church of Rome, such as took place on the occasion of the Jubilee celebrated in MCCC Anno Domini, for example. Many were convinced that even wicked deeds were part of the higher divine plan, but the Curia, the Senate and the people of Padua had decided to support a different theory. On 3rd December 1315, Alberto Mussato presented his tragedy *Ecerinis* in the City, in the presence of bishop Pagano della Torre and Alberto di Sassonia, Rector of the University of Padua. The work upheld the theory that Ezzelino was the son of Lucifer and that the application of divine law required him to return to his natural home, which was hell. Law and

Rights were in fact in agreement that children and parents were destined to be reunited according to the harmony of bloodlines, which was inviolable under the will of the Creator. The Senate and representatives of the people of Padua had conferred the poet's garland made of laurel twigs intertwined with ivy on the author of the tragedy. The performance also deserved to be given wide appeal, as it served as a warning against Cangrande della Scala of Verona, who was belligerent towards the Veneto region. On 21st December 1317, following a performance of the tragedy, there appeared a commentary to the detriment of the City of Padua, written by Guizzardo of Bologna and Castellano di Bassano, professors of grammar. Francesco Petrarca and the other students travelling in the cart knew the tragedy was due to be performed again in December that year, and were thrilled at the thought of being able to hear the whole work, convinced they had a lot to learn in terms of both ethical content and oratory style. Martino listened to their conversation and was enchanted by the beauty of the landscape. A view of some unusual pointed hills emerged through the Ferrara mists, covered in dense, dark vegetation; neat rows of vines with yellow, purple and orange leaves stood guard across the valley of the Bacchiglione river. They crossed a stone bridge beside the river port, buzzing with the activity of unloading fish; the Petrarca brothers and Sette paid the carter, who stopped at the inn to sell his barrels of wine. The students continued on foot and Martino joined them, leading Pegaso as far as Lago della Costa. Leaving the horse at the water trough, they approached the ancient thermal basin. Martino recognised a small frog as what his grandfather used to call a najas marina and imagined that if Francis kissed it, it would turn into a maiden deserving of the dreamer's love. Amongst the vegetation he was intrigued to discover dense marsh reeds, narrow fishbones and thick marsh grasses, as well as waving rushes and hemp of the aquatic type, which he had only seen in drawings in his grandfather's archive.

Leaving their clothes beside Pegaso, the friends dived naked into the warm waters, which was refreshing after their journey and beneficial to the seasonal chills they'd been suffering from for a few weeks.

Towards evening they climbed halfway up the banks, breathing in deeply and glad to hear that the brackish waters had had such an immediate effect. They walked past the ruins of the castle, which had been destroyed during some conflict the previous year, and were welcomed as guests at the House of Contarini. The patricians were in Venice, engaged in the secular gatherings of autumn and winter, but before leaving they had left the farmer with a list of noble persons to whom they could extend hospitality. The nobles of Familia Contarini would be returning to the hills in late spring, but only if no raids were expected by armed gangs.

Francesco was very pleased with the village; he was partial to red dates and said he'd never seen so many of his favourite fruit trees as there were in the village of Arquà, and would love to live there. Martino left three days later, bidding goodbye to the three students whose intellects were too poetic for his taste.

Martino slept with Pegaso in the barn at the Battaglia sul Canale inn, near the river port. He was not in the mood for the commotion and mirth of the patrons, and was displeased with the insolence of the maid who served him at table with a mischievous grin, inviting him to drink wine that was not watered down.

"If you do it, I will too," the girl had proposed, with a smile that revealed rotten teeth. The new wine went well with the pumpkin and boiled chestnuts, but the nobleman didn't trust her outmoded approach and replied that it was better not to do to others what you would not want done to yourself. ...or that you wouldn't want to suffer, he added, with a severe glance at the young woman, who told him to go to the landlady to pay and informed him that water would cost him more than wine, according to Venetian tradition.

Relaxed and happy with his decision, Martino slept peacefully on the litter with Pegaso, who moved up close to him contentedly.

When he returned to Bologna, lectures on becoming a notary assumed a steady pace, allowing him no time for any amusement other than looking after Pegaso, exercising him and going out for walks every other day.

Martino listened to his subject teachers and took notes on wax tablets with a metal stylus, which he carefully transcribed in his independent study hours then refreshed the tablets by melting them and spreading more wax on top.

He had an agreement with two other students to meet up on Wednesday afternoons to repeat what they had learned out loud, each of them pretending to teach the others what he had learned when it came to his turn.

He was so focused on his studies that in February he realised he was chanting the regulations for notaries in the morning whilst he was washing.

He often went to the tavern to eat with other students from the Student Nation to which he belonged. He willingly shared food and drink with some external students from the Natio Germanorum too. As this was the most numerous of the University Nations, it was subdivided into subnationes so that Portuguese, Spanish, Provençal, French, English, Bavarian, Dutch, Flemish, Belgian, Polish, Lithuanian, Hungarian, Serbian, Ukrainian, Romanian, Czech, Slovak, Slovenian, Croatian, Austrian and Bavarian students could be represented and engage in dialogue with tutors and the city.

The Latin language was studied by all, and to obtain his degree every student had to demonstrate that he could translate both the letter and the meaning of texts in his own subject, whether that was medicine or law.

Marcolino left for Venice in February to take part in a masked ball organised by a merchant famous for having very attractive and well-endowed daughters.

Martino was awarded his degree in the profession of Visconti notary at 10.45 in the forenoon of Monday 19th March of the year 1324 AD, in Bologna.

The new graduate celebrated with his friends at the House of Ghisilieri, built on the river Aposa, near the ancient circle of selenite walls. Silvano gave him a gift of 49 bolognini coins, and Aligerno sent him a scarf made of soft white wool that Meb had embroidered with a three-strand plait in gold thread in the form of a shield bearing the House of Bellini bear's paw. On presenting Meb's gift to Martino, Aligerno expressed a wish that love would flow for them like the Aposa from Felsina: from mother to daughter, not common women but women from the Province. Entering the porticoed courtyard, the guests and hosts went upstairs to the hall designed for social gatherings with allied families.

Gherardo Ghisilieri entertained the guests on the third book of *De Architectura* by Vitruvius, inviting Martino to be his model. "Lie down, Messer Notaro, here in the middle of the hall," said the jurist, his tone somewhere between serious and jocular. The graduate obeyed, mindful of stories he'd heard about the customs of the Gaudenti knights, and accepted his forthcoming humiliation with forbearance.

"Good. Now, lying on your back, put your arms up against the sides of your head and cross them to form a perfect X. Now spread your legs, as if you were about to be crucified on the cross of St. Andrew."

Martino sighed and obeyed, depending on the good heart of his father's friend.

"Antonia, bring rope and chalk. Tomaso, blindfold the eyes of the Visconti notary lying here," Gherardo commanded. "To demonstrate the truth of the classical tradition, Grandfather Lippo will proceed with the experiment."

Grandfather Ghisilieri held one end of the rope above Martin's navel, tying a knot in it and securing it to Martino's robes with an ivory brooch in the shape of a dragon with rubies for eyes.

"Delphicus Apollo Socratem omnium sapientissimum Pythiae responsis est professus. Autem memoratur prudenter doctissimeque dixisse, opotuisse hominum pectora fenestrata et aperta esse, uti non hoccultos haberent sensus sed patentes ad considerandum. Utinam vero rerum natura sententiam eius secuta explicata et apparentia ea constituisset."

Little Antonia walked around him clockwise, drawing a chalk circle that started from the tip of Martino's left hand; then stopped, leaving a compass on the ground, and sat down beside her mother.

Gherardo continued, explaining the proportions of the human body according to the writings of the architect Marcus Vitruvius Pollio. He recited, "...item corporis centrum medium naturaliter est umbilicus. Inamque si homo conlocatus fuerit supinus manibus et pedibus pansis circinique conlocatum centrum in umbilico eius, circumagendo rotundationem utrarumque manuum et pedum digiti linea tangentur." He then turned to Martino. "Your hands and feet are touching a circle that circumscribes you; thus, becoming a Visconti notary circumscribes your range of activity. To complete the system of multiple loyalties that determines harmony in the universe, now extend your arms and bring them down on the outside. Keep still in this position."

Addressing the son of his son, he said, "Tomaso, draws a square such that the sides are touching the top of Martino's head, his hands and his feet. As it is written: non minus quemadmodum schema rotundationis in corpore efficitur, item quadrata designatio in eo invenietur. Nam si a pedibus imis ad summum caput mensum erit eaque mensura relata fuerit ad manus pansas, invenietur eadem latitudo uti altitudo, quemadmodum areae quae ad normam sunt quadratae".

While his initiation was taking place, Martino imagined Meb was with him and felt he was ready to live in the world, though he didn't belong to it.

Antonia smiled as she removed his blindfold, and Tomaso handed Martino a parchment.

The sheet was drawn with an idealised human figure without sexual organs, neutral like the noun *homo* of the neutral gender: the Human Being is selected as the unit of measure in the planning of roads, durable constructions, temporary buildings, and public and private services; even including ships and carts: the humanised universe according to Greco-Roman tradition.

Animal rearing and agriculture, on the other hand, were specialist subjects, to be analysed depending on the place and the work to be done. But Martino knew this already, as he knew the importance of the *genius loci*, the vital essence that makes every locality suitable only for certain purposes and excludes all others.

For example, in the case of a funereal *genius loci* it is appropriate to avoid building houses and work places there, since a place inhabited by the souls of the dead is not healthy for those who are not of their direct line, by blood, law and right, that is. Tradition taught that territorial issues and wars are started by the fault of those who control the law, bending it to suit their own superficial thirst for power. When the law is respected, however, harmony will prevail.

There were also two sons of Aimo degli Equi among the guests; skilled flautists who played a merry tune to accompany a dance in the form of a one-way labyrinth.

The young guests were happy moving in the pattern of the old dance, and had fun weaving coloured ribbons that tied up the guest of honour at the end of the dance.

Grandmother Ghisilieri went up to Martino, standing immobile with the woven ribbons of green, white, red and blue wrapped around him clockwise from neck to thigh. The new practitioner kept his eyes on the coffered ceiling, patiently tracing the vine tendrils painted on it.

"Novello Sebastiano," pronounced the elderly lady, turning anti-clockwise around him, holding the ends of the ribbons in her left hand "may the flame of faithful love illuminate your testimony. May the water of friendship quench your thirst and that of those from whom you wish to benefit. By virtue of true faith, I release you."

Freed from his sentimental bonds represented by the allegorical colours, Martino hoped the ceremony was now over, but grandfather Ghisilieri motioned him to kneel down where he stood, so he obeyed, his heart pounding.

Martino knew that the custom of investing new knights by dubbing them on the shoulders with a sword and presenting them with a gift of iron, silver or gold spurs was taking hold in Bologna. It was a questionable but no doubt spectacular custom from across the Alps.

"Knight Martino," said the noble Giulio Azzoguidi, "I do not carry a sword and you will receive no gift of spurs from me, since our lineages were destined for another."

Antonia gave Giulio what looked to Martino like a folded blanket, and whilst acknowledging he had no idea what he would do with a pair of spurs, he was nonetheless disappointed.

Giulio opened the bundle and placed a cloak of pure white around his friend's broad shoulders, with a hood that fell softly down his back. The women sighed; it was beautiful.

Some of the men were astonished by the pure whiteness of it, but the knight understood the honour and the burden of the challenge of San Martino, which he accepted with his right knee on the ground and with his left leg bent as if to rise, bowing his head and kissing the hands of his godfather.

Then an Augustinian friar from the monastery of San Giacomo took the place of the godfather and anointed Martin's forehead, chest and hands, uttering the benediction, to which the young man replied:

"And with your spirit."

"Rise and be merciful," said the priest, "according to the laws of faith, hope and charity. For Christ our Lord and for his mother Mary, conceived by Joachim and Anna without stain of sin. God willing, blessed is He throughout all generations."

After the ceremony, everyone embraced the young knight and kissed him fraternally on the cheeks. Aronne Nahmiel came up to greet him, and Martino shook his hand warmly, saying in a low voice: "Master, if I were a shepherd I would give you a lamb, and if I were wise I would make the crown shine. But I'm just a man: gratias tibi ago". The Hebrew teacher replied, "if I were religious I would go to Jerusalem, but I'm just a student and I shall stay in Modiin to ask for information."

Like other people in the room, Martino had studied with Aronne the theses of Levi ben Gershom ben Solomon Catalan on the theory of grace and acquired intellect, written to unite the Jewish system of Maimonides with the Aristotelian thought of Averroes. In this context many were convinced that the relationship between birth and the constellations allowed the exercise of free will, without preclusion. They were convinced that divine knowledge of the possible choices an individual can make does not imply knowledge of which choice a person will make in practice. In the opinion of that cultural circle, even though the movements of the planets and genetics may affect our nature, every human being remains free to decide which path to take and is therefore responsible for his own actions. Among other things, these humanists considered it inappropriate to say take leave by saying "addio" since no living person can be sure the encounter will not be repeated. Therefore, when taking leave they shook each other by the right hand and bade each other "ad maiora!"

Stepping out into the night on Via Val d'Aposat, Martino set off alone, and arriving at the end of the portico he looked up to the heavens, still thinking about the mystery of creation and personal freedom.

Aligerno and Rebecca had lingered to walk back with Aronne; Ruth had stayed at home. By the time they arrived the sky was starting to get light beyond the eastern towers of the walled city. The almond tree in the vegetable garden was in bloom and the married couple were full of gratitude for the wonder that every new spring brought with it.

Silvano spent the next day looking after Pegaso and exercising him, knowing that Martino would be in dreamland longer than usual. Rebecca had gone to the herb market with a friend, so Aligerno invited Silvano to take a walk with him to see the Ark of San Domenico. As they walked along together they discovered they had many affinities and many differences of opinion, but above all a sincerity that ensured mutual esteem.

"The problem is to be and not to be," said Silvano.

"To be cannot be the problem" Aligerno protested. " Io ero and sarò - am and will be, tu eri and sarai - were and will be, egli era e sarà - he was and will be, noi eravamo e saremo - we were and will be, voi eravate e sarete - you were and will be, essi erano e saranno - they were and will be. Now-here is no-where, as an Englishman would say."

"For me, lei is a daughter and not a son; I am a son and I am not a daughter" explained the tutor. "Every relationship changes depending on expectations, and that's the problem."

"A matter of identity? ...or gender?" Aligerno wondered.

"Identity depends on the activity," replied Silvano. Identification with a gender should imply possibilities and not preclusions, don't you agree?"

Aligerno explained earnestly; "I think you have to be betrothed to become masculine or feminine. As with all covenants, individual ability to give and receive trust must be put to the test."

But Silvano replied, "I'm not referring to the level of adult relationships. I mean on a spiritual level. The problem is managing multiple loyalties and the free will to exist, according to a rightly-formed awareness of the common good ".

Aligerno said, "I don't think there are any gender differences, for a tutor."

"For a riding instructor, gender differences are essential," Silvano said in a peremptory tone, and went on, changing the subject: "perhaps I'm just treating scars that are still bleeding... but even here I think there's a big scar, in the location of the little church dedicated to San Nicolò delle Vigne!"

"Domenico di Guzman died here in Bologna on 6th August 1221, in his monastery," Aligerno explained. "The body was initially laid in the altar of the church of San Nicolò delle Vigne, adjacent to the monastery. But it was put in a cypress wood coffin in 1233, when construction of a basilica was begun to replace the church. Since Domenico was canonised by Pope Gregory IX, the number of visits has increased steadily. To the delight of pilgrims, the sarcophagus was lifted and decorated by Nicola Pisano, Arnolfo di Cambio, Lapo, Donato and the Dominican lay-brother Guglielmo da Pisa."

The two friends fell silent as they entered the consecrated place and went to pay homage at the tomb of the illustrious theologian. Aligerno gave Silvanus a rosary made from rosewood and taught him how to recite it; a Marian devotion that the riding instructor observed for the rest of his life.

"I met Arnolfo in Florence, when I visited the site of the Palazzo della Signoria," Aligerno recalled. "He'd made a model of the basilica of Santa Maria del Fiore in wood: a splendid project of rare geometric precision. His statue of the Crowned Madonna was also commendable: the woman sits looking upwards, her back and neck well supported, without any rigidity. The child sits on a small chair, leaning against his mother's left leg; in his left hand he holds a rolled-up manuscript against his leg, and his right hand is held up in benediction. His mother is supporting him so he doesn't lose his balance. A non-hieratic work; I remember it as an example of classical dignity, softened by delicate feelings, typical of people who are devoted to Mary. Here in the Ark of San Domenico, the style of the master Nicola Pisano is more apparent."

After their pious visit they proceeded to Piazza Maggiore.

"San Domenico was involved in Cumania, the region of Europe that extends from the Danube river to the Carpathian mountains and was invaded by nomadic

Mongols in 1237," said Aligerno, to bring the dialogue back to a subject useful for gathering information.

Silvano understood, and added the story of Bologna to their agenda. "Enrico and Susanna became attached to the Cumans who arrived as refugees on the banks of the Tiber, and were welcomed in that part of Pannonia by the Hungarians, who were the dominant group at the time."

"Susanna's maternal family has Tatar and Jewish ancestors, who were tradespeople on the Amber Road, in the crown lands of Santo Stefano. They probably developed trading relationships with their Cuman customers."

"Susanna's aptitude for learning languages is one of the qualities I admire most in her," Silvano remarked, and went on, "will you come with me to the monastery of Santo Stefano? I'd like to offer you a bottle of the friars' digestive liqueur, which is made with 23 different herbs left to steep in pure alcohol for two weeks, then diluted with boiling water."

"Certainly, but first I want to offer you pasta and beans at the Lamma inn, where teachers and students take their meals!"

After eating and drinking well, the two men were convinced they could trust each other, and in the afternoon they made arrangements to meet up in Oleggio before November was over and took leave of each other as good friends.

THE RETURN

Martino went ahead on Pegaso, while Aligerno travelled with Rebecca and the trunks, paying for their passage on a goods cart.

The young knight stopped at watering places, the stops becoming more frequent as the season grew sultrier.

He didn't take any diversion via the hills as he knew he had some diplomatic missions to fulfil before he could go home. He ascended Via Consolare Emilia to where it crossed the Consolare Postumia, and stayed for three weeks in Cremona, which had been under the control of Galeazzo I Visconti for two years. As the guest of Suardino, a boy his own age from Casa Suardo, Martino was fascinated by the quantity of works planned by the Viscontis for the common good; the digging of the Dugale Delmona canal and the many other irrigation canals in the agricultural territory reminded him of his beloved Piedmont hills and the canals to drain off the rainwater that his family had always helped to keep clean.

In the city he visited the Loggia dei Militi, the bell tower of the Torrazzo and the construction site for the transept in the episcopal cathedral.

He abstained from entering the church of Saint Francis as he did not share the oratory style of these preachers.

Instead he went to meditate at the tomb of St. Omobono, the first layman in the history of the Church considered worthy of being canonised. Pope Innocent III had defined him as a *pacificus vir* less than two years after his death, in the papal bull *Quia pietas* of 13th January 1199.

Suardino and his brother Orichino had an excellent relationship with Casa Visconti and with Ludovico di Baviera, so the Cremona residence was the venue for useful meetings of the notary profession to which of Martino belonged; he was put to the test when they asked him to draft of some deeds in Val Brembana and at Romano, a Lombard castra belonging to the Diocese of Cremona.

It was displeasing to Martino to find that the casa Visconti was inclined to support the expansionist aims of the Republic of Venice; he felt this would reduce the freedoms of the Alpine cities and castles as far as the sources of the Serio and Tranquillo rivers, territories ruled by houses bound to his own by indissoluble alliances. He did not take part in any of the numerous hunting trips with falconers and dogs since they were organised during the breeding season, which was forbidden both by tradition and by logic, as it is dangerous for hunters to kill adults and their newborn young.

The young notary rode along the canals of the river Po river in the early hours of the morning, when the air was still fresh; around eleven o'clock he returned, stopping to clean Pegaso and give him a good feed of hay and oats before letting him graze on grass inside the enclosure with the other stallions. Then he went on foot to the lute-makers' street, where expert craftsmen were making and repairing complex musical instruments using various types of well-seasoned wood. He had paid a coin in advance to have an instrument made that was "lauto", or magnificent in tone and handsome to look at, to present to Meb as a wedding gift. The coin that Martino paid to commence production of the lute had been coined by the mint of Cremona, and the notary reflected that it would have been auspicious to adopt a unique paper currency in the future, as they had apparently done in the Far East. One day, the lute maker invited his young customer to eat with him at the Bissone inn, where they enjoyed an excellent onion omelette and a white sweet called torrone, or nougat. It was made from chopped almonds and hazelnuts mixed with honey and egg whites and whipped with a fork; it thrilled Martino's taste buds, he had never before tasted such a delicacy.

In May, on a visit to see how much work had been done on the lute, he met a scholar from the Babylonian Talmud who astonished him with the depth of his analysis and how he associated numerical values from one to four hundred with the twenty-two consonants; values that made it possible to translate the text of the Bible mathematically.

When the lute was ready, Martin collected it and set off for Genoa on Pegaso, with a few pieces of nougat in his bag, following the road that the consul Postumio Albino had ordered to be built 605 years after the founding of Rome. As he was walking along the Via Consolare built 1372 years earlier, Martino remembered his grandfather Bellini telling him that the Ginami family of the upper Val Seriana were military surveyors, experts in the construction of imperial roads using stakes and an instrument called a groma for drawing right-angles on the ground. The architect-surveyor marked points on the ground and traced reference lines. He thus constructed a grid for the roadway; where the *libratores* dug pits, to a depth of six metres. Each pit was filled with layers of materials that varied in thickness and consistency, to ensure good discharge of rainwater. The young knight also recalled that the Ginamis had given their castle on the river Serio the name Gromo, where they forged blades for special swords in fire and icy water; swords that he now understood could be extremely useful. The small number of swords they made were not intended for use by the infantry nor horsemen, but for surveyors, who used these excellent blades to mark reference lines in the ground, and only to defend themselves in the event of extreme necessity. As he rode along, Martino imagined that the Ginamis, the Bellinis, the Spinolas and the D'Orias became allies during the building of the consular roads that linked Genoa to the Alps, connecting the Italian peninsula with the rest of the continent of Europe and the Amber Road. Satisfied with the idea that the old houses faithful to the ideal of the Res Publica had for many centuries preferred the *Roman pax* techniques to warlike enterprises, he started trotting, giving Pegaso the opportunity to observe the surrounding landscape as far as the Nure river, where the cultivated plains of the Po Valley gave way to green hills and the steep Ligurian Apennines. At Ponte Albarola, Martino lodged at a guest house belonging to the Augustinian friars of the church of San Giacomo, in the churchyard of which was a large market of olive oil for both for the table and for lamp fuel; he also found linen, soap from Marseilles, honey, cheese, beans, salt, cedar, lemons and bitter oranges for sale. There he met with Giuseppe Celesia, an apothecary from the Casa Bellini, and some Genoese, allies of the Spinolas. With his diplomatic mission complete, Celesia returned to Oleggio, while Martino was invited by Lancillotto Anguissola to the castle he'd purchased in 1323 from Oberto Del Cairo for 5,600 lire. Pegaso was accommodated in the wing set aside for stallions of the main stable, inside the triangular courtyard, while the knight visited the chemin de ronde, a semicircular tower and the two square towers at the top of the isosceles triangle surrounded by a moat. Martino admired the strategic position and defensive structure of the castle, including the south-east entrance protected by a heavy drawbridge and portcullis. The captain of the guard showed him an auditorium on the first floor, where the young man sat whilst waiting to meet Lancillotto, who was apparently ill-fitted for diplomacy and especially eager to recite the verses he composed himself in the "dolce stil novo" style favoured by the students with whom Martino had visited the Euganean Hills near Padua.

Lancillotto had a melancholy nature; he tried to involve Martin in the study of madrigals - polyphonic rhymes to be sung in the vernacular, which Bellini did not like.

On Saturday 7th July 1324 AD, they dined together in the vast courtyard of the castle, listening to a bard singing of the heroic but unfortunate enterprises of the Genoese in Caffa. Then they admired the full moon shining down on the crossing place known as *Ianua Italiae*, between Piedmont, Emilia, Lunigiana and the Republic of Genoa.

Tired of the pointless days he had wasted in the shadow of the walls listening to lyrics, Martino mounted Pegaso once again and galloped across the drawbridge. He stopped at the confluence of the Tanaro and Bormida rivers, at a place called Alessandria, known as Alessandria in the marsh, perhaps to distinguish it from Alexandria in Egypt. He stayed at the House of Bergoglio, where he met a scholar in the Jewish tradition who invited him to meetings at their house, named after the Greek synagogue or by transliterating from the Hebrew beit knesset. There the Visconti notary opened the teaching closet and was able to admire the scrolls written in Hebrew. He was impressed to discover that these scrolls could not be touched except with special indicators, and was shown one made of ivory and gold, carved in the shape of a hand with a pointing index finger. As well as a show of respect, the notary understood that this was an excellent way to preserve the precious documents. He decided he too would adopt this system when flipping through the oldest of the manuscripts in the library at home.

Another excellent habit was not to throw out or burn parchments that were no longer used, but bury them all in one place.

On the Thursday following his arrival in Alessandria, the nobleman Umberto Eco took Martino to the herb market where stalls were set out with exotic foods such as Catalan paella and the sweet cannoli that they ate at the court of Federico II of Swebia; crunchy shells filled with ricotta and green pistachios that had a mouth-watering aroma.

Then the two knights took part in a wake in memory of Raimondo, Francesco and Lorenzo Ruffo; three brothers from Alessandria who became Franciscan monks and had gone to the lands invaded by Tartar tribes as missionaries and had been imprisoned and killed by them early that year.

Then, weary from the heat of the city, Martino resumed his journey and stopped at the House of Aleramici as the guest of Teodoro Paleologo. Teodoro was born in Constantinople in 1290, the son of Andronicus II of Byzantium and Violante, daughter of William VII

Aleramico. He landed in Genoa in 1306 and had inherited Monferrato from his maternal uncle. In the same year of 1306 he had married Argentina Spinola, daughter of the Doge Opicino Spinola. In 1307 the Emperor Henry VII of Luxembourg had recognised his right to govern the territory he'd inherited from the female line, in preference to opposing claims from the House of D'Angiò. The argument over who should govern was between Piedmontese feudal lords and the communities, who were preparing their own statutes, but not the clergy who were exempt from paying taxes. In spite of this, the clergy were divided between sympathisers of the Church of Avignon in the vicinity of Casa d'Angiò and those faithful to the Curia of Rome.

Martino listened to the issues put forward and tried to understand without judging. He tactfully avoided adopting any position and his hosts avoided putting pressure him, allowing him to strike up a friendship with Giovanni, the eldest son of Argentina and Teodoro. Giovanni was twelve years old and bombarded Martino with questions. Martino appeared heroic to him, travelling alone and taking care of his own horse. When the boy discovered that Bellini lived below Monte Rosa, he was excited and asked his parents if he could go with him, but they refused permission due to the continuing unrest in Piedmont.

The young Bellini confided to Giovanni that he had confidential messages to deliver, and took the opportunity to leave. On the strength of his seal and his degree as a notary, which guaranteed him right of passage through the warring territories, he decided to visit the lands occupied by Roberto D'Angiò, who had been declared Lord of Genoa in 1318 and demonstrated a despotic nature ill-suited to the people of the Ligurian Res Publica.

After visiting the remains of the Roman aqueduct and baths, Martino bathed at length along with other visitors, who seemed overly convinced of the beneficial effects of the waters to counteract the gastronomic and other extravagances they allowed themselves in the convivial inns around the place.

After the full moon in August, Bellini set off again to pay a spiritual visit to the abbey of Santa Maria in Lucedio, where he studied the system that the monks had devised for managing the territory. To release the brothers from care of the land and allow them more time for prayer and spiritual study, the monastery's territory had been divided up and given over to converts, who returned a profit from it by employing peasant farmers to work the land and periodically report to the cellarer: the monk who managed the abbey. Of course, thought Martino; cultivation at intermediate levels was possible in territories that were highly fertile and had good trade links, but the poor hills of Oleggio would never yield enough to feed people who were so unaccustomed to physical work!

The young man left at dawn on Pegaso to visit the agricultural communities of Montarolo, Darola, Leri, Montarucco, Ramezzana and other monastic properties in the Monferrato and Canavese areas. Arriving at Castelmerlino, he slept outdoors with Pegaso beside a water trough in the woods. He admired the beautiful stone basin decorated with an engraved woven pattern, the crystalline quartz in the stone glistening in the sunlight. Then he galloped towards the Piedmont plain, ascending to the high ground of Candelo.

A small castle stood beside a ford across the winding Cervo river; it seemed to observe the approach of Bellini, who was welcomed by Franco Alciati with the simple dignity typical of mountain lords. Martino was made to feel at home here; he ate a relaxed meal of polenta and cheese with wild honey, and afterwards he told Franco and his wife Ilaria stories from Dante's *Divine Comedy*, Ezzelino's tragedy set in Padua and the expansionist ambitions of Casa D'Angiò. Two daughters of the family competed to attract the young man's attention, but after three days of failed attempts to seduce him they decided he was unmanly and went back to their habitual pursuits: one working in the kitchen garden and the other looking after the ford. Martino noticed that a toll was levied for goods to cross the ford designed for deer, and thought it was a legitimate system that should be adopted on the Terdoppio, to obtain a partial return at least for the cost of maintaining the embankments.

On 22nd August he went on foot, leading Pegaso, to the church of San Martino in Campiglia.

On the way he met some shepherds returning from the summer transhumance and stopped three days to teach them to recite the rosary. Before taking his leave he bought some well-tanned sheepskins from them.

He continued his climb into the beech forest as far as the cave that the shepherds used in summer, and stayed there in seclusion for forty days with Pegaso, studying and meditating on the writings of St. Jerome. Enrico had given him a small manuscript of the life of this Father of the Church and a fragment of his Latin translation of the Song of Songs. Born in Stridone in Illyria, Jerome had studied rhetoric in Rome, Treves and Aquileia, where he dedicated himself to the lifestyle of an ascetic under the patronage of the bishop Valeriano. Disillusioned by the cravings and jealousies of those who should have been contemplative, he went east and spent the years 375 and 376 AD in the desert of Chalcis, living as an anchorite. Disillusioned too by the lack of friendship among anchorites, he became a priest and continued his studies in Antioch, Constantinople and Rome, where in 382 he became secretary to Pope Damasus I. His Vulgate was adopted as a liturgical text for the Latin mass. Among the manuscripts, Martino was struck by the tale of the lion, written by the Blessed Jacopo da Varazze of Liguria. The tale was of a lion that entered the monastery where Jerome was sitting; it was limping. The monks ran away in fear, but Jerome stroked the lion without fear, and discovered a thorn stuck under pad on its paw. He treated the lion and after it was healed the monks kept it to guard the donkey that worked for them. One day the lion fell asleep while the donkey was grazing, and some merchants stole the beast to load it with packs and merchandise. When the monks saw the lion was alone they thought it had eaten the donkey, and ordered it to do the work that the beast of burden had done before. One morning as the lion was walking along, loaded with packs and wood, it saw a caravan of nomad merchants passing by, and recognised the donkey. To get the donkey back and rid himself of his burdensome task, the lion roared and attacked the caravan. The merchants fled and the donkey and other beasts from the caravan followed the lion quietly back to the monastery. When the merchants saw where their caravan loaded with goods had been taken, they introduced themselves to the monks and asked forgiveness of Jerome, who returned their goods to them with the recommendation not to steal any more, not even a donkey from a lion. Martino smiled as he read the story and decided he would have a fresco of St. Jerome and the lion painted behind his work desk in the study his father was building for him.

On 30th September, *dies natalis* (the day of bodily death) of St. Jerome, Martino and Pegaso went down into the valley. Stopping to drink at a farmhouse where some carpenters were working, Bellini noticed they were depicting the devotion of Giovanni Battista and his parents Elisabetta and Zaccaria there too. One of the carpenters was carving their names at the base of some statues. It pleased Martino to hear of the motives that provoked this kind of family piety, and he decided to speak to Meb about the possibility of using their names for some of the countless children that would no doubt be born of their union. But he put aside thoughts of his betrothed, knowing he had other missions to fulfil before he returned home.

At the same time the young nobleman was visiting Casa Cossato to conclude an alliance with the eldest son of his own age, Meb took an excursion to Lake Orta with Silvia Negri. The two young women took a small, narrow ferryboat to the convent on the island. The boat was fitted with wooden arches alongside the outriggers, to which tarpaulins of raw waxed hemp were fixed to shelter the occupants from sun, damp air and rain. The ferryman was a trustee of the abbess, who welcomed Meb and Silvia, pregnant with her first child, in silence, according to the Rule of the Abbey Mater Ecclesiae.

Martino and Fecia di Cossato quickly formed a friendship, and trotted along together to the tower of Buccione to inform the guard of the city of Gozzano of the agreements that had been reached. Weary from the journey, the two young friends stopped for the night with the men of the corps of guards, and drank wine in greater measure than they were used to. Sinking into sleep, Fecia dreamed that a man calling himself Onorato met some noble representatives of the Houses of the North in the meadow below the tower. But a knight with a large dog wearing an embroidered mantle betrayed both sides and allowed the territories to be invaded by a tribe of barbarians, to his own personal advantage. They set fire to the surrounding woods, killing everyone who lived there. He woke up with a start and told Pietro, the guard on night watch, about his dream. Peter told him that 16th of January was Saint Onorato's day, and that a bishop in Novaro by the name of Onorato had restored the tower, but couldn't tell him anything more about it.

Meanwhile, Martino came running up in a panic, saying he'd dreamed about a big brown bear that told him in a deep voice, "he who truly loves honey loves the place it springs from." The guardsman commented that honey doesn't come from a spring because it's not water. Fecia di Cossato said nothing.

The guard then told Martino about Fecia's nightmare and Martino reasoned, "*Nomen omen*- the name Onorato is often given to the firstborn of noble lineage. This son is not intended for military service; anyone bearing the name is usually trained in the honorary field, in other words at home. The sacrament of marriage and providing defence are suitable for a nature thus acquired. My grandfather Bellini told me about an Onorato worthy of remembrance for the excellent surveying work he carried out in the territory. I saw a manuscript depicting him with a groma for surveying settlements in his right hand."

"I know about road surveying; is surveying for settlements different?"

"Yes. Different instruments are used to draw straight lines for the consular roads and right angles for regular squares. Even though the foundations for military encampment buildings were set on an orthogonal cardo and decumanus crossing, as for roads, a different instrument was used for the operation... "

"The sun's coming up," his friend interrupted; "can you explain the units of measurement and how the measuring instruments are made while we have breakfast; I could eat a horse!"

After breakfasting on rye bread and fried eggs with the people who worked at the tower, the young men bade each goodbye and went their separate ways.

Proceeding at walking pace on Pegaso, Martino reflected on what the bear had said and what meaning the words might have for him; he decided to go and see his cousin Laura at Casa Speroni, who raised magnificent saddle horses. The ancient villa was surrounded by a dry stone wall built from square-shaped stones stacked up without any mortar. Arriving at the heavy wooden door, Martino took out the hunting horn he carried on his shoulder along with his gourd of water, and blew it loudly three times to make himself heard by anyone inside.

A few minutes later the stableman opened the door and took charge of Pegaso, while Martino went into the orchard, where he saw his cousin standing on a ladder, passing down the last apples of the season to a girl, who was placing them carefully in wicker baskets.

"Laura, I'm Martino, Susanna's son," the nobleman introduced himself. "Martino Bellini? But surely it was only yesterday you were born!" said Laura, coming down from the ladder. "This young lady is Arianna, our youngest," she said; "her sister is probably in the kitchen, and the boys are out on the moor with Vittorio, moving the herd of mares and foals. To what do we owe the pleasure of your visit?"

"I'm on my way back from the tower of Buccione, where I was with Fecia di Cossato to discuss the continued alliance between our families for our generation," explained the knight, helping Arianna carry in the baskets of apples. They entered the kitchen, where they found four other women working. "I'm a Visconti notary; I have my degree from Bologna. I shall be married to my betrothed Meb on 6th December, and I'd like you to come to the celebrations," Martino announced. "I remember coming here with my grandfather Bellini, and I'd like to ask a great favour, as a wedding present."

"This fine knight is our cousin, Martino Bellini," said Laura, introducing him to the women in the kitchen; "this is Isabella, who is engaged to Giovan Battista Beldì; grandson of the founder of the brick kiln on the road to Borgomanero. Carla, water, wine, bread and cheese for everyone! Arianna, keep a dozen apples for us and put them in the pantry. Well, Martino; tell us what gift you and Meb would like."

"I'd like to leave my stallion, Pegaso, with you."

"For breeding? Certainly, if Vittorio agrees. But what does the gift consist of?"

"First of all, it would give me peace of mind to know he was in your care for the winter and next year, when we will be busy travelling wherever Enrico sends us."

"Yes, that's something we can do, apart from any breeding; it depends on whether he's suitable," said Laura.

"Thank you. Just knowing you were taking care of Pegaso would be a most welcome gift," said Martino, "but if it's possible, I would be happy to have a foal from him in a few years' time, because he's been a faithful companion to both me and my instructor. Healthy, strong, intelligent and well-adjusted."

"There's no such thing as perfection. What's his vice?" asked Isabella, offering Martino a goblet of red wine, to which he added water so it wouldn't set his head spinning.

"He's not used to being alone or with other stallions for long periods in the stable," Martino replied, pensively. "The first winter he was in Bologna, we left him shut in for several days, and although there were cats and a goat with him, he became quite restless, tossing his head and champing. When I noticed this I started taking him out in the meadow at least two hours a day, and he stopped doing it."

"That's good to know." How does he behave with people he doesn't know?" Laura intervened.

"Silvano, my instructor, told me that when Pegaso was two years old he would sometimes bite..."

"...that's quite common among two-year-old foals," Isabella commented.

170

"The same as with children. Between the ages of two and three they seem to try the patience of everyone they come into contact with! But foals and babies bite because their teeth are painful when they're teething;" said Laura, and went on, "does he walk backwards when he's frightened, not looking behind? One of our horses went over the cliff into the Ticino like that. Or does he rear up on his hind legs?"

"He never walks backwards, as far as I know," answered Martino; "he's light; he doesn't put his head down when he rears up, even for fun, as if he's performing. He has a lot of stamina both walking and trotting; he doesn't break into a sweat easily. You have to keep him at a steady pace for galloping; if you loosen the rein when you're not used to him, he might throw his head back and run off wildly. I don't know if he bites or kicks other horses because I don't let him get close enough when I'm in the saddle, and he moves away from other horses when he's in the pasture."

"Well, that seems like normal behaviour for a horse. Vittorio and Gianpace should be back soon; we have a mare about to foal for the first time, and she'll need help with birthing. Go and see Giacomo in the stable if you'd like to help."

Martino was glad of the opportunity. He made himself useful carrying buckets of water from the well and straw ready to clean the new foal.

When the experts arrived, the first-time mother was in some difficulty.

Her nipples were swollen but she didn't want to lie down, so Giacomo brought an old, quiet mare to stay beside her, which succeeded in relaxing her. Martino noticed that the mare was a rather heavy animal, a half-breed, and remembered from when he was a child in Mezzomerico that new mothers of this type were considered at risk because of the size of the foal.

By the grace of God the Speroni experts managed to deliver the first-born successfully. Giacomo and Vittorio taught Martino how to dry the foal by rubbing it with dry straw, and clean its mouth and nostrils of amniotic fluid. Then Giacomo helped the baby find its mother's nipples to drink the colostrum, the first maternal secretion essential for cleaning the intestines and passing on important immuno-active substances for protection against infections, as well as vital nutrition.

The Speronis congratulated each other, noting that Martino didn't vomit, which had happened to plenty of brave men when they witnessed a birth or the distended womb of a new mother. Martino was given the honour of choosing a name for the foal, and he decided on Joselino.

At dinner they ate slices of black bread with salted anchovies in oil seasoned with garlic, and a savoury pie made from chickpeas, onions, sage, rosemary and eggs in a soft cheese dough.

Giacomo played the flute and Isabella the lute, while Arianna sang in a clear voice a song she'd learned from the bard Renato Rascel, a man who loved horses more than riding.

These are the words to the *Lullaby of the little horse*:

Through the pastures of heaven, little horse fly
Your coat shines gold in the blue of the sky
Old moon above, show him the way
Sing a chorus, golden stars through the streets of heaven

And walking, walking
the little horse came to a cloud of pink and stopped
"What do you seek?" asked a little star
"I'm looking for my master, but I'm so tired"
The little star called many other little stars, and together
they drew a map in the sky to show him the way, singing
him a lullaby.
As soon as the little horse fell asleep, the Great Bear
said:
"Old stars up here, sing no more.
Sleep, sleep, Dream sweet dreams"
Goodnight to you"
And the rest of the family answered, singing in chorus:
Good night my love."

The ambiance in the kitchen was serene and a little
melancholy, but it was certainly more lively in the horse
enclosure for Pegaso, who had been given on loan and
placed with the female herd, separate from the other
stallions who were shut in the barn.
The young Bellini remained as a guest at Casa Speroni
for a week, during which time he learned a lot about life
as a horse breeder. It was hard for him to leave Pegaso,
even though he knew he was leaving him in good
company with the beautiful mare Bonadea and the more
experienced Eurinome, who had been renamed after she
gave birth to the third female foal. The names of her first
two fillies had been renamed too, after the third was
born, from a beautiful classic story that Vittorio and
Laura wanted to pay homage to. The mare was only
named Eurinome after giving birth to her third filly, and
her daughters were Eufrosìne, Talìa and Aglaìa. Martino

didn't recognise the names, and Laura was happy to tell him the story.

"Hesiod describes Eurinome in his *Theogony* as a daughter of the ocean; she was radiant in appearance and had three daughters with beautiful cheeks. Eufrosìne, the beautiful Talìa and the resplendent Aglaìa were here daughters, and from their eyelids dripped the love that can liberate from all suffering. Their eyes were enchanted."

Martino smiled and told them a story in turn: "The names of all sea creatures lend themselves very well to horses' names; they are animals by nature, but inextricably linked to the water. Hesiod also described another ocean creature. Oceanus and Tethys gave birth to the beautiful Europa, sister to 2999 seas and three thousand rivers. Oceanus and Tethys were the only ones who didn't participate in the war against Zeus, who upon conquering Titans, his controversial antagonists, left them the government of the waters. Europa married Poseidon, who ruled the Mediterranean Sea and became the mother of Euphemus, one of the Argonauts."

"Who were the Argonauts?" asked Arianna, who had no tutor to teach her Greco-Roman classicism, just her mother Laura, who was usually too busy with her daily affairs for intellectual teaching.

"Fifty heroes who went to bring back a fleece, perhaps made of gold," replied Martino, not realising the girl would take his words literally.

"I've always liked the idea that they set sail with just one sailor on board. Only the helmsman was a man of the sea; the other forty-nine were young - brave but inexperienced!" the nobleman continued, thinking to himself, *just like me*. He went on:

174

"In his fourth Pythian ode, Pindar wrote that Era kindled the desire in each of the fifty sailors to set sail on the ship *Argo* because he didn't want to leave them all rotting at their mother's house, preferring them to confront the trials of life with other young people."

Arianna sighed, gazing at Martino with a dreamy look, then cast a challenging glare at her mother Laura, who pretended not to see. Isabella asked Martino to list the names of the Argonauts, and prepared to write them on parchment with good elder ink so she could learn them by heart and make a good impression on her betrothed.

"Acastus, son of Pelias

Admetus of Pherae

Ancaeus of Tegea

Ancaeus of Samos

Amphion, a soothsayer

Argus of Thespiae, who built the ship

Ascalaphus of Orchomenus

Asterius

Atalanta, a skilled huntress with a bow

Actor

Augeas

Butes of Athens, a beekeeper

Calais, son of Boreas the wind

Canthus of Euboea

Castor of Sparta, one of the Dioscuri

Cepheus

Caeneus

Coronus of Thessaly

Echion, son of Hermes, a messenger like his father

Heracles or Hercules, of Tiryns

Erginus of Miletus

Euphemus of Tenaro

Euryalus

Eurydamus from the lake of Siniade

Phalerus, the archer of Athens

Phanus, son of Dionysus

Jason, head of the expedition

Idas of Messene

Idmon, son of Apollo

Iphiclus of Etolia

Iphitos of Mycenae

Iolaus the Dryope

Laertes, who became the father of Ulysses or Odysseus, the eponymous protagonist of Homer's epic work and husband of Penelope, the great weaver

Lynceus

Melampus, son of Poseidon

Meleager the Calydone

Mopsus

Nauplius, son of Poseidon

Oileus of Locri

Orpheus the poet

Palaemon

Poeas

Peleus, the future father of Achilles

Peneleos

Periclymenus

Pirithous

Pollux, a boxer from Sparta and Castor's twin brother

Polyphemus

Staphylus, brother of Phanus

Telamon, brother of Peleus

Tiphys the helmsman

Zetes, brother of Calais."

"How dull!" said Arianna and asked Martino to tell them the exciting story of their adventure to make up boring them with the tedious list.

"The first island they came to was inhabited only by women, who wanted to marry the sailors and produce a new generation of inhabitants for the island. Jason didn't want to, but the islanders got them drunk over dinner and took advantage of them, to conceive many children. The only ones to remain on board were Atalanta, a woman, and Hercules, who was on guard duty. The two of them intervened and forced the sailors to get back on the ship. Near to Thrace they waited for night before skirting the coastline; they knew the Trojan king Laomedon didn't allow free passage to Greek ships like the *Argo*. After several vicissitudes, a kingfisher landed on the prow, and Mopsus, who was an expert at interpreting omens, explained that the bird was sent by Rea, the Earth, who was incensed by the turmoil their voyage was creating. They placated Rea by fixing a carved wooden statue of her to the prow. The young sailors were restless, being aboard the ship for such a long time. Do you know what they did next, Arianna?"

"How would I know... maybe they went fishing?" said the girl, taking a bite from a shiny red apple.

"They challenged each other to a rowing race," explained Martino, "during which Jason collapsed and Hercules broke an oar. When even the Dioscuri twins finally tired, they realised they had arrived at the island of Chios and disembarked. Hercules went off to look for wood to make a new oar, and when he returned he found his trusted Hylas was no longer waiting for him. I should explain that Hylas was his lover as well as being his squire, so Hercules was furious at his disappearance."

"In what way was Hylas his lover?" Isabella inquired.

"In the sense that they cared for each other very much and looked out for one other, both in war and in peace," answered Laura, who was busy shelling peas; "what happened next?"

"Hercules and Polyphemus went to look for Hylas on the beach, where they found him in the arms of some nymphs. They tried to persuade him to come back to the ship, but he wouldn't; he stayed there with the young women for eternity, apparently. The weather changed overnight and the next morning Jason decided to set sail without the friends who had gone ashore, because the wind and sea were becoming dangerous and he didn't want to risk staying in this place with so many dangerous women."

"Go on, Martino!" the Speroni sisters exclaimed in chorus, enjoying the story. The knight took a long drink of water and went on.

"After many setbacks, the *Argo* arrived where the Tibareni people lived, which was unique for the fact that the husbands the shared labour pains of their wives. The sailors then had to defend themselves from an attack by some birds, but were advised to scream at them, which scared the birds away. The advice came from Phineus, who had discovered that the birds were afraid of loud noises. After more adventures and a violent storm, they sighted a raft with four survivors from a shipwreck, and took them on board.

These were the sons of Phrixus and Chalciope: Cytisorus, Argus, Phrontis and Melas, who accompanied them to Colchis, their destination. King Aeetes guarded the golden fleece jealously and imposed terrible conditions on Jason before he was allowed to take it, but the king's daughter, Medea, decided to help the young man because she had fallen in love with him. In short, although Jason managed to succeed in the trials he was given with the help of Medea, Aeetes refused to hand over the golden fleece and threatened to burn the Argo.

Medea then took Jason to see the dragon that guarded the oak tree from which the golden treasure was hung. Medea put the monster to sleep. Jason broke off the branch with the golden fleece and together they went back on board the *Argo*, where they found five of their comrades wounded after being attacked by the inhabitants of the region. Medea treated them and Argus, Atalanta and two other comrades recovered, but Iphitos died. The *Argo* sailed across the Black Sea away from the sun, on the advice of Phineus, pursued by Aeetes' ships. There are many different versions as to their return, but I think they all agree that Medea helped kill her stepbrother Absyrtus in order to slow her father Aeetes down and prevent him catching up with the *Argo*. The Apsyrtides islands rose up in the Adriatic where Absyrtus' body parts were thrown, and are named after him."

"Did Jason marry Medea? And did they live happily ever after? And what happened to the golden fleece?" Arianna wanted to know.

"Medea helped Jason and they got married, but he forgot the sacred alliance he had agreed with her and suffered dreadful consequences," Laura interposed, and told them about a legend that said there were jewels at the bottom of the lake in Val Devero, and wondered if there was a dragon guarding this treasure too.

"Once upon a time there was a young man who got engaged to a beautiful girl who loved him," said Isabella.

"But the man was still in love with his old flame, who demanded more and more of his time and attention. His fiancée was hurt and jealous; she sat crying by Lake Devero, until a sorceress who lived nearby approached her. Moved to pity, the woman advised the girl to dive into the lake to discover her true nature. The young girl followed the woman's advice. As soon as she came into contact with the water, her legs fused together and formed a long tail with two tips and covered in scales. She swam around for a long time, and when she came out of the lake she turned back into a girl like before. When she asked the sorceress to explain, the woman told her she was a Melusine. Lake Devero had revealed her true nature, and from that moment on she would turn into a mermaid every time she came into contact with water, whether it was lake, sea, river or even a bathtub. As well as that, her words would have the power of persuasion, but she would also be at risk from people who were afraid of her and would try to kill her. The sorceress went on, telling her to watch the surface of the lake carefully, and suddenly two men's faces appeared side by side. One was the face of her betrothed, which grew old and turned into a skull with empty eye sockets as she watched. The other was an unchanging face with strong, regular features and a gentle look about it. She also saw many magnificent jewels at the bottom of the lake, and the sorceress told her that if a Melusine were to dive down she would be able to gather them, and the man with eternal life would take her with him. The wise young woman understood that the sorceress had promised her neither jewels nor eternal life, and replied that she would rather return to her normal life. She thanked the sorceress for showing her the beautiful face with the profound gaze, and the jewels that were so magnificent she would remember them forever. She thanked the woman by giving her the carved rosewood clasp from her hair, and went home, where her fiancé was waiting for her anxiously. Whilst she was away he'd realised he loved her more than anyone else. Seeing her hair loose about her shoulders, the young man gave her a clasp of amber and ivory which she wore on their wedding day. They lived together happily for the rest of their lives, and their bodies were buried next to each other so that the memory of their love would endure over the centuries."

Arianna had heard the story before and gone out to feed the rabbits. When she came back in for dinner, she asked Martino to tell the story of the only woman on the Argo, so the young man told his hosts what he knew of Atalanta.

"The name Atalanta is Greek and means 'in equilibrium'," said Martino. "She was the daughter of Clymene and Iasus of Arcadia. Disappointed because he wanted a son, her father abandoned her as a newborn child on Mount Pelion. A bear nursed and weaned the infant until it was found by a group of hunters, who took her to their village. When she grew into a woman, two centaurs tried to take advantage of her, but the young woman defended herself by shooting deadly arrows at them. When she found out the *Argo* was about to sail, Atalanta asked if she could join the crew, but Jason didn't want any women on board and refused. One of the trials for selection consisted of capturing a boar, so she took part in the trials and was the first to wound the beast, so they gave her the bear skin as a token of honour. Her father was proud of her but wanted her to marry, which she had no intention of doing."

"Why didn't she want to get married?" asked Isabella and Arianna in unison, astonished at the idea.

"Because an oracle had warned her that she would lose her skills in archery and running if she got married" Martin replied, and went on with the story. "To show her father she wanted to please him, Atalanta said she would marry whoever managed to beat her in a race. But she killed every suitor who won. Hippomenes was in love with her and asked Aphrodite for help before challenging the girl he wanted to marry. The goddess of love gave him three golden apples picked from the garden of the Hesperides and told him to drop them one at a time during the race. The young man did this and won the race because Atalanta was fascinated by the gems and stopped to pick them up. They married and had a son, Parthenopeus. In his *Metamorphoses*, Ovid writes that they were making love one day in a temple dedicated to Cybele, and were turned into lions as a punishment."

"What a lovely story!" exclaimed the hosts.

Vittorio raised his cup of red wine and proposed a toast to lovers of all ages, present and absent, saying that it was better to live as a lion than to live without love.

After dinner some of the sons played and Gabriele sang the *Ballad of the lost horse* in his tuneful voice:

A thought for the knight,
who without his horse is just a man.
The swollen river does not respect the living
the swollen river does not respect love.
A thought for the knight,

182

who without his horse is just a man.
The horse now gallops through pastures in the sky.
The poor man looks up in hope.
A thought for the knight,
who without his horse is just a man.

It was the evening of 8th of November. Arianna had fallen in love for the first time in those few days and suffered at night the sweet pains of a newly-kindled love that was already lost.

When she woke up, she used the pot and washed her face in the basin of icy cold water in less time that it normally took her, then

quickly put on a camisole and skirt scented with lavender, her work apron and a woollen shawl. She put on her wool stockings and wooden clogs too, and ran down to look for the young knight, hoping she could sneak up next to him before anyone noticed. The words of Matthew the evangelist (8:8) came to mind, in which a Roman army officer said to Jesus: "I am not worthy to sit at your table, but say only one word and my servant will be healed." Just as the soldier was certain the Lord's words would be good for his servant, so Arianna was certain that listening to Martino would be good for her heart, because listening to him meant being with him.

Martino was not in the kitchen. Arianna took a slice of corn bread with some cheese for breakfast, and two apples which she put in her apron pocket, then went out to the courtyard.

The turkeys were pecking and scratching, Laura was cleaning out the litter in the rabbit cage and the dog was busy eating ripe persimmons that had fallen from the tree near the kitchen garden. Fog was rising from the ground as Giacomo was hoeing, preparing for the winter sowing. She saw three men standing near the open door in the perimeter wall and her heart sank; one of them was Martino. She ran towards them, and when she drew close she was glad that Martino was the first one to speak to her, and didn't comment on her being so red in the face.

"Hello, Arianna," said the knight; "I'm going to the blacksmith's house. I'll be back tonight, could you give Pegaso an apple for me? Good day to you." He turned around and set off with Giancarlo the blacksmith, without looking back.

Vittorio placed a hand on his daughter's right shoulder and went to check how Joselino had spent the night. Arianna gave Pegaso both apples because her stomach felt tight.

Martino returned at sunset, bringing a rolled-up parchment in his leather bag to give to his father from the blacksmith. The next day he left for home on foot.

When Bellini took leave of the Speronis they were all looking forward to the wedding; it would be an excellent opportunity for them all to meet up again, eating and drinking together; people who work with horses are averse to solitude, unless they're out galloping wildly in the wind. Arianna felt weak, but she was content knowing Martino was happy. She went over to the rabbits sadly, and sang them a strange little song that went something like this: "I'm happy I'm dying but I'm sorry; I'm sorry I'm dying but I'm happy..."

In Oleggio, work was underway to build the new quarters for the newlyweds. Enrico and the masons from Bergamo were completing the new home for the betrothed couple, following their instructions. The perimeter wall was already there, as it formed the rear of the shops and the portico on the market square, in front of the bell tower that called the people to assemble in emergencies. A second perimeter wall had been built with bricks, and the cavity between the two walls packed with stones and mortar. Other walls were erected, leaving gaps for doors and windows. Oak beams of varying thickness were brought from the carpenter of Casa Bertaccini and erected skilfully into place. In short, the work comprised a single entrance door that opened onto the square, a two-storey residence with three wings, and the door that connected the kitchen of the old house with the Meb and Martino's new quarters left free.

The staircase to the first floor was built of bricks; the steps themselves were made of grey stone brought down from the mountains, and were greatly admired by the local people, who were accustomed to stairs with wooden railings that creaked and caught fire easily.

Martino had decided on a study similar to his grandfather's, on the ground floor with direct access to the courtyard. Meb had a large room on the first floor that she would use for writing and sewing; arts in which she excelled. She had asked for large windows that opened wide, with no decoration, like the ones in the "Casa Grande" library. And just like the ones in the big house, Enrico had arranged for them to be protected with strong window bars.

The ground floor windows also had diagonal iron bars fitted in the jambs, to prevent prowlers from bursting in on the unarmed family.

Other changes had also taken place in the meantime. Sara had died, leaving Paolo a widower, and Cesarina had gone to live with Giacomina, Filippo and Juanìn at the small farmhouse in Mezzomerico. Filippo's marriage to the blacksmith's daughter was imminent, and joyful preparations were underway in the hills.

Susanna brought up her two daughters herself, and shared with them her passion for embroidery. The mother encouraged her pupils to try everything, from designing models to choosing which coloured threads to use and composing the actual stitches, trying to set them a good example of consistency and precision. One point about which she was very punctilious was fixing the threads by weaving them into the work before cutting them off, which she considered much neater than tying knots at the back. But Margherita preferred to knot the threads and cut them off in spite of what her mother said, because it was quicker. In the little girl's opinion, the lack of neatness was not important because no one looked at the back of the work in any case.

"I look at the back of your work," Susanna pointed out. "But you're my mother so you don't count", replied Margherita with a little smile. Clemenza carried on with her embroidery without comment, although she did consider it important to always make her mother happy, not to mention the fact that her mother would give advice without making judgements, and never meted out punishment like her father did if she disobeyed.

They worked in the large room between the library and the twins' bedroom on the first floor. When they tired of sewing they could look out of the window at the kennel, the tower and the irises, silhouetted against the sky.

Lino had married Grazia after being betrothed for two years, and the couple had come to live in the room that Cesarina had vacated. The young man of twenty helped his father and was still taking care of the dogs for the Viscontis; Grazia did the shopping and cooking for the whole family. Three times a week another married couple came to clean the house, and stayed in the quarters next to the kennel.

The City had organised a laundry service that was paid for with a tax on the price of goods produced locally. The laundry carts came every Monday at mid-morning to collect dirty laundry from the houses within the walls and take it to the washerwomen, who boiled in special tubs and hung it out in the meadow near the southern walls, or if was raining under the roof of the large shed in the market where live animals were sold on the last Thursday of every month. Each household embroidered their own unique mark on their linen to make sure the right items of the clean laundry were delivered to the right owners, like fire-branding animals to mark who they belonged to.

The houses outside the walls had no need of a laundry service because they had enough space to wash and dry their own linen.

Apart from that, farmers were not used to paying taxes in their own homes, and it was best not to upset them because they used their tools as weapons when they thought they had to defend themselves.

Susanna was sitting with Margherita, known as Verde, and Clemenza, known as Balsamina, in the vast cloakroom on the first floor embroidering Meb's wedding dress, when they heard Martino's voice as he entered the courtyard.

Mother and daughters left their sewing and locked the cloakroom door behind them, as the future husband should not see the bride's dress before the day of the wedding.

Their embraces and kisses were sincere but were not prolonged; Enrico was eager to take his son to the construction site to see the new house. The two of them didn't return until the afternoon, when the women pressured the young man to take a long hot bath and change his clothes for the evening.

They all dined together in the hall; the parents at the head of the table with Martino on his father's right; Clemenza next to her brother and Margherita facing her. Places had been set for Rebecca, Meb or Aligerno, and their chairs were vacant. Silvano's place and the one facing him were vacant but set with plates, cutlery and pewter goblets. This was a novelty and the girls asked the reason for it, since they usually had to wait until all the guests had arrived before they could start eating.

"Uncle Silvano is on his way, but we don't know if he'll be here tonight or tomorrow, and the other place is for Elijah," said Susanna.

Martino explained the Jewish tradition that says a place should be kept free at the table and set for Elijah, the prophet of silence.

"Why should we wait for him, if he's never been here?" asked Margherita.

"Because he defeated the priests of Baal on Mount Carmel," Susanna replied.

"And killed all 450 of them on the banks of the river Kisom," added Enrico, who knew how massacres piqued his daughters' imagination.

"Even though we've never met him, we believe in the one who passed down this story to us, and in the prophecy of Malachi," Martino continued.

"What does Malachi's prophecy say?" Clemenza inquired earnestly.

"Elijah was a pious man who ascended to heaven in a chariot of fire and will return before the messianic era. That's why we should always be prepared to welcome him."

"Pious like Aeneas who fought for his homeland, and when he lost, carried his father Anchises on his shoulders whilst holding his son Ascanius by the hand?" asked Margherita with renewed interest.

"Yes, *piety* demands the same behaviour whatever sky you're born under," replied Susanna, adding that study enables you to avoid at least some of the mistakes that those who preceded us made.

"Why did we adopt the tradition of saving a place for Elijah?" Clemenza asked.

"Because Meb is Jewish, and Martino is going to marry her," Enrico explained.

The next day Martino gave his father the parchment the farrier had asked him to deliver, and started explaining what it was in his own words. He'd just begun when Silvano arrived, looking too clean to have just arrived after a long journey.

Our of respect for his hosts, he'd taken lodgings for the night at the Locanda del Pellegrino just inside the walls, where he'd had a tub prepared and taken a bath.

189

Martino informed them how he'd left Pegaso for breeding, and noting how happy his old instructor was with the news, he resumed his analysis of the text.

"The blacksmith told me this is a summary of some teachings that have been used since ancient times for breeding and caring for horses. Let's read what it says and discuss how we might try a few of the remedies when we've studied them carefully," said Martino, opening the scrolls out on the table. The opening words were *Hippocratic Civitas*.

The moon's phases and the cycle of the four seasons were given as determining factors for when females were on heat, and depended on variations in climate and therefore location.

The recommended procedure for helping mares give birth for the first time was the one they used at Casa Speroni, but treating the hooves with olive oil infused with certain herbs was a procedure unknown to the three men, and they spent the whole morning in the study that once belonged to the grandfather and was now Enrico's.

"Sanguis quando superhabundat in equo fanne il cristere, once a day and it will heal," Martino read aloud. Then there was a knock at the door and Clemenza announce that lunch was on the table.

When everyone was seated (except Elijah, who had not yet been seen in those parts), Silvano handed Martino a wooden casket covered in purple-red velvet as a wedding gift for the new family residence.

The casket contained a glass bowl. Before shaping it, the craftsman had inserted a filigree gold medallion between two strata of transparent glass, depicting an ancient caduceus. From the bottom rose a vertical element that emerged as two serpents entwined in a dance around a staff that was part of the same vertical element as themselves. At the point where the staff ended, the serpents were joined to form a pair of wings open in flight.

The serpents continued their labyrinthine dance into the wings, which ended with their heads directly facing each other; between their open mouths was an egg, which in the figurative language that Dante Alighieri also used, was the symbol for the cosmos.

"It's a saltcellar," said the riding instructor in his usual straightforward manner.

"Thank you, Silvano," replied Martino. He showed the gift to the diners then put it back in its casket. "It's beautiful, I'm sure Meb will be delighted and keep it under lock and key to avoid breaking it."

"It's only a saltcellar for the table," Silvano insisted. "I hope you'll use it for salt, whether you have guests or not."

After dinner, Martino took his instructor's gift to his own room and placed it in the finest of the trunks, next to the lute he'd brought for his bride.

The following three weeks were very demanding for those who had work to finish before the wedding and those who were travelling.

Silvia Negri gave birth to a boy at Giacomo and Irene Mainieri's castle beside the river Agogna, which flows from Lake Orta into the Po valley. Speranza their cook helped to deliver the baby, and Meb gently washed it in a basin of warm water prepared by the lady of the castle.

The scions of the house, Leonardo and Maddalena, were older children and Irene was not pregnant, so she was happy to let Speranza go, taking her son Ilario with her, who became milk brother to the Casa Negri infant.

191

Welcoming Speranza into the castle had been a benevolent act by Irene, as the poor woman had been widowed the month before Ilario was born and everyone thought it was fitting to give her the job of cook, even though Irene herself liked cooking.

Giacomo Mainieri sent a man to inform Casa Negri of the happy event and the schedule for the following week, when the women and children would be accommodated at the convent on their way home, for the baptism. A covered cart drawn by two mules was set up, and Giacomo put the women and children in the charge of his attendant, Guido. As they were saying their goodbyes, Irene gave each of them, including Meb, a small amber pendant to hang around their necks. The cart followed the Via Francisca connecting the Alpine passes of the Valdossola to the roads to Rome, as far as the convent, where they received a warm welcome from the abbess.

On their arrival she confirmed that everything was ready, and Guido transported the women and the abbess to the parish church of San Michele, where a procession of carts and horsemen was arriving from Oleggio for the solemn celebration of the baptism of little Ilario della Speranza and Francesco Negri. It was the first day of December. Enrico, Susanna and the twins from Casa Bellini took part in the event; they brought a gift of a puppy called Otto, who remained a faithful companion for over twenty years.

Martino arrived unexpectedly as they were having lunch at Casa Negri. He came in wearing leather boots and trousers of soft, well-tanned calfskin, a voluminous cotton shirt and a leather jerkin engraved with a bear's paw on the breast, which demonstrated Martino's enduring attachment to the tradition that his grandfather had kept alive. The scarf that Meb had given him around his neck and the pure white cloak on his shoulders completed the attire of the knight devoted to San Martino and spiritual love, which was also enhanced by the "dolce stil novo". As soon as he heard about the event, he'd decided to make a grand entrance; he wanted to make Meb proud of the man she was going to marry in five days' time.

Margherita and Clemenza ran to embrace their brother as soon as they saw him advancing with long strides through the courtyard of Villa Negri, between the village and Via Francisca.

Silvia complimented Susanna on Martino's gentlemanly style, and Meb bent down, pretending she'd dropped her handkerchief, so as not to reveal her emotion at seeing her fiancé wearing the scarf she'd given him. The young people danced until nightfall in the light of the stubble bonfires left burning in the corners of the courtyard. They all said goodnight when the Negri farmers put the fires out, and Meb went home with her hosts while Martino returned to the village, walking with some friends, holding their castor oil lamps high. Along the way, Giuseppe Gagliardi told them about a race he'd witnessed on a trip to Padua. His friends the Scrovegnis had organised a chariot race in a meadow reserved for winter pasture, taking advantage of the absence of cattle, which had been taken up to the higher altitudes of the Asiago plateaux for the summer transhumance.

"Each driver wore a different colour of shirt so you could tell them apart," said Giuseppe, "and drove a two-wheeled vehicle pulled by a single mare."

"Were they chariots like the 'birocci' used in the Apennines?" Martino inquired.

"Biroccio is a word from their dialect," said Filippo Grassi. "It comes from the Latin bi-rotium or bi-roteus, which means two wheels."

"Birocci are more manoeuvrable than four-wheeled carts," Martino went on. "Unlike the ancient Roman chariots, they have a platform above the wheel axis and a small bench where a passenger can sit as well as the driver."

"Exactly," Giuseppe agreed; "some of the drivers were Slovenian and they called their carriages *kolesa* ; Gabriele Scrovegni told me this means 'two wheels' and is translated as 'chariot' in the vernacular."

The story continued with a description of the competition and the lavish feast at Casa Scrovegni, but Martino wasn't listening, he was dreaming about designing a chariot for the new house, for him and Meb.

Martino took his leave of his friends as soon as they entered the village, leaving them no excuse to prolong the night with a visit to the tavern.

"Here we are on this beautiful night of the full moon in December, in the year 1324 AD. The chill of the afternoon has been consumed by the warmth of friendship. Let us now bid each other a peaceful goodnight in this absolute tranquillity, under the light of the moon and with our lamps still full of oil. In the embrace of the firmament we give thanks to those who armed us with the weapons of faith, hope and charity to protect the lives of our loved ones. For the sake of St. Christopher, let it be so."

The noble Bernardo Balsari repeated, "let it be so". The knight Giuseppe Gagliardi also agreed, "let it be so". His friend Filippo Grassi added: "May the moon bring us good dreams in all its phases. Let it be so".

But no one answered because they were not experts on the moon's phases and its influence on the living.

On Thursday 6th December at dawn, the Bellinis decorated all their windows with branches of red beech and oak as an omen for prosperity.

A group of friends beating drums made of wood and leather made their way along the cardo and decumanus of Oleggio - the two main streets, with Enrico and Silvano walking behind them: the start of the wedding procession.

Meb walked solemnly, holding up the hem of her long, pale silk dress gracefully in her hand, a white rabbit fur cape around her shoulders. Her plaited hair was piled high on her head and decorated with a wreath of intertwined willow and rose twigs woven by Silvia and Speranza; they had removed the thorns but left the plump, juicy rosehips in place. Aligerno walked beside his daughter, her left arm through his right. Behind them came many friends of the family and the farmers from Mezzomerico.

When they reached the end of the portico they were joined by four musicians in the square, who accompanied them with flute music to the door of their new residence, where Martino stood waiting on the threshold. Aligerno presented Meb to Martino, who swept her up in his arms and carried her across the threshold into their house. Enrico joined Meb's father and led him, followed by the other guests, into the courtyard of the old house, which was now known as the "Big House" to distinguish it from Meb and Martino's residence, although in terms of its footprint the opposite was true.

Lino, Grazia, and Paolo were busy stoking the fire that crackled in the kitchen fireplace. Long tables had been laid both inside the house and in the courtyard. As the guests gradually trailed in they helped themselves to bread, walnuts, cheese, roast duck and turkey, spit-roast chicken, carrots, slices of leek and pumpkin pie, millet pancakes, eggs seasoned with thyme, and slices of honey and spelt cake with hazelnuts, cubes of quince and grape jelly for dessert. Aligerno helped Enrico to tap copious amounts of red wine from barrels, which were set up in the courtyard where everyone could reach them. It was the farmers who drank most, accustomed as they were to drinking their wine undiluted, but water was supplied in elegant pewter carafes on the tables. Susanna and Rebecca were good company for each other, although both complained of strong migraines and were feeling a great deal of stiffness in their backs and at the point where the neck joins the shoulders.

"It's strange," said Rebecca, "I was alright yesterday when I got back from Lake Maggiore with Aligerno, and up until tonight..."

"Me too," Susanna confided, "I was going round checking everything was in order right up until dawn, and I felt fine, but my eyes are burning now. It feels like I have a tight band around my forehead and my head is throbbing." Grazia was nearby; she brought them each a goblet of wine and water, and told them it was this that made her own mother feel better when she got married to Lino.

A few hours later the couple appeared in ceremonial dress and the party continued. Their friends had not succeeded in gaining entrance to their apartments to play pranks on them, which was commonplace in the country. Everyone laughed at Lino's account of what happened when he got married. After the wedding, he and Grazia were to sleep in the barn at the house where her parents lived and where the wedding ceremony had been held.

Unknown to the newlyweds, their friends had offered to set up the bed for them; an offer that had been gratefully accepted by house owners, who were busy with preparations for the wedding breakfast and celebrations.

The pranksters had sewn two sheets together on three sides to make a kind of sack for the bed, and filled it with straw. So when the newlyweds retired exhausted and a little inebriated, they'd had to first empty the straw out of the sack, which had cost them some effort, and had still gone to bed fully dressed to avoid been prickled by the straw still left inside. Their wedding had been in wintertime too, so they couldn't sleep out on the grass; their first night together was a nightmare. "But after that first freezing cold night," Lino concluded, handing Grazia a goblet of wine, "a stupendous honeymoon followed, all because of my Grazia." Then, turning to the newlyweds he said, "a toast to your happiness!"

"To the newlyweds!" everyone shouted, raising their cups to toast them.

Then everyone went home, satisfied with how the wedding had gone and without the slightest cause to accuse the Bellinis of being over-ostentatious.

The following day many wedding gifts were delivered to Meb and Martino's residence, including fruit preserves, sacks of flour, good quality parchments and inks of both types, vanishing and indelible. The two young people spent the day looking around the place, relaxing and having fun, left alone together in the big house as they were for the moment. Paolo, the Casa Bellini cart driver, came into the courtyard at midday with an unexpected gift. The faithful old servant handed Martino a handwritten letter from his grandfather, and a mare called Niamh, who was accustomed both to being ridden and pulling light vehicles. There was a goat too, which had been an inseparable companion to the mare ever since she was taken from her original herd. The newlyweds shared their midday meal of bread and cheese with Paolo, and gave Niamh some carrots and apples. When the frugal meal was over, Paolo offered to help Martino and Meb arrange the litter for Niamh and the goat in the stable belonging to the new wing of Casa Bellini.

"Noble Martino, my son Lino and I looked after Niamh all the time you were in Bologna," said Paolo, going back into to the kitchen where Lino and Grazia were. "I'll be happy to continue taking care of her daily needs if you need me, and drive the carriage. Signor Bellini told me I should treat Niamh like a princess, because she comes from the excellent herd in the northwest and was raised under our own Monte Rosa!"

"Thank you, Paolo," Martino answered, smiling; "I'll be glad of your help. Please continue to feed Niamh. We'll take care of her drinking water and the rest, and look after her as if she were a noble princess from an allied clan." Paolo was satisfied; he bowed his head in assent and left.

"What was that talk of clans and noble princesses?" asked Meb as soon as they were alone.

"Paolo knows lots of stories, even though he can't read!" replied her husband. "He inhabits a mysterious world where the only things that appear in writing are the milestones carved in Latin along the imperial roads. The Bellini ancestors for him were noble knights and magicians, like that Merlin that some bards sing songs about. There are two female bloodlines in what constitutes our "clan" for him: his and Lino's ancestors are ordinary people who cannot read or write. Mine are noble because they know how to read and write, like you, or because in ancient times, as they say, they were naiads or dryads: wild creatures that could assume human form if necessary, or princesses of the herd, like Niamh, if they incarnated as mares. When a female horse is called an *equa inter pares*, it means she's a sentinel."

"Niamh is a beautiful creature," Meb commented, cutting Martino's explanation short; it was getting a little too technical for her. "The fact that she was a sentinel doesn't make any difference when she's being ridden or pulling a carriage, does it?"

"Niamh is not as submissive as other horses, but she's totally committed to the common good. You'll see, when you get to understand the qualities she has that make her so precious to us too."

"Maybe the same goes for males, with the myth of the centaur Chiron, the teacher of heroes. He was an *equus inter pares* too," Meb remarked, with a smile. "Forgive me if I desert you now; I'm tired and I'd like to rest before we go to the big house for dinner."

Martino knew how delicate his wife was. He kissed her tenderly then lit the lamp and read the words that his grandfather had written for his wedding day, the only date recorded on the Bellini family tree with the first name and surname of the bride.

His grandfather explained that their territory was a place of transit, but was safe in its role as a link in the north-south axis road, and well protected by both the Oleggio and Castello militia and the splendid Res Publica of Genoa. Movements in the east required more attention, both in the valley and along the imperial roads across the uplands between the Amber Road and Munich in Bavaria. Preservation of the local juridical and administrative apparatus was the responsibility of Cavalier Enrico and his peers in the municipality, while Martino would receive diplomatic assignments up until the age of thirty-three. He should be sympathetic to with the traditions of imperial soldiers, who after serving in the army often married girls from the places where they had been posted and became the progenitors of new dynasties; he should do this by granting rights to local populations who were accustomed to living dignified lives as free persons. When they were abroad, the soldiers were accustomed to intolerable abuses of power in undefeated territories where the empire had been accepted in exchange for administrative autonomy. The difference, difficult to explain to anyone who considered themselves strong, was that a free people could never accept slavery because they were not willing to obey other men, only comprehensible laws.

Subscribing to an alliance without conflict was essential because it led to good governance, i.e. the intention to assert a valid legislation within defined territorial borders to allow free movement to those who agreed to respect the dignity of individual lives. Grandfather Bellini concluded by urging his grandson not to deceive himself; demanding respect for the rule of citizenship would be a constant struggle, not a dialectical exercise.

"Martino, do not be content with simply carrying out the duties attached to your position," his grandfather said. "Remember to pass on this advocacy to anyone who declares that the people are just a mob and that it is dangerous to control their will. All forms of government must serve their own people without affecting the rights of other peoples in the territories to which they belong; peoples with whom reasonable alliances had to be agreed in the past, and will need to be agreed again in the future."

After reading this spiritual testament by the man who in his mind was the one most connected with the world, Martino placed it in the archive, then he went up to his room to ask Meb to help him look after Niamh. The mare had been moved that morning; there was only the litter to clean out and the water trough to fill before nightfall. The task was pleasanter than the young woman had imagined, in spite of the goat greeting the two strangers with a series of kicks in an attempt to eject them from his little territory. Perhaps it was the smell of Niamh and the warmth of her body that made the place feel so hospitable, thought Meb, adjusting her skirt. Martino's natural scent heightened by the savage edge it acquired came to her through the aroma of the leather harnesses and clean straw, arousing in her the courage to try new caresses and kisses she'd never dared before, and became another reason for her to repair to the horse's stable on occasion with her husband.

After sundown they emerged dressed as if for a trip to market and presented themselves at the big house. They knocked three times on the main entrance door with the heavy knocker of burnished iron before entering, as a sign of respect for the privacy of the residents. Enrico was seated at the head of the table in the hall, with his back to the door of his study. Martino took his place at his father's right, with the window to the courtyard of his own house behind him, and Silvano, Clementina and Rebecca came next. Facing the head of the family at the other end of the table sat Susanna, with Meb, Margherita and the empty place set for the prophet Elijah on her right, followed by Aligerno who for the first time was struggling to find the appropriate words for the occasion. Grazia had placed water, wine, plaited loaves, black cabbage soup, boiled swiss chard, cheese and roasted river fish on the table. Apples, pomegranates, pears and bunches of white and black grapes were piled high on white ceramic dishes on tables in the corners of the room. Beeswax candles burned in two pewter chandeliers, and between them in the centre of the table was a large white oval dish with painted ivy tendrils decorating the border, full of small almond paste and honey sweetmeats.

A lovely aroma of beeswax, bread and fruit pervaded the air.

Rebecca broke the silence by expressing thanks for the hospitality and announced that she and Aligerno would be leaving the following Monday to go to a new pupil in Gromo, where they had been summoned by Gianpace Ginami dei Licini and his wife Marzia de Piccoli. Aligerno explained that Marzia was the daughter of one of the soldiers who collecting the toll duty on the imperial Alpine road beyond Folgarìa, going towards the Venetian territories. He had accepted the position of tutor for their first-born, Palmiro Ginami, who was about seven years old, informing the Ginamis in his letter that his wife Rebecca could help Marzia and little Teresa, who was two years old. He'd specified in his reply that Rebecca was a Jew who followed the Judeo-Christian religion, and the Ginamis had replied that recent imperial rulings advised against entrusting the education of girls to Jewish women. Gianpace and Marzia had considered it fitting to transfer Aligerno's appointment to a family who lived in Folgarìa, above Rovereto, who could provide lodgings. With the approval of the family in Folgarìa, the appointment letter gave directions for the journey and no further communication was entered into.

The silence that ensued was broken by Enrico, saying that Martino and Meb could go up to Folgarìa in the summer for their honeymoon. Meb went around the table filling their cups with wine, her eyes glistening with tears. She poured just a little for Verde and Balsamina and filled up their cups with water, and when she returned to her seat Martino raised his cup and proposed a toast to friendship and freedom.

After dinner Rebecca helped Susanna put the twins to bed, and told them an old story entitled *Nivella*. "Once upon a time there was, and will always be, Winter and Snow," Meb's mother started. These two young people were in love and decided to get married, for their health, at a time when the air was freezing cold. Sun and Moon, the groom's parents, didn't attend the wedding for fear of overheating the atmosphere. Accepting this precaution, the couple had set their wedding date for a time of year when it was cold and there was a new moon: a moment that happens about once every 29 days, when the Moon declines to reflect the light from the Sun and stays indoors to read and write, and observe the Earth. The bride's parents however, Cold and Frost, did attend the wedding, and took advantage of the absence of Sun to adorn their daughter with magnificent jewels made of frozen water, which would melt in the slightest heat. Snow's brother, Ice, formed a thick layer on the surface of the lake in front of the couple's large house, and all the guests had fun skating on it. The groom's father, Sun, remained hidden behind large grey and white clouds for the entire day of the wedding. Since he was unable to see what was happening himself, he asked an eagle to soar high above the festivities and report back on what he observed every six hours. The Moon, who had repaired to her sitting room at sundown the day before the wedding, watched the ceremony and the festivities from behind her curtains; it seemed a joyous occasion. The first born of the union was a daughter, who was given the name of Nivella. But I don't remember what happened to Nivella; perhaps you could write Nivella's story yourself." Susanna finished brushing her daughters' hair and thanked Rebecca, while Verde and Balsamina embraced her affectionately, then went to bed and dreamed peaceful dreams. Before they left the room, the two friends held hands and Susanna whispered a blessing.

WINTER

"The snow has melted with the swallow's arrival," announced Arianna Speroni; "blankets of violets and yellow crocuses are blooming on the forest floor, along the path between here and the kennels!"

"Describe it," said Meb, "but keep still while I try the dress on you. I'll prick you if you keep fidgeting, I won't be able to help it."

The morning light shone through the window and lit up the wedding dress that Arianna was trying on in the first floor dressing room of the house they called the Casa Grande - the big house, to distinguish it from the Casa Piccola. The two residences shared a common wall and portico facing Piazza Martiri della Libertà in Oleggio, where the community lived closely packed together on a hill in the region of Novaro; a good position for both people and merchandise.

"Aunt Meb, how do you do it?" said Clemenza, who they called Balsamina. She was draping a remnant of cloth around a doll, trying to imitate her aunt, who was an expert seamstress.

"With great passion and patience, because you can't do it if you don't have them," answered the dressmaker, smiling at her niece.

Balsamina's twin sister Margherita, who they called Verde, now entered the room and entirely monopolised her aunt's attention by handing her a missive that had just been delivered to the study on the ground floor of the old building. It was a parchment, folded and sealed with the seal of Aligerno and Rebecca seal, Meb's parents; they had left two months earlier to work with the family of little Otto, whom Aligerno was teaching to read and write. This was the first news she'd had.

The dressmaker read in silence, paying close attention.

"Folgarìa, 12th January MCCCXXII Anno Domini

Dearest,
You are with me every day like my own shadow, in my thoughts.
Think of me as I think of you, so when the light falls on one of us, the other will feel it too.

Otto, my current student, requires practical exercises because he gets too distracted to just study intellectual work. I hope we shall be able to move on from this soon, so I can start teaching him to read. It seems that Emanuele and Clara, Otto's parents, have invited an English teacher from Robert Grosseteste's school of apophatism.

See you soon,
Aligerno"

The letter continued in a different handwriting, and Meb read on.

"Dear sweet Meb,
Do you remember the myth about Sappho and the truth?
I could write to you about the cycle of the moon, or lyrical poetry.
But I prefer to write in friendship, woman to woman. Sappho was born of a family that took care of her education, teaching her in such a way as to instil the

values of both her father's land and her mother's land. Her ancestors, both male and female, should still thank them for this, over all the generations! According to Greek tradition, the people were separated from the aristocracy into which Sappho was born. It is not our custom to separate any person from others, leaving it to posterity to judge who deserves to be considered *primus inter pares* o *nobilis*, as they used to say in Lombardy; 'noble' referring to anyone respected for the accomplishment of works worthy of remembering. So remember never to neglect your studies.

Your father is very busy with his teaching. Otto is not used to listening, so it's good for him to do work that obliges him to put what his teacher tells him into practice. Yesterday they went to the mountains on a sled pulled by Pioggia, a gentle mare on whom I've been out riding a few times myself. Papa drove the sled, explaining what he was doing to his pupil. On the way back he changed course, so the mare wouldn't recognise the road and return to the stable of her own will. Then he handed the reins to Otto, telling him which way to go every time they arrived a crossing of two, three or four roads, and how to guide Pioggia. At dinner, Aligerno told how they'd reached the first hut outside the village within half an hour on the way there, but the return journey took four hours. Otto was so tired that he went to bed as soon as he got home, without any dinner!

In you fall pregnant you could stay in Oleggio, and I'll come if you write to me. If we don't hear from you we'll arrange quiet lodgings for you next to our own, with a separate entrance.

Big kisses
Rebecca"

"Everything's fine," Meb reported, rolling up the parchment and tying it with a purple ribbon. She told them the story about Aligerno and Otto going out for a ride with Pioggia pulling the sleigh, then continued with the fitting for Arianna's wedding dress. As she was pinning the bodice together, Meb reflected with wonderment on her mother's words; she'd never thought in the three months she'd been married to Martino that she might soon become a mother herself. When the dress fitting was over, she left her young guest playing with the little girls and went downstairs to Susanna, who was helping Grazia to wash chard in the kitchen. Once they'd been washed they would be steamed in a basket over a pot, in which onions, lentils, beans and a chicken's leg were already bubbling away on the fire. The chard would be ready in half an hour, and served with bread, cheese and nuts; the broth would be left to simmer until evening, then served for dinner with a spoonful of olive oil.

Meb told Susanna that they were expecting an English teacher in Folgarìa, and Susanna was thrilled with the news, hoping Martino would be able to get there in time to meet the luminary.

"Opportunities to converse with any English teacher are very rare, let alone a teacher of the Thomas Becket school," said Susanna at dinner. She was sitting at the head of the table with her back to the kitchen door; Arianna was on her right and Meb on her left. Enrico sat at the other end of the long table, with his son Martino on his right.

"Meb says he's a follower of Robert Grosseteste" said Arianna, and enquired "what's the relationship between Grosseteste and poor Thomas Becket, Susanna?"

"Thomas Becket lived in the Kingdom of England," said Susanna. "He studied law in Paris, Bologna and Auxerre, and when he returned to London King Henry II made him Lord Chancellor, in the year 1154 AD. During his religious career he opposed the reduction of ecclesiastical privileges, to the detriment of the barons who complained about him. He was killed for this in 1170. Becket's tomb in Canterbury has become a destination for English Catholic pilgrims, who consider him a martyr for the independence of the clergy from the secular government.

Robert Grosseteste was born five years after the assassination of Thomas Becket and followed him in his studies and his intent. He came to terms with the economic interests of the English barons, however, who had been alienated by Becket's intransigent position. Grosseteste affirmed that the people, the aristocracy and the local clergy must remain united and enter into dialogue with the government. He then started to favour the nobility, the bourgeoisie and the local communities over the Curia of Rome, which he considered too greedy and closed to any discussion with the Government. Adam Marsh was a close friend of Grosseteste; he was in correspondence with Simon di Montfort on ways of protecting the government from any threat of tyranny."

"We would like to know the content of that correspondence and what English scholars currently think," Martino explained, "and also about the apophatic philosophy."

Susanna had got up and was pouring water into Enrico's cup, pensively.

"Thought is a form of energy, the original source of which is unthinkable to the human mind," Martino went on, addressing Arianna.

"Apophatism is the philosophical discipline that refuses to define divinity, considering it to be impossible to understand," Enrico continued. "The School has adopted a negative theology: logical thinking reaches its limit when it perversely demonstrates the existence of truth by stating that all that is true cannot exist."

"In Greek philosophy, if we adopt the deductive method of Parmenides, the dialectic of Plato and the rationality of Aristotle," Meb interjected, "we come to perceive the unity of pure thought. Reality emanates from the original unity, and as humans we can only study the manifestations of it. We can study anything from the nature of light to any imaginable thing; as long as we accept that we cannot know the first principle, which it is impossible to understand or communicate."

The diners also reflected on the importance of silence, to make space in one's own mind. Martino was not a supporter of abstract intellectualism; he brought the evening to a close by advising Arianna to study the manuscripts *De aquarum conductis et ingeniis erigendis* by the Alexandrian and *De virtutibus alimentorum* by Galen, which were in the library on the first floor of the Casa Grande. After dinner, Arianna went up to bed with Balsamina. The little girl was singing lullabies to her doll made of hemp cloth stuffed with wool and a painted face. Arianna told her how the adults talked about Greek and Latin philosophy over dinner, and politics too. "It's important for you and Verde to study too," she advised the child, "so you'll be able to make wise decisions and join in with similar conversations suitable for ladies and sympathetic gentlemen."

Balsamina wanted to know more about this but understood practically nothing.

"If I had a choice," she confided later to her doll, under the blanket, "I think I'd keep quiet at the table and work hard in the kitchen. I want to learn to choose foods that are not bad for you but infuse you with energy, which is the source of every virtue. Like Mamma does, although I don't quite know how eating a fig can be bad for you and eating an apple can increase faith, hope and charity. Heaven knows what we're supposed to eat for generosity, modesty, temperance, patience and harmony."

Before she went to sleep, the little girl decided she would study the subject of nutrition in more depth.

In the weeks that followed, Arianna helped Grazia with the shopping at the market, along with Verde and Balsamina, and with the cooking, learning the secrets of the Oleggio diet. They learned that eggs and meat came from the farms less than an hour away. Fresh fish was caught in the river Ticino that flowed like a green ribbon across the plain towards Milan; bottles of olive oil, salted anchovies and sardines preserved in oil came from Liguria and the sea there. Arianna was eager to learn, and told Meb she was hoping for a honeymoon that would take her to this region. Meb listened but made no comment on her young friend's dream; she was torn between curiosity to discover new horizons like the sea, and her desire to see her parents again. Unable to arrive at a decision by herself, she went to her husband's study to talk to him about it a few days later.

"Both propositions are interesting," said Martino.

"I think so too," said his wife. "We would meet relatives and see new things either way."

"In Folgarìa I could study the Constitution of the Magnificent Community and compile a summary of it to discuss with our fellow citizens here. I could also discover the current philosophical stance of the English School," the knight went on, meditatively. "But in Genoa we could visit the doge's palace that Obizzo Spinola had built so he would no longer have to hold public meetings in urban residences. That would be an interesting possibility to introduce here too, if the cost is not too much for our municipal finances. We could also travel along the coast from Mount Portofino to Santa Maria, where my maternal grandfather has his olive groves."

"Do you have relatives you would like to introduce me to?" asked Meb.

"Yes, I'd like to introduce you to two children I met last year on my way back from Bologna, both sons of Teodoro del Monferrato. Teodoro was born in Byzantium thirty-one years ago to the Byzantine emperor and Violante, the sister of Giovanni Aleramici who appointed him as his heir in his will. Teodoro landed in Genoa in 1306 and married Argentina, daughter of the doge Opicino Spinola."

"Is Argentina the daughter of Violante di Saluzzo?"

"Yes. She's the only daughter of Violante's union with Opicino Spinola. When Opicino died in 1315, Violante married Luchino Visconti of Milan."

"I remember; it was a magnificent wedding. Sadly, Violante died that same year, didn't she?"

"She did. Luchino Visconti, Violante's widower, married Caterina, daughter of Oberto Spinola, in 1318. Sadly, Catherine died too in the first year of their marriage; the air in Milan is apparently lethal for Casa Spinola!"

"The deaths are more likely to have been caused by poison in the Lombard water; the thirst for power in that place is constantly sparking war!" Meb remarked sadly.

"Azzone Visconti was born in Milan on 7th December, the day dedicated to the Father of the Church of St. Ambrose, twenty years ago," Martino went on; "I met him when he was a student and I consider him to be a person of good sense. St. Ambrose is the patron saint of Milan; God willing, Azzone will be a model of good governance!"

"Let's hope so," said Meb, unconvinced.

"I told you last year that I'd met two children I wanted to introduce to you," said Martino, getting back to the point. One of them is Violante, who's about three years old. They say she had grey eyes like her maternal grandmother when she was born, which is how she came by her Christian name. Her elder brother is called Giovanni, and at nine years old he's already a war-hungry knight, more fitted for fighting than administration. Argentina Spinola, their mother, was not receiving any visitors at the time. I remember she had to rest as she was expecting another child, which must be born by now. As for Teodoro, the Emperor Henry VII of Luxembourg called him to the marquisate to invest him. Teodoro continued convening the parliaments that Manfredo IV of Saluzzo set up in 1305, in order to govern the territory under his jurisdiction without dissent. These parliaments are meetings that the Marquis holds with feudal lords and representatives from the community; the clergy are not involved since they are exempt from paying taxes. At these assemblies they discuss land management, duties to be levied and military defences, to ensure the safety of residents and travellers. In 1319, Pope John XXII asked Teodoro to act as mediator to repair the schism between the Church of the West and the Church of the East, by virtue of his contacts with the court of Byzantium. Unfortunately, although the Eastern Emperor Andronicus II Palaeologus was willing, the Church of Avignon sided with Casa D'Angiò, which put an end to the negotiations."

"We should perhaps not seek personal meetings where our family owns agricultural land," observed Meb cautiously, "since we don't hold any political office."

Martino agreed with his wife, and stood to embrace her. Her scent of lavender uplifted him and he thanked her, whispering words that tickled her and sent shivers of pleasure through her.

Two days later, Meb returned to her in-laws' residence for Arianna to try on the dress again, and found Enrico lying in bed, in pain. Susanna explained he was suffering from an attack of gout; there was swelling in his knee and toe joints, and he had a high fever. "Other members of his family used to suffer from this affliction," Susanna confided to her daughter-in-law. "If Martino shows similar symptoms in the future, remember that the apothecary advises avoiding raisins, seasoned salami and wine. But I won't bore you any further; let's go and see what Arianna is doing with the girls."

They found them in the kitchen, helping Grazia prepare the bagna cauda. She was cutting up edible thistles and removing the filaments, and explained that she would leave them to boil while the Rosary and the Angelus were recited at midday. She would them put them in a pan with butter and garlic, add some anchovy fillets and crush it all down with a spoon until she obtained a creamy mixture, which she would serve for dinner with fresh ricotta. Meb waited till they'd finished preparing the vegetables before asking Arianna to come to the dressing room to try on the dress, which was finally ready. The families of both spouses were very fond of tradition, so Arianna had chosen purple wool for her cloak and airy, white muslin for her dress. She would wear white shoes on which her mother Laura had embroidered two silver horseshoes woven with a four-leaf clover entwined around them. Satisfied that the dress was a perfect fit, the two friends spent the rest of the morning in the library and returned to the kitchen for the ritual prayers with the cook. The following day, the majordomo Lino took Arianna back to her parents' house, with the dress as a gift.

As soon as Enrico felt better, Martino invited him into his study to discuss a report that had arrived from the Bellini family in Venice.

"Emperor Henry VII," Martino read aloud, "wasted no time playing music as they do at the house of D'Angiò and in Burgundy; nor did he go hunting for wild birds like the young Swabians. He did not even recite the prayers theatrically as Casa d'Aragona husbands often do.

For over ten years, the Roman emperor has established a robust fiscal network, substituting power and captains of the people with vicars loyal to his empire; in urban centres in particular, since it is easier to collect duties and state taxes in cities using tax collectors from outside the local area. This was a blatant violation of the Peace of Constance drawn up between the cities and the defeated emperor, Barbarossa; he nonetheless had supporters in some of the cities and thus managed to stir up discontent and agitation against scapegoats that had goods to be requisitioned. Federico II, Manfredi and D'Angiò tried too, but in a less systematic way; perhaps because they are more open to distractions and have less determined allies.

Genoa, Rome, Florence, Padua and Bologna resisted.

Milan, Bergamo, Brescia, Cremona, Parma, Reggio, Modena, Piacenza, Pavia, Tortona, Asti, Verona, Mantua, Lodi, Como, Vercelli, Novara, Ivrea, Canavese and the territories of Crema, Chieri, Borgo San Donnino, Monza, Reggiolo and Valcamonica surrendered and accepted the vicars appointed by the empire. Only half of these spoke Italian; among them, Enrico VIII of Genoa nominated Manfredo Grillo to stand in Pavia and Alberto Malocello in Novara. Hugues de Bresse was appointed vicar in Vercelli; he came from Burgundy bringing twenty knights loyal to Casa Savoia. Vicars were also appointed in Como and Lodi: two vassals from Savoy; in Ivrea, Jean De Luysiel, the castellan of Saint-Laurent de Pons and a subordinate of the Savoys, translated his name into Latin and became Johannes de Sancto Laurentio, but behaved in an uncivilised fashion. All those from across the Alps were distinguished by their tendency to prefer absolutism to mediation. In particular, the imperial vicars proved to be dominated by the courts of Chambery and Vienne, As a clear sign of the transalpine umbilical cord, Jacques de Boczosel was rewarded with the appointment of vicar of Grenoble, castellan of Nyon and Prangins, visdomino of Geneva, castellan of Versoix and bailiff of Vaud, on the strength of having held the vicariate of Lodi, and now appears to be one of Count Edoardo's preferred advisers.

Perhaps the emperor favoured Savoy for his nominations because his sister was married to governor Amadeus V, who was loyal to his wife's family. Even the notary Bernardo de Mercato, perhaps the most active and cultured of the elected emperor's collaborators, was born in Savoy. At least, he doesn't appear to have burned or forged any documents! Although there's no trace left after documents have been burned, it's true...

The king of the Romans supported the men of Amedeo, who was the first to appear before him, across the Alps or in Turin, and rewarded the loyalty he demonstrated in the *iter romanum* with a trip to Rome. The problem is that these people were not interested in managing cities and abiding by the needs of the various territories. For these foreigners the *genius loci* is an unknown soldier, dead and forgotten on the ancient republican battlefields.

We might recall Tommaso of Enzola as an exception: captain of the people at Bologna in 1274 and the podestà of Modena in 1278, Reggio Emilia in 1279, Cremona in 1284, Lucca in 1285, Siena in 1289 and Perugia in 1303. Apart from Tommaso, the only vicar to present a classic *cursus honorum* was Lapo degli Uberti, rector of Mantua in 1296, 1297 and 1299, then of Verona in 1301, 1302 and 1306. Apart from these two officers, the rest proved to be neither professional nor helpful.

Henry VII supported his imperial choices in the name of *pax romana*, but transalpine ignorance of Italian dignity is unacceptable. In Milan they describe the Flemish vicar, the royal marshall Jean de Calcy, as an *arrogant, ignorant, rude person.*"

"I agree," said Enrico. "The transalpine vicars have shown themselves to be superficial and incompetent. Their behaviour is determined by personal interests, not by concern for the common good. The life of our communities and our cities is more complex than foreign kings and emperors understand!"

"Listen, Papa," Martino continued, reading again from the Venetian document: "Magistrates must govern in conjunction with representatives of the people. The imperial vicars of Henry VII, however, burdened the residents with an *onerosum iugum*, an expensive tax, without rendering them any service. Moreover, during the years of royal administration, no effective administrative apparatus was formed because most of the nominees made their careers across the Alps. Francesco da Cocconato, Spinetta Malaspina, Vanni Zeno dei Lanfranchi and Lamberto Cipriani followed Henry into Tuscany but were given no government office. Niccolò Bonsignori was Luigi di Savoia's vicar in Rome in the summer of 1312, but was expelled in October of the same year after a pro-European uprising led by the House of Colonna. Following this rebellion, the vicar of Bergamo was one of the few to be spared in the popular uprising; he barricaded himself in the town hall, refusing to announce imperial orders regarding the spending of public contributions on the Roman expedition. Henry was more cautious in nominating the second round of royal officers, and selected politicians and experienced administrators who preferred to wield their authority at local level rather than pursuing the sovereign's ambitions. When he left Lombardy to go to Genoa, he left the government of Milan to Matteo Visconti, who was also an imperial vicar and captain of the people at that time. In Verona he nominated Cane della Scala, in Mantua Passerino Bonacolsi, and in Parma Ghiberto da Correggio."

"True," said Enrico, and went on meditatively: "These appointments, however, have given rise to despotic forms of government."

"So, father, how shall we continue to safeguard our traditions and our freedoms?"

"By adopting the system of multiple loyalties, son."

The older man continued, explaining what he meant: "Better to be silent than to say or write falsehood. Where there is danger the use of any means of avoiding an unnatural transfer is permissible, provided you don't put a single life at risk in order to save your own. The end does not justify the means.

"Outside of politics and diplomacy, if you had to choose between the life of the child and the life of the mother during childbirth, which is it better to save, father?"

"*Primum non nocere*, as Hippocrates teaches us. You must try to save both the woman and the child, because if the child cannot be born, the woman too is condemned to certain death. At the moment of conception the organism turns the woman into a mother, a condition that can only change when she is no longer fertile. When I was a magistrate in Garlasco, a woman in an advanced state of pregnancy fell into the Ticino and was almost drowned, sucked into one of those eddies that form into funnel-shaped whirlpools. She was saved by some fishermen and immediately went into labour. The village midwife stepped in, but had to call the apothecary, who delivered the infant by caesarean section because the uterus did not dilate after the waters broke. The child lived, but the woman died a week later and the widower accused the apothecary of voluntary homicide. A reconstruction of the facts and the testimony of other patients convinced me that it was his intention to save the lives of both mother and child; having done all he could to save them both, I declared him innocent."

"How did you demonstrate professional integrity?"

"The midwife and other patients testified that he boiled the tools he used for every operation in water, and treated the wound he inflicted in the conventional way, with compresses and bandages. Unfortunately, the woman's body proved to be too weak, but the apothecary prevented infection and tried to help her recover, using tonics known to be effective. This behaviour saved him in my opinion, and in that of his fellow countrymen in particular, who still give him work."

Martino listened to his father, with heartfelt gratitude that he had chosen the profession of notary, which did not involve him in any magistrate's duties.

He changed the subject and showed Enrico a dispatch he'd received from Lionello Nicolussi di Luserna, a man he'd met in Bologna and with whom he had continued to correspond.

The two men were distracted by the sound of the bell announcing it was time for dinner. Meb served them lentil soup to break their fast, and thinly-sliced apples spread with honey the way Martino liked them, greedy as a bear.

In the afternoon Enrico and Martino went back to the study.

Lionello wrote that Thomas of Lancaster had been imprisoned. Accused of serious crimes that fell outside the honourable combat expected in war, it was possible he would be beheaded. In this event, Edward II of England would request sanctions against the bishop of Trento, who was a Bavarian appointed and protected by the kingdoms of Bohemia and Hungary.

"With the conquest of England in 1066 by William, Duke of Normandy, there began a dispute that cannot be resolved by peaceful means, since a vassal of the king of France became king of England, claiming to be the head of a nation independent of Europe," Henry reminded his son.

"What nonsense!" Martino commented. "Nothing is further from good governance than those who seek to challenge documents and oral traditions in their own favour."

"The people will be a good witness in generations to come," Enrico hoped. Martino suggested writing to the Ginamis of Gromo to order a new sword for defence purposes when travelling, and in case the clashes should spread from the cities to the villages.

"*Si vis pacem para bellum*" said Enrico with a weary smile.

"Yes, father," Martino agreed, "classical teaching is worthwhile for every generation, if those who are born free wish to leave their freedom as a legacy."

*

At the horse-breeding farm belonging to Arianna's parents, preparations were underway to celebrate the marriage of their daughter to Enea of Como. The bride and groom would live in rooms built specially for them on the first floor above the stables. The external staircase, the gallery and the remainder of the structure consisting of A-frame and joists were already completed, as the autumn had been mild. The terracotta roof tiles and shingles had arrived from the Beldì kiln in early November and had been installed during the "San Martino" summer between the 8th and the 11th of November, when it had not rained and the temperature had risen, as every year. Over the winter, Enea had decorated the apartment with frescoes; he was an artist. He had painted festoons above the doors and windows of all three rooms. The windows looked out over the garden encircled by a dry stone wall, and as far to the hills rising up to the Monte Rosa that stood out magnificently on the horizon. The gallery led into the first room, where there was a fireplace and a table and four chairs. The decoration in this room was dedicated to the favourite kitchen garden products at the farm: apples, pears and carrots. The wall that housed the fireplace also contained the door to the bedroom, where Enea had painted intertwining branches of wild rose, bramble and ruscus aculeatus, also known as butcher's broom. The branches were weighed down with red berries and juicy fruits; gifts of nature that were considered auspicious. A small door to the right of the bed led into the third room, which he'd decorated with a lake scene: reeds bending in the wind and two ducks swimming, and a robin observing them from a blooming chimonanthus bush in the foreground. The only window in the room looked out over the farmyard. The carpenter had already delivered the oak bed, table and chairs, and the day before the wedding three trunks with clothes and linen were also brought in. Laura spread out the sheets and blanket with the help of Enea's mother; they worked in silence, each dreaming of cradling a grandchild within a year.

SPRING

On the morning of Saturday 13th March 1322, the Speroni family welcomed the Visconti notary Martino Bellini and his family. Martino recorded the marriage in triplicate; one copy for his archive, one to be delivered to the magistrate Pietro Caccia, and one for the bride. The master of the house then opened the first of many bottles of wine to animate the festivities. The women gossiped, deciding that Martino's sisters would do well to spend the summer there on the farm with the stableman's children and all the jobs that were to be done in the open air. "They're so pale compared to the children who live here," Susanna conceded. Laura Speroni was glad her friend was willing to leave the twins in her care and changed the subject quickly, thinking she might change her mind if she prolonged discussion of it.

"Our son-in-law Enea was at the workshop on Lake Como for two years," said Laura. He did an apprenticeship at a famous studio. There were two rooms for painting miniatures and three for sketches, cartoons and frescoes. Other rooms were reserved for architectural projects."

"What did he specialise in?" asked Meb.

"He knows how to prepare powders and mixtures for decorating walls and woodwork," explained Enea's mother, who had said nothing up until then.

"Can he copy too? And draw freehand without copying? And colour?" Meb persisted.

"Yes," answered the groom's mother; "he gave me some parchments with some of his studies on them. There are decorations that he copied from the masters and drawings that he did himself, from his observation of nature."

"He did the frescoes in the new rooms," Laura added. "Let's go and see them while there's still light and the newlyweds are busy with their friends!"

The group of women went off to look around, content to distance themselves from the pranks and the rhythmic singing that made them feel like dancing.

Vittorio Speroni took Enrico and Martino Bellini to see their stallion Pegaso, and the mare selected to mate with him.

"This will be the first time this mare has been mated, so if she's impregnated by Pegaso, all her foals will have some of your stallion's characteristics. She's called Aracne; she was born of our own Mercurio and Erica, both healthy animals. Erica is a good trotter too, ideal for pulling a cart. When Aracne was a filly, she was in the enclosure near the moor with her mother and the other trotters, so she learned to hold that pace without breaking into a gallop."

The old magistrate and the young notary listened with interest as they knew nothing about horse-breeding methods, even though both were expert riders.

"Has Pegaso already mated with Aracne?" Martino inquired.

"Yes. Mares come into season regularly," Vittorio explained. "The duration of daylight hours is an important element for stimulating oestrum. Mares are stimulated visually to accept the male, and become excited by his readiness, which they recognise by his eye contact, aroma and body movements."

"When did you put them together?" Enrico asked.

"As soon as Pegaso arrived we left him with Bonadea and some other mares, but he didn't take to them. We've been putting the two of them in the enclosure beyond the vegetable garden together for a month now, on fine days when the ground's not too muddy; near the water trough bordering the path up the hill. So far I've seen Aracne urinate to indicate she's ready for mating, and lift her tail. Pegaso was excited at this sign; he wasn't able to penetrate her but he ejaculated and his semen had no smell of urine."

"Is that good?" asked Martino, puzzled.

"Yes, it's fine," Vittorio replied. "Pegaso has a good reproductive organ, suitable for depositing his seed in Aracne's uterus. Like I said, I've checked and his testicles are still producing quality seed. The penis is usually flaccid and stays in the sheath that you see under his belly; but being hollow, it increases in volume when he gets excited, when the blood inflates the corpora cavernosa. The erect penis varies in size between animals; in horses it can be more than an arm's length and four inches in circumference. But it's not the size of the individual that's important for successful mating, it's the balance between their sizes, their suppleness and female's lubrication. During the first stage of the erection, the top of the penis is no different from the rest of the shaft; but before ejaculation it swells and increases in diameter by up to three inches. In jargon, we say it's gone pink."

"That happens in dogs too," said Martino. "Lino says that the male does the 'flower', remaining attached to the bitch so as not to disperse the seed."

"Actually, the dog always remains attached during coitus, he can't help it," Enrico pointed out. "The male and female sometimes try to separate but they can't, then they start yelping and you have to keep them still to stop them injuring themselves."

"Horses are more patient," Vittorio went on. "The semen is ejaculated in a series of spurts stimulated by pelvic movements, swinging of the tail and anal contractions. If you put your hand under the stallion, you can feel the pulsating wave that signals the passage of the seminal fluid. When I examined Pegaso, the quantity, concentration, white colour and smell of his semen was good. Aracne will probably be impregnated by spring."

"Before we join the others," Martino suggested, "I'd like to show you the horse we came with in the cart."

They went to the stable where the mares were kept and Vittorio stood to the left of Niamh. He opened her mouth with a steady hand and announced that her teeth were normal for a four-year-old female and would be permanent by the end of the year. Then he looked at her eyes and touched them gently. "Healthy, her neck's not too muscular and she has a delicate musculature. You can rely on her to pull the cart, and she may be good for your wife to ride, but only if you're with her because she's nervous and it wouldn't take much to scare her."

Two tables had been set up for dinner in the large kitchen and dining room of the farm. Large earthenware pots of barley soup, plaited rye and spelt loaves, platters of polenta, sliced cheese and roast turkey had been prepared for the guests, and they could also help themselves to red wine and water. Apples, pears, walnuts, hazelnuts and shelled almonds were arranged on the kitchen worktops and cupboard. Dried medlars, red dates and grapes were served in pewter bowls to end the meal with something sweet.

When Susanna told her daughters that they would be staying until the autumn, the little ones got excited and no longer felt sleepy, so they stayed up for the evening festivities. A bard from Borgomanero sang for the pleasure of the guests, who would have been more generous if the artist had risen to their expectations. The young man began with an ancient song about Lago Maggiore:

Oh Giorgio, Giorgio, Giorgio
Wine, barley and polenta!
Oh Giorgio of Lago Maggiore
I'll be happy if you take me there!
But if you go to Arona in summer
And Angera in winter
I'll stay at home with mother!

The lyric was a transposition of the saying "If you want to suffer the pains of hell, go to Trento in summer and Feltre in winter" and provoked general hilarity. Delighted with the reaction, the bard carried on in a colloquial mood:

I was walking down the street at one thirty-three
when I came across a heifer worthy of a king.

I whistled.

227

What a doll!
The dress she wore was fabulous
and her curves were like no other
Charming feet peeped out below her dress
dainty, small and bare.

I whistled.
What a doll!

Hey, hey, baby said I
don't be shy, come here and kiss me!
If you go, you'll miss your chance.
Stay here and give me a kiss!

She turned and looked me up and down like a tramp.
Then suddenly she turned on me and landed me a
champion punch!

But she was so scared
She went all pale and breathless
and then, well she was worried
she hugged me and cried in grief!

You know how it is; I decided to go
I pretended to swoon
and what did she do?
Sorry she said and planted a kiss on my mouth!

I whistled.
What a doll!

The bard paused for a cup of wine, then sang a song
dedicated to Arianna and her bosom friend, the beautiful

Caterina di Bellinzago, who was at the party with her new husband.

Two women, two women, two women
whatever will they talk about?

How many hints will they have for each other
when they go to the river to bathe!
They'll tell each other secrets because they're such good friends
When they look in the mirror they say they look good together
But since they married, the playing has stopped
A total change has taken place and each one for her man!

Two women, two women, two women
since they married, the game will never be the same again.

Susanna clapped and the other women followed suit. Then she asked the bard to sing the *Ballad of Kublai Khan* and started humming it; then the young minstrel joined in:

In Xanadu did Kubla Khan
A stately pleasure-dome decree:
Where Alph, the sacred river, ran
Through caverns measureless to man down to a sunless sea.

So twice five miles of fertile ground
With walls and towers were girdled round;
And there were gardens bright with sinuous rills,

Where blossomed many an incense-bearing tree;

And here were forests ancient as the hills,
Enfolding sunny spots of greenery.
But oh! that deep romantic chasm which slanted
Down the green hill athwart a cedarn cover!

A savage place!
Oh holy and enchanted!
As e'er beneath a waning moon was haunted
By woman wailing for her demon-lover!

But a hazy mirage
appeared to the man one day.
And Kublai Khan had to leave that paradise.
to never, never, never return again!

The newlyweds asked him to play music they could dance to, and the evening continued with the airs of graceful madrigals and many toasts to their conjugal bliss.
At the close of the evening, Enea presented Arianna with a poem that he'd composed and penned himself, illuminated with a miniature bust of a woman as the initial:

A so strong, enough for me to fall in love
since this is the initial of your graceful name
it fills my heart like a portrait in a frame
it is surely the first of all letters, the place it deserves to hold!

A greater honour than pearls have I

painted for your gratification, dear.
Your faithful servant, that I may be
the one to receive your love!

Another grace I ask you of, my love:
allow me to paint you with my brush
so your beauty may be remembered for all time
and I am happy to leave but this sign!

Because you alone, gentle Arianna,
have led me out of the labyrinth!

Everyone applauded and the bard promised to put his composition to music to add to his repertoire, to the greater glory of the couple. Then holding hands they went up to their new apartment.

The guests lay down on makeshift beds in the house and the bard slept on clean straw in the barn, lying next to the sacks of oats and flax seed for the horses. Martino showed him to the stable and patted Pegaso fondly. The horse that Martino's tutor, Silvano, had given him as a graduation gift had been left at Casa Speroni for breeding, and was now sleeping upright beside the goat that inseparable from him. The nobleman of Casa Bellini lay down next to the bard and covered them both with his cloak before falling asleep. When the last lamp was turned off, the silence of the starry night finally replaced the drunken singing, and left even the householders to sleep. It was pouring with rain by the time the cock crowed to announce the beginning of a new day. Martino, the bard and the newlywed couple who were sleeping in the room above the stable, woke up when Pegaso whinnied. Martino didn't want to get his white woollen cloak wet that he used for official visits, so he just shared a few apples with the young minstrel, the goat and the stallions. They chatted as they waited for Enea to come down.

"What's your name?" asked Martino, biting into an apple.

"My name's William, but you can call me Sam. I'm the son of Antoine Vert Monts, who's been called Mal Green Mountains ever since he went to England. My mother's name is Anna Drunemeton; she travels along the Brittany and Normandy coast with her family."

"Have you been to Burgundy, Savoy and Provence too? And Avignon?" Martino inquired. He was starting to think the bard might be an interesting person to talk to.

"I passed through Burgundy when I left my mother's clan, and fell in love there with the graceful and slender Eline. She skipped like a fawn and loved taking her brother's flock out on the plateau of Bresse! Her family were shepherds, they put me up for a few months in exchange for some wooden instruments, which I've learned how to carve. I left before I got too involved, because I really liked her. I crossed the Alps and stayed in Geneva for a few months; the covered market there is wonderful. And now here I am, talking to you, and it's raining 'cani e gatti' outside."

Enea came in then to clean the stables out, fill the water troughs and feed the animals.

"...raining cani e gatti?!" he said, repeating the last words he'd heard with evident curiosity.

William gave a rather bizarre explanation of the expression: "my family is as free as the wind and as powerful as the rain. Our men go hunting in packs like wolves, the animal that's most like the wind. Our women are as powerful as the rain and bring up their children like cats, with no men around. So when it rains we say it's raining cani e gatti. But it's probably just a play on words they came up with when they went to England, and heard someone in the market say *it's raining catadupe,* meaning it was raining heavily."

"How do you say it in English?" Martino asked. He'd known lots of English-speaking students in Bologna but he didn't ever recall hearing the expression before.

"It's raining cats and dogs."

"It's raining *catadupe*... it's raining catsa... or cata... d... "Martino mused out loud.

"In Greek there's an *unusual* expression *katadoxa,*" said Enea. "Giannis used to say it a lot, a Byzantine icon writer who used to teach methods and formulas to the masters in Como. It was a criticism of our way of drawing; the Orthodox Greeks considered it too subjective and too far from the iconographic canon."

"Of course!" exclaimed the other two in unison, delighted they'd discovered where the strange little saying came from.

"People in the British Isles must have overheard it in Greek conversations at the market or the baths, not knowing what it meant," Martin surmised. They wouldn't know how to translate the words into their own language, so they just repeated them their own way, like our own people do when they hear the Jewish merchants speaking Hebrew in the market. The Romans spoke Greek when they traded with the Celts - it was the universal language at the time of Alexander the Great - and it would certainly be *unusual* for anyone from the Mediterranean to see the rain they get in the North!"

The spring rain fell lightly and persistently throughout the day, which ended with a dinner enlivened with some new songs from the bard William, known as Sam. The tables were laid with cheese, poached fish, steamed wild artichokes, rye bread and fruit. Verde sat with Bastet, the kitchen cat; the girl ate her dinner curled up as usual under the table, claiming the cat needed her company. Balsamina passed food down to her twin sister, who split it with the graceful tabby with eyes as green as the stagnant pond in the birch wood that bordered the moor. After eating and toasting the health of the guests, Sam dedicated a little song to the horses, thinking of Pegaso.

Wild beast from the West
when you eat oats
drink water and sour cherry!
I will ride only you
On your back I would be
more powerful than a king!
Long live the fury of the West
the strongest beast that lives
I will ride only you!
I will ride only you!

Balsamina clapped her hands, and so did Elio, the stableman's youngest son, and the two of them galloped around the kitchen table together for a few minutes. William had to repeat the song four times before the company transferred to the hall. The bard then quietened the mood with something more soothing:

I want to give you a present tonight
so you'll remember

the one who cannot forget.
This is my loving thought
for you, for you.
Sing whenever you feel the need
and think of me, of me.
If my love you do not want
or you cannot, cannot accept
this at least you will cherish, cherish
When you are alone
it will keep you company
since I shall not come back.
I shall never come back to you.
But any time you want to sing
think of me, of me.

He continued with more songs from his sentimental repertoire, seeing the children had fallen sleep and the couples still listening to him had their arms around each other.

Dark eyes
You no longer want me
in your heart.

Dark eyes
And I cannot
stop.

I'll feel like
crying
if you leave.

Dark eyes

dark eyes
go with him
but he is not love.

In the meantime
I shall die
but you may not
know it.

Dark eyes
dark eyes
I feel I'm
all at sea
a sail
with no wind
and the sun
has gone in.

Dark eyes
dark eyes
I lived only
for you!

For his finale, William known as Sam told his audience that his Christian name was Etienne, but his maternal grandparents called him Mal. He dedicated a song to Casa Speroni in his mother tongue:

J'ai un père et j'ai une mère
Que j'appel papa et maman
Mais moi dans mon vocabulaire
Je croix qu'ils sont plus que mes parents.

Ils sont mon ciel et ma terre
Et moi un cheval sans fer
Qui a besoin de leur lumière
Oui, j'ai besoin de leur lumière.

Ils sont ma nuit et mon bonjour
Et moi le fruit de leur saisons
Je porte les couleurs de leur amour
De leur visages
Et de leurs noms.

Ma chanson soit comme une prière
Pour une église à tous les pères de la terre
Une synagogue à toutes les mères qui entendront
Nous vous aimons.

Nous vous aimons
Avec l'espoir comme seule promesse
Que dans nos coeurs
Sacrifier toutes les passions.

C'que vous avez laissé derrière.
C'que vous avez laissé derrière.

After this melody the guests said goodnight and slept peacefully.

The next day Vittorio, Enea, Enrico and Martino retired to the Casa Speroni archive, where the head of the family kept the bloodlines of his herd and ownership documents that established their succession.
"Eight years ago, after the death of Henry VII," Martino recalled, "some electoral princes put their emperor

Ludwig Wittelsbach on the throne. But other princes elected Frederick of Habsburg. Pope John XXII officially refrained from siding with either faction, but the request for Ludwig's right to accede to the throne was ignored, and this convinced the Pope to disqualify him. Ludwig in turn did not consider the pope to be above the parties, and wanted to continue electing princes to the office of bishop in the territories under his control. These decisions of his explain why he was called Ludwig the Bavarian: the Habsburgs and the pope used the term pejoratively, to indicate that he was from the Province of Bavaria, bound as a villein to his turf of origin. But for us this does not indicate a shortcoming, as it also reveals a manifest attention to the needs of the environment and the people."

"Who was the rival to Ludwig the Bavarian?" asked Vittorio.

"Frederick of Habsburg," answered Martino; "born in Vienna in 1289 to Albert and Elizabeth of Carinthia, who brought the Tyrol and Gorizia as her dowry. Frederick became Duke of Austria and Styria after his father was killed in 1308 and his elder brother Rudolph died. He was raised alongside his cousin Ludwig, and they were bosom friends until Frederick was given the tutelage of the Dukes of Upper Bavaria, a role to which Ludwig aspired, and was offended because Frederick - who was not Bavarian - had been chosen above him."

Enea interrupted Martino to fetch fruit and water. When they had taken refreshment, they listened with renewed energy to the background events, which they needed to know before they could settle their plans for the future.

"Henry VII died and both cousins accepted the candidacy for succession to the imperial throne. The election for the new emperor was held in October 1314. Peter von Aspelt, in his youth a personal physician to Henry VII and supporter of the Bavarian, had been elected archbishop of Mainz. He could thus help his candidate by giving him the deciding vote. Ludwig, in fact, obtained four votes in the election to Frederick's three. But the death of Peter von Aspelt in 1320 made the situation equal; even though the Knights Templar were in support of the Bavarian, who protected them."

"We breeders," Vittorio intervened "were alerted."

"What did they ask of you?"

"They wanted horses for battle."

The news was greeted by a stunned silence; the thought of the valley being turned into a bloody battlefield was bleak.

"Damned civil war," muttered Enea, and was shot a warning look by his father-in-law, who for professional ethics avoided commenting on the use of weapons.

" ... Let's hope the fighting is confined to the Bavarians and Austrians," said Enrico, meditatively.

"It probably will be, Father," Martino tried to reassure him. "The struggles for the imperial succession don't affect the Lombard territory."

"We are neutral in the struggles for dynastic succession and must avoid taking sides, even with those who are fighting for local power," the elder magistrate reflected. "We are older than any adventurer or pretender to power that we know to be illusory. The actor, the protagonist of the moment, moves on, and we restore harmony in the relationships between nomadic and sedentary peoples, between the living and the undead. We are conscious interpreters of the relationships that animate the world! We are all like Joseph of Arimathea."

"So, Enrico," Vittorio intervened from a practical standpoint, "should I be feeding my battle stallions more oats? Should I train them?"

"Yes Vittorio," said the old sage, coming out of his philosophical reverie. "And you, Enea, can you ride a battle horse?"

"No. I can drive carts and tame animals; I can't jump over obstacles or control a battle stallion."

"We'll take that into account," Martino reassured him. "The women and children must stay away from the town because they get sick more easily within the walls, between spring and autumn. They must be guarded in places away from the passage of armed men; regardless of whether they're imperial soldiers, Guelphs or Ghibellines."

"By the sea?" asked Vittorio, who had never been to Liguria and hoped he could go with his daughter and son-in-law.

Enrico laughed bitterly and explained that the Apennines and coastal areas were exposed to constant fighting.

"The houses that control the passes across the Apennines are unstable, and the maritime republics are in a constant state of war; they even arm and finance pirates to carry out raids where diplomatic treaties are impossible. Unfortunately, Genoa, Pisa, Amalfi and Venice cannot live together in peace and are consequently laying waste to the entire Mediterranean. Not to mention the continuous raids by non-European marauders who take advantage of internal discord."

"Let's get back to discussing horses," Martino proposed. "Is there one ready that I could buy?"

"Your own is ready!" Speroni exclaimed. There were three knocks on the door as he spoke. This was Laura's usual way of telling Vittorio that the horses were ready. She greeted the men kindly as they passed through the kitchen.

"I've prepared some cheese and biscuits for you, and gourds of water. That way you won't be famished before it's time for dinner."

"Thank you, Laura," said Enrico, taking his bag. The others followed suit and went out to the farmyard, where Martino's horse, the only one not bearing the Speroni brand, was standing. The horse had been bought for Martino by his paternal grandfather, and was branded with an oval pierced by a triangle, one corner of the triangle hitting the centre of the circle; this was the personal device of the knight, Martino Bellini. Gianpace, the eldest son of Vittorio and Laura, greeted them cordially and praised the horse, describing it according to the teaching of Xenophon:

"The hooves have a thick wall and the fetlocks are high off the ground. The pasterns are robust and oblique, good for sustained galloping. The knees are flexible, which reduces the risk of stumbling and falling. The back was well-formed when he arrived, but I've strengthened the muscles with targeted exercises and now it's more well-developed: more flexible and comfortable to ride, and stronger too. His deep, rounded flanks indicate good digestion and will make him easier to ride without a saddle. The short, wide loins increase his ability to recover, indispensable when the horse has to lift its front legs and put its weight on its hind legs to jump over obstacles. The hocks and shins are well separated; do you see how wide the base is?"

"Yes I see," said the knight, going up to the magnificent animal to stroke it. Enrico was pleased with the high withers, the high posture of the neck, the small ears, the prominent eyes, the wide nostrils, the broad chest and the thick mane.

"The testicles have both dropped and are not too big," continued Gianpace. He described other anatomical details, and when he'd finished Martino demonstrated the horse's slender head with its prominent bone structure to Enrico.

"The jaw is small and the teeth are healthy. How I wish I could thank my grandfather! The only thing I can do to honour him is try to be worthy of such a gift!"

Without further ado, Martino got into the saddle and started towards the exit gate, followed by his father and friends. They warmed up their mounts, first proceeding at a walk, then a trot, and finally a full gallop when they reached the main road. Then they slowed down to turn onto the uphill path. They spent the rest of the day going up and down the slopes and through the streams in the dales, which the horses crossed obediently. Gianpace and Martino also jumped hedges and ditches, while Vittorio and Enrico rested under an old oak tree, deciding how to advise the young men. After the trials, Martino named his horse Bonaparte, since it was the 'best part' of the inheritance he'd received from his grandparents. On the way back, the older men took the main street again, walking side by side with their sons in the mellow glow of the sunset. Before dinner the knights joined their respective brides to tell them what they'd agreed. Giacomo from the stable groomed the horses to remove the dust and mud from them, asking his eldest son Aldo and Enea to help him. Enea agreed, but later told them he was an artist and refused to use clean the hooves with a hook.

"Sorry, friends, but if I damage my hands I won't be able to do my job," he explained, going off to have a wash.

The women were sharing the housework that day. The younger ones went to the wash house and hung out the linen, while Laura, Susanna and Giacomo's wife took the children to pick herbs and did the cooking in the afternoon. For the evening meal, Arianna and the little girls had decorated the two long tables in the hall and kitchen with daisies and violets. After dinner the bard sang a new repertoire, this time dedicated to horses. Martino was pleased; it would give him time to relax before telling his wife about the plans for the summer. He knew Meb was hoping to spend the summer with him, but he would be leaving without her. After singing a number of songs, William known as Sam changed the mood and introduced a farewell theme.

Hello my friend.
Hello, it's me!
And if I say it
so it must be
that you recognise me again.
It's been years, but tell me you'll come now!
Don't give me excuses or ask my pardon
there are no issues between us!
Oh my dearest Tammy
you cannot but greet me!
Kiss me my sweet one
and I will caress you!
Sweet Irene I shall go out of the door
'cause you're an ancient story to this heart of mine!
I will write to you as another page in my diary.
Or on a leaf that will remain solitary.

Sweet Irene, you cherished me too much,
and now I can hardly catch my breath!

You're an ancient story to this heart of mine!

Meb jumped up in irritation, while Enea put his arm around Arianna's shoulders, protectively. They didn't join in with the refrain for this song, which they were happy to do when the well-travelled young man sang the Song of the Horse, *Le Chant du Cheval*:

"Tu es un cheval qui aime galoper," Sam began softly, as if he were whispering in the animal's ear.
"Dans les champs et dans les prés!" everyone shouted, clapping their hands and stamping their feet like galloping hooves, glad to return to a more playful mood.

Martino took the opportunity to get up and join his wife, who had gone out to the farmyard to calm her nerves. The large hood of her cloak was pulled down over her face, but seeing how agitated her movements were, Martino realised he must try to calm her. When Meb noticed he was there, she suggested they give their home up to Grazia and Lino, the majordomos at the big house.
"Enrico and Susanna can tell them of our decision when they get to Oleggio. I'm going with you, wherever you go. I like travelling; don't ask me to stay on my own!" she said in some agitation, then taking his left hand she kissed it passionately.
"We're not school children anymore, my love. You might fall pregnant; you won't be able to ride. Think about it," murmured Martino, kissing her cheek in return. He went on: "You can go back with Enrico and

Susanna, close up the house and move back to your old room next to the library. I'll ride Bonaparte and Niamh will ride alongside me carrying the bag with our clothes; I'll be able to go faster without the cart. I'll be back in the autumn, I promise."

Meb began to cry and took refuge in his arms.

"I'm tired. Very tired and confused," she said, and closed her eyes, her lips slightly apart as a sign of acceptance. Martino kissed her for a long time in silence, then took her to see Pegaso and Bonaparte standing in their stalls. Thus reconciled, they went back to the other guests in time to say goodnight. Meb retired to sleep with Susanna, Laura and the children in the master bedroom, which was warmer than the other rooms as it backed onto the wall with the fireplace. The men retreated into Gianpace's large bedroom clad in aromatic pine wood, and William was invited to sleep in the room that used to be Arianna's; a small room but homely with its embroidered curtains. The stableman and his family went home to their residence at the bottom of the garden, after the young married couple had gone to their rooms above the stables.

The following week the discussions were a series of quarrels, as if the changing season were influencing all their moods and thoughts. Susanna only refrained from putting forward her opinions when her son advised her to shut up and not interfere between him and Meb.

Enrico ruled that every generation must learn to live with disagreements they couldn't resolve, but couldn't help reminding Martino of the time he spent with his grandfather while he and Susanna were travelling. There had been no ill effects in that case, for example, judging by how well he'd turned out being brought up in Oleggio, and the twins too who were born along the banks of the Tisza.

On Wednesday, however, a knight from Vallagarina came galloping up with news that swept all else aside. Giacomo recognised the rampant lion crest and opened the farm gate; he took charge of the horse and Gianpace went to call Vittorio, to whom the knight Michele of San Cristoforo was to deliver a dispatch bearing the seal of the Castelbarco house. Aldrighetto Castelbarco was asking the Speroni breeding farm to send six horses back to Castel Beseno with Michele, upon payment by cash that the envoy carried with him.

Vittorio immediately made provisions to this effect, and had Enrico and Martino called so they could be introduced, while Laura set the table with rye bread, cheese, apples and red wine. The men were left alone in the kitchen with the laid table and the cat Bastet lapping up a bowl of milk, while the women took Verde and Balsamina to pick wild herbs.

"Which region will you be taking the horses to?" asked Enrico, to find out in which areas armed clashes were to be expected.

"From the Adige riverbank, we'll follow the course of the Rio Cameras and the Rio Gresta to stock up on carrots, courgettes and cabbages grown in the valley of Gardumo. This is an important area for us; the climate is mild and the land is easy to cultivate due to its proximity to Lake Garda," Michele replied, referring to the route he would take on his return, saying nothing about any armed clashes. Martino asked if the area and the access to Vallagarina were safe enough to travel through with their women. Michele thought carefully before

246

answering; he knew trust was important in the relationships between Houses and the imperial militia.

"Vallagarina is safe," he said. "Aldrighetto Castelbarco controls Lizzana, Rovereto, Pietra and Beseno, and is allied with the Lodrons who have extended their influence from the Valle del Lago d'Idro across the Storo plain in the Valle del Chiese, as far as Castel Romano and Val Rendena. It's safe to take women there; no one would dare attack in the valleys or on the passes beyond the Lago di Lavarone towards the Venetian territories."

Gianpace came to announce that the horses were ready for inspection and took Michele to the stable. Two hours later they returned to the others and announced that the knight from San Cristofero would try each horse calmly. Martino said he would gladly accompany him on Bonaparte, so they could practice in the open field and get to know each other better before the journey.

Before the following week was out the most suitable horses had been purchased and branded with the Castelbarco rampant lion with its plumed tail. The heraldic lion of the Castelbarcos differed from that of the Lodons only by the lion's tail, which for the Lodrons was an ascending double spiral.

"The Castelbarco and Lodron clans are descended from the *milites maiores*, the auxiliary infantry of the Roman army from imperial times, Enrico explained to Martino. The lion indicates their decision to serve the government and the imperial law as free-born men, accustomed to using weapons and with no deep territorial roots."

"Warriors," commented his son; "men used to living by the rule of the fittest; dangerous, if they really believe that all human society can be organised like an army."

"*Societas: oratores, bellatores, laboratores servique*-male society, which says nothing about knights and women."

"*Oratores, bellatores and laboratores* do not think highly of us, but they tolerate us because they could hardly manage without us," the son observed bitterly, "as if we were women."

"What do you mean, *as if we were women*?" His father was shocked and put on the defensive.

"The military act as if we didn't exist, yet they use us in every relationship. We Knights of the Houses are the element of mediation between the people and the feudal lords, who often profit from us like the clergy do at the expense of taxpayers, without providing any useful service in society. It's no coincidence that both those groups live shut up in castles and walled buildings, while we live in houses and farms in open contact with our people."

"It's the limits of imperial organisation. It would be logical to declare equality of rights and duties, but all despots favour those who support them in power in exchange for protecting their lives."

"We on the other hand, like women, strive for the common good *for nothing: giving freely what we receive*."

"You're right son, but I don't agree with the comparison you draw between us and women, who are equal to men in both vice and virtue. We're trained to think like mothers, empathetically," Enrico observed. "A mother feels the flow of energy between herself and each of her children, just as every knight is able to share the same vital energy with the first horse with which he is matched. The important thing is to learn by yourself how to live in harmony with each other, in mutual respect."

"We're like the Bear of Raimondo Lullo," Martino went on. "When I was studying in Bologna, there were some Spanish students who followed his Aristotelian ideas. I liked his method of research and his imaginative style..." He brought his train of thought to a close; his father had dozed off.

After the final dinner before their departure, the bard Sam sang:

As evening descends more sadly
everything seems like it was.
I sing and repeat the eternal song
hope is a vain illusion!

With you, without you
we sing to the stars and the moon.
Who knows but
good fortune may smile on us!

If the reason for those drums should change
our destiny could change in one turn
Will it come, will it not?
It may be right here and nobody knows!

Arianna was moved and asked him to repeat it. She took Enea's hand and led him in a graceful dance facing each other. Their steps were like those from the old European ritual of dropping pebbles along the path of a maze, or those made by children weaving coloured ribbons around a maypole. The spontaneity of Enea and Arianna was pleasing to Martino, and he took Meb by the hand to follow suit. The bard smiled and sang the song again. Then he changed the music:

The first stars were already shining in the sky
among the hawthorns the wind murmurs and departs.
The wood beneath the moon is like a charm;
passionate fairy tales for you!
Come, there's a path through the woods.
I know its name: do you want to know it too?

Come, it's the path of the heart.
Where love that never dies is born.
There among the trees, entwined in the blossoming branches
is the simple nest your heart dreams of!

Come, there's a path through the woods.
I know its name: do you want to know it too?

Then William known as Sam bade them goodnight and made to go to bed, but Vittorio asked him to dedicate a song to Laura, and Sam sang flippantly:

What a wonderful day it was today!
What happiness!
My lovely wife has gone away
and left me all alone, free.
I am once again the master of my life.
And will enjoy it to the full!
Living!
Without sadness.
Living!

Without jealousy.
Without regrets
without ever knowing what love is.
Gathering every beautiful flower,
enjoying life and silencing my heart!
Living, always so joyous.
Laughing, about the follies in the world.
Living!
As long as there is youth.
Because life is beautiful; I want to live it to the full!
It is often beautiful women who recite the comedy of
love.
Then I shall become a fine actor
And say what she wants me to say.
When the evening finally ends, reality returns.
And the comedy of love, a passionate farce will seem!
Living! Without sadness.
Living! Without jealousy.

Susanna applauded loudly, laughing. Laura did the same
as her friend, but understood the embarrassment of the
other guests and sang a madrigal dedicated to Vittorio:

Together we dreamed dreams.
Among six peacocks I saw one white
with a high crest and soft plumage
he spread his tail like a pageboy.
In showing thus his beauty
he honoured each colourful friend
in a graceful vision of true love.
His partner stayed constant by his side
and while he sings she will not leave him!
And cast off all her arts

and though other enchantments may end
the beautiful sight is worth the role and mantle.

"We dreamed memorable dreams. And we shall continue to do so, I promise," said Vittorio, standing up; a sign that the evening was over.

At dawn the women prepared bread and scrambled eggs for everyone. Arianna brought Niamh and another mare and attached them to the cart, ready for the journey. Two small barrels of drinking-water barrels and two baskets packed with spelt cakes and cheese preserved in fern leaves were loaded onto the cart, as well as the bags containing their clothes. The cart was covered with waxed canvas, tied down with ropes passed through metal rings attached to the sides. The canvas was stretched over bent willow branches fixed to the cart at regular intervals to form supporting arches. Laura kissed her daughter and handed Meb a wooden box full of horse-shaped blocks and cubes.

"When Arianna came home with the wedding dress you'd made for her, she told me about the letter you'd received from your parents. So, I had these toys made for Otto."

Meb thanked her and put the gift in her bag; then she sat on the bench next to the driver. The two women took turns to drive, chatting as they went along.

Michele, William, Enea and Martino climbed into their saddles, leading the battle horses for the Castelbarcos with ropes.

Martino's cart was left behind in Vittorio and Gianpace's storehouse, where they studied its construction in detail to copy it and improve the design.

252

Along the journey, few stops were as memorable as Como. Enea had done his apprenticeship as a painter here, and did the honours of the house with the attention of a good (future) father of a family. He kept the cheerful little party away from the drunken gangs in the local taverns, and took Meb and his wife to the apothecary's house, on the main street, towards Camerlata. As they passed through the town, the women peered at tailors' shops and tanners, where leather goods were made to order. The workshop that impressed Arianna most of all of was the bow maker's, because she'd always dreamed of learning to shoot with a bow and arrow ever since she was a child.

"When I went to the Festa dei Ceri in Gubbio as a little girl," Meb recalled, "I was fascinated by men with crossbows competing outside the walls, on the market square."

"I've never seen a crossbow," Arianna admitted, "but look how elegant this little bow is! I don't think there's a finer way to hunt!"

William pointed out that if she'd ever seen a falconer she might not be so sure.

"I know a family of Catalan descent who live in a farmhouse on this road, and breed falcons for hunting. I can take you there," said Enea, "as long as you give me time to meet up with my masters and introduce them to William."

Michele and Martino said they would be working with the local authorities for a few days, and assured them they would come to the apothecary's house the day before they were due to leave. They watered the horses then walked along leading them, as they may have to inspect the local area as well as work in the village.

253

Arianna and Meb put the cart in the courtyard and took the food to the kitchen. Then they went with the apothecary's sister to pick herbs and flowers to be used in the laboratory, mixed with olive oil or animal fats. Arianna taught the apothecary's eldest daughter how to style her hair in a Burgundy-style plait, the latest fashion at knightly tournaments. Meb taught the youngest child, who was about three years old, the days of the week, using the various stages of a brood of chicks:

On MONDAY he's all closed in
On TUESDAY he breaks the egg
On WEDNESDAY he leaves the egg
On THURSDAY he goes cheep cheep
On FRIDAY he's a fluffy chick
On SATURDAY he pecks a grain
And by SUNDAY morning he has his crest.

William helped Enea take care of the horses, then followed him to the workshops of the Como fraternity. They saw master Villar de H. balancing perilously on a wooden scaffold. When he saw that Enea had returned and was pointing at a hooded stranger, he raising his hand in greeting and climbed down cautiously.

"Some shingles got broken over the winter. I have to fix them before it rains again," he explained without preamble.

"Master Villar, this friend is the bard William, known as Sam."

"Let's have a drink and something to eat; *anyone who doesn't drink in company, is either a thief or a spy!*" the master proclaimed, in the serious-jocular manner that was one of his main character traits. During the frugal meal, William told his story until the master tired of hearing it and took the floor himself to deliver a lecture on the history of art.

"Two thousand years ago, four hundred years after the walls of Rome were first built, the Gauls destroyed it. The Eternal City was then rebuilt according to a very complex planimetry, very different from the simple urbanism of the colonies that grew up in lands with no building tradition. It seems that at the time of the Res Publica, there lived in the city a thousand free-born adults, who lived in villas on the hillsides and the urban insulae," Villar began.

"In the colonies, villages sprang up as they evolved from military encampments, along the cardo and decumanus axis roads," Enea recalled, while in the Provinces the orthogonal pattern of the Roman roads was built on top of the pre-existing urban conglomeration, with the roads converging on the market square."

"Three hundred and fifty years after the founding of Rome," continued Villar, "Julius Caesar proclaimed the *Lex de Urbe augenda* and the *Lex Iulia principalis*, in addition to arrangements for reclaiming the Pontine Marshes, the opening of an emissary from the Fucino, the isthmus of Corinth and improvements to the imperial road system on the plain."

"Did the violent death of the emperor put an end to these plans?" asked William.

"No. The emperor has died...long live the emperor," Enea replied.

"Octavian Augustus continued the expansion towards Campo Marzio, but abandoned the idea of diverting the course of the Tiber and dismissed the Greek architect who had devised the project," continued Maestro Villar;

"Augustus stopped informing the senators and expanded Rome by annexing the suburb, without consulting them. He divided the public administration into regions and promoted the construction of new aqueducts. He left in marble the situation he had inherited in bricks. A thousand years after the founding of the city of Rome, an edict by Valentinian forbade the construction of new buildings at public expense. It was decided that the *Forma Urbis* must be as solid as in Greek cities; it went as far as prohibiting the reuse of ruins, which had to be restored or treated with respect. Twenty-five years after the Edict of Valentinian, the Vandals visited havoc on Rome; the marble and stone were stolen and reused, scattering their secrets."

Enea sighed and took a long drink of water; he was thinking that the same fate had been visited on Troy, even though it was by Greeks and not barbarians. William looked at him and, perhaps sensing his thoughts, pointed out that although the Romans considered human works to be eternal, the Celts did not make the same error. In fact they revered natural things like air, stone, bodies of water and oak trees, caring only for the invisible unity inconceivable to the human mind. Villar said nothing. He took them to see the rooms open to the public, with items for sale.

"These are plans," the master explained to William; "two-dimensional geometric diagrams that describe different types of three-dimensional building spaces. The footprint of the structure can be monodirectional; for example, if the longitudinal dimension prevails over the other dimensions, such as with a gallery or access porticoes to a prestigious space. Structures that are two-directional, on the other hand, are those with two equal poles, as with arcades where both openings are important."

"Could we define bidirectional works as *elements of mediation*?" asked Enea.

"As you like, but not at the moment," old Villar silenced him, trying to pick up the thread of his discourse; "alternatively, there are footprints that define a hierarchy, an order. The crossings in a network can come together from two, three, four or more directions; hierarchical systems on the other hand must focus their attention on the fulcrum of the work, the geometric centre or the most important functional point. These plans are useful for choosing which type of footprint to work on. You have to know how to read and reason in two dimensions, then move on to designing a space and the potential movements within it."

William examined the sheets ordered by architectural theme, then asked if there were any plans for openings too.

"The architect must sleep in the place where the building is to be built," explained the teacher. "The position relative to the prevailing winds and the sun's cycle determines the orientation and the openings. As for their shape, we follow tradition."

"What the master means is that the Como school does not agree with the Gothic architecture from across the Alps, and tries to contain the vertical rush towards the sky, judging it too far from logical reasoning," Enea whispered.

"I imagine you refrain from studying grotesques here, or decorative dragons or spires or pointed arches; things they're partial to across the Alps," William commented, as Villar walked towards the pile of sheets with doors and windows.

"An image," resumed the master from Como, "is useful as a key to interpretation. If it's carved, for example, on the keystone of a round arch, above a door in the entrance walls, or at the time of the Roman Empire, on a triumphal arch."

"Now I come to think of it, I've often seen heads carved above arches from the Roman era. Who is it meant to be?" asked William.

"Usually Hercules," replied Enea.

"I won't go into technical details," Villar continued, undaunted. "It's enough you understand, in a general sense, that the keystone is special because it brings two semi-arches together at the highest point. The shape of the keystone is different from the other stones, and allows the force to be distributed, carrying the tension into the ground and keeping the whole structure balanced. The other blocks are also shaped, at least when building arches without using mortar."

The three men spent the afternoon looking at sheets of plans for structures based on rounded arches. They studied drawings of relieving arches to be placed inside the walls. They discussed the spatial extension of this constructive principle: from the circular cupola to the barrel vault, from the rise and extrados to the rib vault, the sail vault and the cloister vault.

"The dome vault on a circular base is my favourite," Villar enthused, "because there are no corners to weaken it and the cylinder keeps the horizontal thrusts in balance, transmitting vertical pressure evenly to the ground."

"Where can you find such a marvel, master?" asked William.

"At the Pantheon in Rome, a building based on the circumference, in plan and in elevation. A perfect system: constructed in such a way as to generate opposing thrusts that work together to keep the entire structure stable. Similar to the harmony that we imagine reigns the celestial spheres."

"Maestro Villar, it's late. Thank you for your hospitality," said Enea. But William was given permission to stay, in exchange for his assistance with some small manual jobs and a few songs after dinner. So they agreed that Enea would call back for his friend in the afternoon of the day before their departure, and they said goodnight.

❋

In Valsassina they were joined by a few soldiers sent by the Ginamis of Gromo, who delivered Martino's sword with its blade tempered with fire and in the icy waters of the river Serio, and Michele asked the soldiers to accompany him to Castel Beseno. The company made its first official stop at the castle of Vezio, which boasted a stupendous view of Lake Lecco from the windows. The women withdrew to the gynaeceum, and Meb was enchanted when she looked down on the olive grove from the first floor window above. The silvery leaves of the trees, pruned back to encourage the olives to grow, enhanced the twinkling silver tones of the lake landscape. Marzia, the castellan's daughter, explained that they were able to cultivate olives here as the lake waters made up for the climate, which would otherwise be too cool to grow this Mediterranean species. Arianna noticed some cages in the stable courtyard and asked what they were for.

"We breed birds of prey," said the girl proudly; "Papa chooses them depending on what creatures they prey on."

"Like my own papa when he chooses horses according to the work they're required to do," Arianna replied.

"Lino too, he chooses breeding dogs according to their abilities," added Meb, recalling the young man who ran the Casa Visconti hunting lodge in Oleggio.

"The goshawk catches pheasants in the woods because it flies low," explained Marzia, "but the peregrine falcon is better at catching prey in open clearings, as it flies higher and swoops rapidly. Papa uses eagles for catching foxes and roe deer; it's difficult and dangerous, and the eagle is the only bird that can do it."

"What animals do you hunt, usually?" Arianna asked.

"Hare, ducks, partridges, pheasants and quails."

"Do you use retriever dogs too?" asked Meb, thinking she would like to introduce Lino to their hosts at castle Vezio.

"Papa has a couple of dogs trained to retrieve; they're tame, but he keeps them in a cage. He says sheepdogs should stay with the flock and hunting dogs should stay in their enclosure, in order to maintain the skills they were raised for. *Everything in its place and a place for everything* - that's his motto!"

Meb thought this was a typical military attitude, but made no comment.

A musical evening was organised for the evening before they left. Tables were set up in the courtyard and flautists and lutists played for them. The castellan asked William for a song, which he sang first in French, leaving the title in Greek.

EGO

Miroir, dis moi qui est le plus beau
Quitte à devenir mégalo
Viens donc chatouiller mon ego
Allez, allez, allez

Laisse moi entrer dans ta matrice
Gouter à tes délices
Personne en peut m'en dissuader
Allez, allez, allez

Tout est beau
Tout est rose
Tant que je l'impose
Miroir, dis moi qui est le plus beau
Allez, allez, allez

EGO

Mirror, tell me who's the fairest.
Even though it makes me vain
stimulate my ego.
Do, do, do

Let me into your world

to taste your delights.
Don't try to put me off.
Do, do, do

Everything is beautiful
Life is rosy
as long as I say so.
Tell me who is the fairest.
Do, do, do

Everyone applauded, each to demonstrate perhaps that he or she could not be accused of narcissism. Marzia's father thanked William for the song, so he dedicated a song to his daughter and the other women present, singing in a deep voice:

Ich liebe dich
Und finde dich
Wenn auch der Tag ganz dunkel wird

Mein Lebelang
Und immer noch
Bin suchend ich umhergeirrt.

Ich lieb dich
Die Welt ist taub
Die Welt ist blind

Nur wind, der goldene Staub
Aus dem wir zwei bereitet
Sind!

Marzia translated

I love you
and you will be with me
when the day grows dark.

For all my life
from this moment
the never-ending journey begins.

I love you.
The world is deaf.
The world is blind.
Just the two of us, golden dust!
We were made for this.
We are!

Everyone applauded and decided to sing the Germanic version together, in honour of the castellan. William listened quietly. After they'd finished their rendition, he stood up and asked if he could sing one last song before going to bed. Marzia offered him a cup of red wine and told him it was a pleasure to hear poetic lyrics from such an enchanting voice as his. Arianna was amazed to hear such bold words from so young a girl, and resolved to speak to her about it before they went to their rooms. William drank and sang spiritedly:

If a thousand are the stories that the wind carries away
This is our story, generation of mine!
Risen from hell with fire in our veins
we shall lift up to heaven, to heaven our chains!

Arise now brothers, it's now or never more

let us play the game of youth the best way we know how
If a foolish curse should hold us back
we will bless them together and it will fall to the wayside
Into the ditch of memories that get carried all away
if we unravel the knots that used to hold us
We shall fly higher, stronger in forgiveness
Listen friends, the sweet sound of freedom!
It matters not if they burn the towers
Friends will find a place in their house for us!
They'll make a thousand schemes but our song will be heard
by anyone who sings of sweet liberty!

The following day they resumed their journey towards Vallagarina, but had to stop after an hour as Meb was feeling unwell.

The young woman was lying in the cart feeling tired, when she had an attack of nausea and asked Arianna to stop. The men got down from their horses and held them by the reins, and as soon as Meb had evacuated her stomach, they proposed continuing their journey as far as the nearest farmhouse, where they could at least water the horses. The women of the farm were busy hanging out washing on the lawn in the sunshine, and the children gathering clover in the meadow; they took fright when they saw the riders approaching and ran screaming to their mothers. The older daughters were in the vegetable garden; the sound of the little ones screaming put them on their guard, but the women knew there was no escape if they came under attack.

The horsemen stopped and waited as Enea approached on foot, leading his horse, with Arianna driving the cart, to demonstrate that they intended no harm and allow

Meb time to ask the women for help. Enea returned shortly after to tell them they could put their horses in the nearest vacant stall, where there was a spring and a water trough. Michele advised Martino not to reveal his true identity and not to approach the farm, then he took up his position in the enclosure with the other soldiers while Enea and William stayed with Arianna and Meb until the following day. Martino's wife lay down beside the fire, propping herself up on one elbow to eat plenty of spelt cakes and a little cheese. The eldest of the mothers at the farm handed her a cup of hot chamomile tea with wild honey, saying softly: "Sciuretta, t'ha gà majaa peu. Fa festa e sta alegher, ch'el tu fiol à da venir ingrasa e fort, poevr cinìn!" Meb followed her advice; she drank willingly and fell asleep wrapped in her own cloak, lulled by the voice of Arianna who was playing with the children of the house. "Give me your hand," she told a little boy of four, "did you know that each finger has a name?"

The little boy shook his head timidly.

"This one is called Thumb and he's always serious. He stands alone, but he can be useful, just like Papa. Index is a mother who sees far and teaches freely everything she knows. Middle is straight and tall like a playful, lively uncle. Ring is graceful and wants to be a bride. Pinkie is little like your nose!"

The head of the family had eaten enough whilst she was cooking, so she set the table with polenta and chopped cheese in cups of warm milk. The others ate in silence, and the old grandmother told them a story in her strange local tongue: a blend of the Bergamo, Lecco and Milan dialects.

"Donca, mì disi in temp del re de Ziper, dopu che Gufreed de Bujon l'ava ciapà Tera Santa, l'è suceduu che 'na bona sciura de Guascogna a l'è 'nda in pelegrinag (*g dolce*) al Sant Sepulcher. In del turnàa a cà, quand l'era ruvada a Ziper, ona manega de lifroch vilan i l'han tolta a perzipità. Lea la se ne casciava col magon, di mò ch'el l'ha pensaa de nà dal re a met giò quarela. Ma quaichedun i gh'han dii che l'eva fiaa traa via, che quel re l'avea 'n por tabalori che, in scambi che fer giustizia, el mandva giò qui balussad che ghe faven anca a lù. E insciì tucc quii che ghe l'aveven su con lù i s'impagaven fasendeghen 'na quaivuna. Quela bona sciura, quand che l'ha sentuù insciì, desperand de utegn giustizia, tant per cunsalass on zich, l'ha pensaà de casciàghela a quel re. Tuta caragnenta la ghe s'è presentada e l'ha gha a dir: – O sciur, mé vegni mica scià a pregàt de utegn giustizia de quii balussad che hoo patii. Te preghi de 'nsegnàm coma te feet mò mai ciapàt su mocc mocc quii che te fan a te; e insci, imparandel de te, poda anca me ciapàm in pas mè fastidi. Che, se 'l pudess, le sa el Signur come i' butaress tucc vuluntera adoss a te, che ti suportet insci cucc e cuntent. El re, che infina alura l'eva staa 'n margnach indurmetaa, el s'è dessedaa fò. Scumenzand l'ha fa giustizia per i birbunad che l'ava patii quela pora sciura; e po' el se metù a farla pagà salada a tucc qui che fasessen vergot contra de lù e del so unur."

After dinner, William told them his name was Lluís Llaach and asked if he could sing a song in his mother tongue, but the signora said it was better if he sang in a language everyone could understand. So Lluìs sang in the language of Dante and Petrarca that now understood from Tuscany as far as the Alps:

Grandfather was speaking
to the spring at dawn
as the sun was coming up
high on the horizon.

He spoke some names
by whom we are bound
like mules to a post
or starlings without wings.

But if we think about it
we are not like fish on the hook
and as if by some charm
our singing is free!

They all enjoyed the song and wanted to sing it
themselves again and again, until they knew it by heart
and could teach it to the shepherds when they returned
from the transhumance. Meanwhile, Martino and the
other riders camped for the night in the enclosure. After
taking care of their horses they lit a fire and sat round it
eating the cheese preserved in fern leaves. They also
munched on the remaining biscuits and drank a few
bottles of red wine that they'd been given by some
representatives of the municipality in Lecco.

"Tears and laughter," Martino exclaimed for everyone to
hear. "The alternation between conceding defeat and
hope for the future: that's the poetry of the Psalms!"

"Losing Jerusalem," Michele remarked, "can lead to
discovering new lands and new skies."

"...or a new way of looking at the sky and the earth,"
continued Bellini, staring into the fire as if hypnotised.

One of the knights from Gromo added: "Occupying a place is unreasonable abuse for a contemplative soul. Occupying and respecting it, however, is a sublime challenge for an active mind."

"In the psalters I saw in Bologna," Martino recalled, returning from his journey into the burning embers, "the relationship between the miniatures and the text filled me with wonder. Both were poetic, but the text was a choral work, while the miniature was an individual interpretation."

"Is a man who dies really gone?" Michele asked, quoting Job.

"In the psalter, the prospect is comforting," Martino replied. "Faith gives grace the opportunity to act, and grants pure joy to those who are faithful in love. Being joined in a relationship is our eternal saviour: an educational relationship is the absolute good, before which bodily death is just a transition from manifold trials to complete happiness."

"We cannot fail to accept the positive commitment of those who love," said the knight from the Castle of Gromo, "as in our *Song of the Exiles*:

Along the banks of the rivers of Babylon
we shall not sit weeping.
In memory of Jerusalem
we shall not hang up our lutes
on the branches of weeping willows.
We shall sing together.
We shall act together.
Wherever there are testimonies
to Hope!"

Mindful of the things they had been taught since their childhood, the brave cavaliers sang an ancient song, and fell asleep wrapped in the their ample woollen cloaks.

Meb woke up feeling good when the cock crowed. She knew what the head of the household had told her was true, but she decided to keep the news that she was expecting her first child from the others. She ate bread and scrambled eggs for breakfast, and some fresh milk. Enea fixed a ladder that had a broken rung, then helped the women climb into the cart and he and William mounted their horses to join the knights.

They passed many shepherds and a few herdsmen climbing up to the mountain pastures from the valleys. The shepherds left it to their dogs to keep the flock together as they walked along, while the cattlemen rode at the sides of the herd to keep their animals in check. In the evening they organised dinners in the fields, roasting game caught by the knights and sharing bread and cheese.

They reached the parish church of San Martino on the hills above the river Sarca at the time when the air was getting warmer and flowers were blooming in the meadows, inviting them to sit down and rest in the afternoon. Enea spurred his horse and galloped ahead because Master Villar had told him he would find Giovanni de Massone there, painting frescoes on some walls. A Benedictine monk came out to meet him in the churchyard and stopped, waiting for him to introduce himself. Enea explained he was looking for a fellow craftsman in the art of fresco, and asked if the whole party could be accommodated. The monk offered bunks in the novices' dormitory for the knights, and two rooms on the first floor of the monastery for the married couples, adjacent to the church. With the cart and horses accommodated in the inner courtyard of the building, Enea went to look for Giovanni, who was putting away his paints and brushes at the end of the day's work.

At dinner, Father Giobatta, the prior of the community, offered a prayer of thanksgiving for the food and drink, then entertained the guests by telling them the ancient origins of the place of worship.

"In ancient times, sources of water were also venerated here," said the prior. "In Greece, many of you will certainly remember that the sanctuary of Delos was dedicated to Artemis, protector of springs, streams, pregnant women and childbirth. In Rome too, one of the woods on the hills around Lake Nemi was consecrated to Artemis, who was called Diana in Latin. In this consecrated place there grew a tree, the branches of which it was forbidden to break. Only an escaped slave could break off one of the leafy branches, but by doing so the fugitive accepted to fight to the death with the priest guardian of the *genius loci.* If the slave was victorious, he would be required to take the place of the dead man, and would be called *Rex Nemorensis*, Custodian of Nemi."

After the meal, Martino spoke to give the prior Giobatta the chance to eat and drink.

"According to the legend, the *pater patriae* Aeneas took a branch from the tree of Nemi on the advice of a Sybil, to travel unharmed into the realm of the dead. We Celts think the branch he took was mistletoe, and the tree *robur* - oak," said Bellini. Enea took up the story, remembering how his namesake Aeneas was able to accomplish the task with the help of his mother Venus, who sent him two doves that showed him where the consecrated tree was by flying over it. He then recited the words that Virgil had written about the exile:

Latet arbore opaca
aureus et foliis et lento vimine ramus
Iunoni infernae dictus sacer; hunc tegit omnis
lucus et obscuris claudunt convalibus umbrae.
Sed non ante datus telluris operta subire
auricomos quam quis decerpserit arbore fetus.
Hoc sibi pulchra suum ferri Proserpina munus
instituit, primo avulso non deficit alter
aureus, et simili frondescit virga metallo.
Ergo alte vestigia oculis et rite repertum
carpe manu; namque ipse volens facilisque sequetur,
si te fata vocant; aliter non viribus ullis
vincere nec duro poteris convellere ferro.

After the meal everyone retired to bed. When they were alone in their room, Arianna confessed to Enea that she hadn't understood a single word because she didn't know any Latin. Her husband smiled and translated fluently, whispering the words to her:

"Hidden in the shady tree
lives a branch with golden leaves and a flexible shaft
consecrated to the woman who is the lady of transformations.
The wood all around grows up to hide it,
the shadow protects it in the dark vales.
It is prohibited to proceed beyond what is apparent
if not to take the golden branch from the tree.
Take it in one hand:
it will come away with ease, if it is destiny.

But if it does not come away,
not by force
will you take it."

Arianna asked Enea in a whisper what had been the enterprise of the father of the nation. He whispered in her ear: "The Sybil told Aeneas to hide the branch under his clothes and offer it to Charon, to placate the fury in the demon's body."

His wife undressed and lay down next to him, asking what happened next.

"Aeneas took out the branch and bathed it in holy waters. Then he placed it at the entrance to the Elysian Fields, as a votive offering to Proserpina *perfecto munere divae*," the young man murmured, aroused.

A few days later on their way to Rovereto, they passed by the Lac de Lopi. On the banks of the lake they stopped at the stone drinking fountain and exchanged some game they'd caught for some fresh fish from a local fisherman's family. On the lake island they saw a consecrated building with a stone cross, and the people who lived on the shore of the lake told them no one went there because of the ancient tombs and evil spirits that would harm anyone who went there. The information troubled Martino, so he and Michele decided to leave this clearly insalubrious place in the afternoon. Before they left, Arianna washed in water that the fisherman's wife boiled up every morning on the hearth and left to cool for a variety of uses. She gave the young woman a mixture of dried soapwort root and sage leaves to remove dirt and sweat, which left a delicate scent on her skin. Meb had gone off to relieve herself amongst the reeds when she saw some toads leaping up to catch insects, and a frog croaking, which drew her attention to the mud, at a point where the sun's rays were shining on something small. Holding her skirts up, she went over and picked up a silver coin which, turned out to be a coin issued from the Mint of Padua some time in the last two years, according to the men. As he was helping her into the cart, Martino explained that Count Gorizia Ulrico of Valdsee had been appointed as the imperial vicar of Padua by Frederick III to oppose the Della Scala armies of Verona; it seemed that only an armed peace could impede Della Scala's intentions to conquer the city. The coin she'd found was a Grosso Aquilino, similar to the Adlergroschen minted in Merano fifty years earlier by Mainardo, the imperial Count of Gorizia. Meb looked at the writing on the *obverse* side, which said + PADUA: REGIA with an eagle facing right, and the cross with arms of equal length and the word CI VI TA S written between them on the *reverse*. She hid the small object in the inside pocket of her robe, thinking it would be a lovely souvenir to give the child she was carrying, then tired and happy she dozed off, rocked by the motion of the cart that Arianna was driving competently.

Michele led the company to Rovereto then bade them farewell to accompany the knights of Gromo to Castel Beseno with the new horses, where they were designated for patrol of the Adige Valley at the fertile Folgarìa plateau and Lake Lavarone, a major Alpine crossing. Enea had received a very tempting offer of work from the Castelbarcos, so Arianna handed the reins to Meb and climbed up in front of her husband in the saddle, handing her bags of clothes to the other horsemen who would continue the journey with them.

"Legend has it," Michele told Enea and Arianna as they proceeded down the main road from Rovereto to Trento, "where Lake Lavarone is now, there was once a lush forest. It was owned by two brothers who were constantly fighting. The mother asked the Lord to reconcile her restless sons, and was rewarded with the sudden collapse of the forest and the appearance of clear springs that still keep the water level constant in every season."

They passed through the guard post within the walls, Martino riding Bonaparte and Meb in the driver's seat with William at her side, and entered the village at a walking pace. The bard looked around in silence, thinking about the next stages of his journey, the people he would meet, and how he should put forward the subjects that were close to his heart to probe their minds and gather information. Their stay in Rovereto was longer than they'd planned due to Meb feeling unwell, and the enormous amount of work that the Castelbarcos had asked Bellini to do in his capacity as a Visconti notary. Their aim was to archive documents from Trentino in the territories controlled by Casa Visconti; to this end they had asked him to draw up some transfers of property in duplicate or triplicate. It was an attempt to safeguard evidence that would be at risk if it was only stored in that area, and thus exposed to the cupidity of the Veronese and the Venetians.

Rovereto, 11 April, MCCCXXII Anno Domini
My dear mother and father,

Martino and I are staying as guests of the vicar of Castelbarco, in Rovereto. I hope you will be able to visit us in this peaceful, hospitable village.
Yours as always
Meb

The young woman rolled up the parchment and sealed it with the Bellini bear's paw seal. Then she entrusted it to her husband, who was about to go up and register a transfer of ownership.

On Monday 12th April, the Visconti notary and William the bard rode up to the vicarial office of Folgarìa in the afternoon, just in time for Martino to attend a tribunal. The defendant was accused of infringing a public asset belonging to the rural community called Magnifica Comunità, since it had decided to write its own social norms seven years earlier, in the form of the Statutes. The Charter of Regulations seemed straightforward, but the municipal authorities were struggling to convince all the residents to accept the responsibility that the change entailed in practice. Martino listened to the accusations and ascertained that the farmer who had planted beets and cabbages on municipal land was an honest man, and that he had thought he could use the land because it belonged to *everyone, which included himself.*

"Common property" explained the judge "is not for individual use. Communal assets are managed by the representatives who are elected by the Magnificent Community, not by individual voters."

The defendant looked at the judge uncomprehendingly. Then he seemed to see the light, and remarked that the judge was right: he too had voted, and said, "maybe I should have spoken to the friend I voted for, before

275

going out to sow. I regret this oversight, truly. I acted as my father would have done; because the soil there has more water than ours, which can't be cultivated it in this drought. So excuse me, your honour, if my ignorance is not equal to yours."

"The Magnificent Community has established that the land is used for grazing in the lower part and cutting wood towards the ridge," said the judge, without commenting on the defendant's ambiguous words. "Aware that your family was used to cultivating - sometimes - even the strip of land adjoining your property, to accustom you to the regulations you shall donate half of your harvest to the May Festival."

After the sentencing, Martino compiled the transfer of ownership for a building plot, then he was free to join his in-laws for dinner. As he was walking along holding Bonaparte by the reins, he observed that the houses in the village were of two distinct types. Those towards the valley were built of stone in the Roman tradition, adapted to the requirements of a mountain climate with round arched doorways and small windows to prevent heat from escaping. He looked round the back of some of them and found that they all had a large, south-facing vegetable garden that opened out onto the broad valley. The houses on the other side of the street were built of wood, like the ones on the other side of the Alps, with external staircases and a gallery. Behind these northern-style buildings were the enclosures rising up the slope of the hill with rabbit hutches and chicken coops. Whilst he was observing one of the many stray cats that roamed stealthily all over the village, William suddenly emerged from the *Osteria di Giorgio* on the side of the street that overlooked the valley.

"I've found a room," he announced cheerfully; "we have to be back by midnight, when Giorgio locks the door."

Martino took the opportunity to rest Bonaparte and tie him up with William's horse in the level enclosure behind the inn; then they set off down the main village street. A little further on they met Aligerno and Rebecca listening to some villagers who were playing music and singing at the end of the working day. Disappointed at seeing the two men without Meb, the couple were concerned about their daughter's health and asked for explanations that Martino could not give, and instead handed Rebecca the missive. She read it and considered the brevity of the message to be confirmation of a pregnancy, but said only that Meb didn't know what to put her illness down to and that she would return with her son-in-law; Aligerno assured them that he would see them in Rovereto for the August holidays, if they didn't return sooner. The tutor then moved the discussion on to local traditions, where the customs of the Cisalpine and Transalpine Celts were not mixed with the customs of the Cimbri carpenters but coexisted alongside them, like three good, clever sisters. They soon reached the end of the village street, where Rebecca opened a wooden gate into a courtyard encircled by a dry stone wall. She knocked and opened the door of the two-story stone house. In the kitchen was a staircase leading up to the first floor, with three large rooms. The householders extended a warm welcome to their guests, saying their eldest son Giorgio had told them they were coming. Otto was playing with his dog on the lawn outside the kitchen; every so often his mother would look out of the window whilst she was cooking.

"It's an honour to meet two eminent intellectuals like yourselves in person, my lords," said Emanuele; Martino was astonished, but the man continued in a most cordial manner. "Cavalier Bellini, I know you are a friend of a cousin of our cousin, Luca Nicolussi of Luserna."

"... Yes. We were students together in Bologna and we write to each other occasionally," Martino confirmed, amazed at how certain information got round.

"Master William," Emanuele went on obsequiously, turning to the other traveller," I hope you will be able to advise our Magnificent Community by virtue of your experience at Merton College, Oxford."

"*Qui timet Deum faciet bona*" William replied, lowering his head in humility.

Martino gulped; the thought that he'd been treating the English philosopher so lightly, mistaking him for a simple bard, was quite daunting.

At dinner, Clara presented a dish that Martino found exquisite. "We call it *peverà*. You chop some onions and fry them in butter," the lady explained, delighted with her success. While they're browning, you prepare a good mince of beef, wild boar and dry bread, and add some whole bay leaves. Then mix everything together, until it's well cooked. Then you take out the leaves and serve it with polenta and beer, or wine if you prefer. The important thing is not to alternate beer and wine; it's not good for the stomach."

After dinner the Visconti notary went to Giorgio's inn with master William, both of them too tired to talk. The following morning Martino returned to Clara's house, who served him a cup of milk and buttered bread with wild honey. Under the kitchen staircase there was a spinning-wheel, and the lady showed him how she used it to weave wool rugs that her husband sold at the Trento fair in March. "I've only got this little rug left now," she said, showing him a handsome *rug* of natural wool that Martino decided to buy for Meb.

William, meanwhile, spent the morning with Emanuele, in the village. Then they ate at the other village tavern, which was owned by an immigrant family from Carinthia, and spent the afternoon playing ball with Otto and some other children on a plot of land belonging to the Magnificent Community. When the sun went down, Martino and William said goodbye to Otto and spent the evening with Giorgio, who had prepared a splendid beef goulash. William noted that it was seasoned with Hungarian paprika, a product from the Kingdom of Charles I of Anjou, which stretched from Transylvania to Dalmatia.

"Carlo Martello D'Angiò" Martino recalled, whose mother was of Hungarian origin on the maternal side;" is the son of Charles of Naples and Maria Arpad of Hungary, daughter of King Stephen V and Elizabeth of Cumania. He was crowned King of Hungary at Aix in 1290, but he never went to his kingdom. In fact, his cousin Andrea III ruled in Hungary until his death in 1301. Since then the local tribes and clans have ruled, who are often in conflict and always independent, in terms of both alliances and managing trade. The king only collects a few taxes to keep the connecting roads and border outposts open."

William intervened to allow his friend to eat; "Andrea III was the last male descendant of Casa Arpad. They called him *the Venetian* because he was educated in Venice with the family of his mother, Tommasina Morosini. During his reign, representing his cousin from the House of D'Angiò, he fought on two fronts: internally, against usurpations by tribes and clans; and externally, against the House of Habsburg that claimed Hungary as its fiefdom and didn't recognise the rights claimed by the Angevins of Naples."

When the goulash was finished, Martino told them that the *Nations* of students in Bologna and Paris distinguished between *Latins* (French, Italian and Hispanic), *Normans* (Breton) *Piccardians* (from the Netherlands) and *English*. The latter was the largest group because it included students from the British Isles and the English fiefdom of Normandy, as well as Germans, Slavs, Hungarians and Finns.

William was very interested in these distinctions and explained that in Oxford, on the other hand, there were only two *Nations*: the *Australs* (Scottish) and the *Boreals* (Irish, Welsh and English), and in the same group a few rare students from the rest of the known world. Hearing their talk of university students, a young man approached and asked if he could join them at their table, saying he was alone in the village. He introduced himself as Riccardo from Bertoldi, a village on the Lake Lavarone plateau. Martino and William were delighted to make his acquaintance, and asked him to describe the place, which they'd heard tell as being an important Alpine pass.

"In summer the laburnum blooms on the shores of the lake, encircled by the aromatic pine forest," said Riccardo, giving rein to his poetic flair. In wintertime it's a joy to hear movements beneath the surface as you walk in the mild midday sun or slide across the frozen water!"

They talked at length, sipping a bitter, herbal liqueur.

Before taking his leave, Riccardo studied William intently for a few seconds.

"You know life?" he said, turning to him with a serene smile. "Our own lives, I mean. Well, I think it's like the hand of a painter that colours the things around us and helps us to a greater or lesser extent to change our own inner colours too."

"What colour are you, now?" William asked him.

Riccardo said he felt like a mirror, but throughout the day that was coming to a close, he'd been orange.

"What about you, William? What colour are you?" Riccardo asked.

"Blue. What about you, Martino?"

"I don't know," said Martino, shrinking back; he wasn't used to these society games.

"Oh, how serious you are!" said the boy from the lake good-naturedly, then added playfully that Martino did honour to his name not only with his beautiful cloak, but by displaying a candid nature.

The next day Martino and William left Folgarìa along with Rebecca, who was given a passage on a cart with a consignment of vegetables on the way to Rovereto market. When they reached the vicar's house they learned that Signora Bellini had moved into the building at the back of the courtyard, near the woods. The vicar's wife showed Martino, William and Rebecca the way, explaining that the wing had been built for the family of the seneschal of the Castelbarco family, who would be in Castel Pietra until the autumn. Putting the cart and horses in the stables between the two residential buildings, Bellini went to looked for his wife while the others arranged their few packs in their rooms.

Martino found his wife asleep under a blossoming apple tree. Kneeling down to admire her serene face, he noticed how her dress emphasised her breasts, which seemed fuller than usual, and her swollen belly. *My angel!* thought the young man, timorously. Meb became aware of her knight's scent, a mix of leather and animal sweat, but kept her eyes closed as she took his hand and placed it on her stomach, confirming the joyous news that she was expecting his first child.

For the evening meal, the vicar's wife had arranged two tables under the portico in the courtyard. It was all white and green, from the embroidered tablecloths to the plates decorated with ivy, to symbolise friendship, bread dusted with flour and white roast meats: turkey, chicken and veal. Vegetables from the kitchen garden and wild herbs were arranged on large wooden platters, alternating with green plates piled up with hunks of cheese.

Jars of honey from the wild bees in that enchanting valley were provided for the sweet-toothed to dip their hunks of cheese into.

Over the next few weeks Martino executed some notary duties for Casa Visconti and the Castelbarcos, William visited the construction site for the castle of Rovereto and made friends with the workers there, while a new generation was being nurtured, beginning to hear the sounds of its mother. Following Rebecca's wise advice, Meb sought her husband's caress every evening, and asked him to tell of his memories from the time he spent with his grandfather, because his tone was especially affectionate when talking about it. The young wanderer slept well until her last dream, which she recalled with clarity and which helped her meditate on her singular point of view with respect to the flow of reality. At dawn she would wake before Martino and prepare a breakfast of wholemeal bread, butter and honey, with milk from the cow that had been milked the day before. While setting the table she watched a couple of great tits as they built their nest in the kitchen garden, in the branches of a budding red beech tree.

On 22nd April, Ugo Maloss arrived at the vicar of Rovereto's house at a gallop, bringing terrible news of a plot that had been perpetrated the day before in Caldaro. Some landowners from Val di Non had carried out an attack on Henry of Rottemburg, the Count of Tyrol's majordomo. Ugo told how Ottolino di Raina, one of the conspirators, had been taken prisoner and had confirmed, "We were tired of German domination in Caldaro. It would be better if we all spoke Italian." But this reasoning did not ring true because of the small number of conspirators and because they were isolated, and since the governing houses and the Bishop of Trento were in agreement to involve the Bavarians. The truth seemed to be that Ottolino had tried to kill Henry in order to take his place. Svicherio di Malosco was another of the conspirators. He was excommunicated by the Chapter of Trent in 1316 for a crime that he committed in collusion with Morando and Roberto da Vasio. "Unfortunately," said the vicar, "a perilous split is emerging in Val di Non between the Prince Bishop of Trento and the Tyrolean counts, who are trying to occupy the great jurisdiction of Melango, Raina, Dovena, Senale, San Felice, Brez, Traversara, Arsio, Ruffrè, Don, Amblar and the valleys of San Romedio, Tavon, Sporo, Cavedago, Segno, Torra, Andalo and Molveno. If the Tyroleans also manage to seize jurisdiction of the castle of Visione, Meldola and Pallade, they would be in control of all connection routes accessible to vehicles. These *domains* have been of conventional descent under *lex romana*, although not Latin law, up until now; but times are changing and I cannot imagine what barbarism we would be subjected to under landowners who are not of our own tradition."

"Let us not give way to pessimism," Martino intervened. "The Roman tradition is strong even beyond the northern border of the Duchy of Trento. Think of southern Raetia, with the Val Badia, Gardena, Castelrotto, Rittena, Sarentena, Merano and Bolzano."

"You're right, notary Bellini," agreed the vicar, somewhat heartened. "Ludovico il Pio's *capitulary* stipulated that the ministers of those valleys must commit themselves to living according to the *lex romana*."

"... On the other hand," Martino went on, "the confusion that followed the division of the Carolingian empire allowed the Saxons to take possession of many territories. The jurisdiction of Chur seems to have been saved; but I don't speak from personal experience, I've never been there."

That evening at dinner, Martino reported part of the conversation to Meb, Rebecca, and William. After considering a number of options, they decided to move to Folgarìa where life was peaceful because of the sense of citizenship that prevailed there with respect to various family traditions.

SUMMER

When the tutor returned with the rest of the family, Emanuele and Clara were happy to make Meb's acquaintance and insisted on accommodating the Bellini couple in the house that had belonged to Clara's parents, on the main road just before their own, towards the mountain. Meb liked looking out of the window at the kitchen garden and woods that rose up to the mountain ridge. Clara and Rebecca competed to bring fresh produce for the young people every day, and teach Meb lots of recipes for simple, tasty dishes that could be prepared economically for what everyone hoped would become a large and embracing family.

Master William of Oxbridge lodged with the parish priest and was often invited to dinner with Emanuele and Clara, where he would meet up with the the Bellini family too. One evening, Meb asked William why the people in Folgarìa referred to him as "of Oxbridge," and the philosopher explained that it was a figure of speech, meaning he had studied at university over the Channel, in the British Isles, in other words. "Oxford and Cambridge," the bard philosopher concluded, "are united in their function as learning establishments, and merge into a single entity in the collective imagination, so together they are called *Oxbridge*".

Martino helped the Magnificent Community officials to formulate some regulations that would restrict as far as possible any conflict between shepherds travelling through for the transhumance, landowners, farmers, and carpenters who cut down woods in rotation. *Dominus Iohannes Baptista* was a landowner, and one of the most insistent that regulations should be put in place to prevent the woods on the border between the meadows of Folgarìa and La Martinella being cut down before Sant'Anna's day. The naysayers claimed it was not a matter of safeguarding a tradition but allowing them to harvest the grapes from their vines, which were ripe by 26 July - Sant'Anna's day - without all the noise and sawdust involved with tree felling. In any case, *dominus Iohannes Baptista* managed to convince the majority of the peoples' representatives, and the decision to wait until after 26th July to cut down these woods was ratified with a regulation in the presence of Visconti notary Bellini, latinised as *notaius Belenus,* and Father Gabriel of the Church of Saint Peter and Saint Paul, who would impose fines on any transgressors.

A beautiful day followed the calm, cold night of the full moon in May, and the people of Folgarìa were able to celebrate the return of spring by raising a pole called the Albero della Cuccagna - the maypole - and setting up stalls with the products from their gardens. Little girls wove garlands of wild flowers for the occasion, and danced around the maypole holding hands. The wooden pole had been smeared with lard to impede the boys in their competition to climb up and reach the food suspended from a metal ring on top of it. When the festivities were over, Rebecca took her daughter's arm under her own, congratulating her on how radiant she looked, and telling her she had a gift for her. Meb was as excited as she used to be as a child, and followed her mother up to the bedroom where she gave her a soft, luxurious cloak of fur that she'd never seen before.

"Mamma!" she exclaimed, "it's beautiful! Oh, how soft and golden it is! And the hood is immense!" She put it around her shoulders and spun round until she was dizzy, then sat down and asked for an explanation.

"When we were travelling last December," said Rebecca, "the centre axle of our cart cracked, so we stopped at the castle of Ala, and had it fixed by a carpenter, Damiano, in Tezzéli; the sawmill is in the village of San Sebastiano, on the road from Folgarìa to the Veneto. This good man had not been able to go back and see his parents and brothers for many years, so he asked us to take some gifts he'd accumulated for them. We honoured his trust in us, and as soon as we arrived we told Emanuele and Clara about it. Following their sound advice, we managed to deliver the parcels during the feast of the Epiphany on 6th January, and Damiano's family gave us this cloak to express their gratitude. As well as being carpenters, they are excellent hunters of martens, and sell the pelts after tanning them. Furs like this one, stitched by their women, are kept for special occasions such as weddings and births, or given as gifts of gratitude. In our case, fate has combined all these motives, don't you think?"

Meb accept the gift gratefully, caressing the soft mantle of marten fur, and asked how they celebrated the 6th of January in Folgarìa.

"Three men wearing long cloaks and fake crowns carry a Star of Bethlehem made of papier-mache around the village, knocking at doors in search of the baby Jesus," said Rebecca; "they represent the Magi of the Christian tradition: Kaspar, Melchiore and Balthazar. The first time someone receives a visit from them, they're entitled to carve the year and the initials of the Magi on the lintel above their entry door. For example, for this year's Epiphany they would write: MCCC + K + M + B +

XXII. They used to carve the millennium and the century, then the initials and finally the decade and the year. Don't ask me why, that's all I know. Clara says it's a northern way of blessing the house, linking the peaceful meeting with Roman legislation and various traditions from around the world. The initials of the Magi form an acronym: K for Kaspar and also Kyrie, which means "lord" in Greek; M for Melchior and also for Mansionem, which is "house" in Latin, in the accusative case which refers to the object of an action; B for Balthasar and also Benedicat, third person singular, imperative tense, of the Latin verb to bless."

"There seems to be a lot of confusion between the various traditions and the different languages used over time and in different places," Meb observed, perplexed.

"Oh darling!" her mother reassured her with a smile, "as long as you're blessing, any poetic licence is forgivable."

*

Enea and Arianna departed from Castel Beseno with two mules and a covered cart to visit the castellans of Weinegg, who had asked the Castelbarcos for a master from Como.

They were accommodated at the farmhouse of Thurnhof which had a large kitchen that provided warmth at night time; the nights were cold there even though it was summer. Arianna like to watch a squirrel outside the window every morning, busy gathering nuts and berries.

"The chapel where I have to restore the frescoes" Enea told his wife as he was cutting wholemeal bread by the squirrel-window, "was part of a castle that was built a century ago *ab dem Turen*, as an extension to a watchtower."

"I noticed some ruins; there were some shepherds taking stones from the ruins and building dry-stone enclosures with them to put their pregnant ewes in, and to store firewood," said Arianna; she was curious to find out what had happened to the castle and the castellans.

"The lords of the house of Weineck who built what is known as Weinegg Castle were officials of the Bishop of Trento in Bolzano."

"What does that mean?"

"The authority in charge, in this case the Prince Bishop of Trento, assigns a task to a trusted servant, who is given a great deal of executive power but no freedom to make decisions. At the end of his mandate, if the *dominus* or *domina* who conferred the assignment is satisfied with his work, he can free the servant with a *manumissio.*"

"I heard my father talking about it with the stableman Giacomo: what happens with a *manumissio*?"

"A *manumissio* can be executed *vindicta, testamento aut censu.* The servant is granted Roman citizenship as well as his freedom; this means that he is free within the boundaries where the system of government of Rome is in force."

"Free to observe Roman laws," Arianna remarked.

"Exactly. More than this it is not possible to grant," Enea agreed.

"So what happened to the Weinegg castle?" asked his wife, getting back to the original topic.

"Mainardo II of Tirolo and Gorizia fought against the Prince Bishop of Trento in 1292; the castle was destroyed and the defeated Weineck was stripped of his appointment. The chapel remained as it is privately owned by the Weineck family, who built it in 1275. Come on, I'll show you the work I'm doing. Be careful not to trip over the scaffolding."

"I've never seen a crest like that before!" said the young woman in astonishment, looking at the emblem carved on the keystone at the entrance, on the belt course cornice, and painted inside the chapel.

"The Weineck coat of arms has an *unusual emblasonment. It has an indented bordure in gules, an outer, embattled ordinary and field in four sections with a ghibelline in argent on a sable field.*"

"The structure looks very old," Arianna observed, looking at the masonry.

"It is. This was a consecrated place as much as seven hundred years ago. When I accepted the task of restoring the family crests and the cycle of the Stories of Mary, they told me that religious signs have been left here in places consecrated to memory since prehistoric times. Places to avoid spending the night in, where there are powerful and mysterious influences."

"Talking of sleep, this fresco depicts a knight...in bed?"

"It's a knight on his death bed. According to the Christian tradition, his invisible soul represented by the small naked body suspended high above the supine corpse, must face the First Judgment immediately after bodily death."

"The First Judgment is based on individual thoughts, words, deeds and omissions; I remember the catechism. So these characters in the almond suspended in the air above the soul - they're the Celestial Tribunal?"

"Yes. The Creator sits at the centre, with Mary on his left and his son on his right. At the bottom, next to the corpse, you can see the devil accusing the dead man, putting more blame on him than he deserves. The infernal creature is trying to amplify the faults of the accused, to get his soul condemned to hell for eternity, atoning for the passion that dominated his earthly life."

"Mary, though, intercedes with her son, who judges by virtue of his unity with the Father creator."

"Don't forget the role of the archangel Michael: see how he holds the scales and is ready to pierce the devil with the sword of truth?"

"What does that mean?"

"It means that Michael is ready to reveal the falsehood of the accuser, in order to guarantee the authenticity of the weight to the dead man's heart. The heart is depicted on the scales that the archangel is holding in his free hand."

"The scales - I don't remember those being there in the Mamma's lessons."

"They're not always there. According to what I learned in Como, it's a device of the Catalan School that came from ancient Egypt after it came under Alexander the Great's Hellenic domination. The dead man's heart is on one side of the scales, and there's a feather on the other side. If the heart is lighter than the feather, the deceased can ascend into the unity of his humanity, redeemed by the passions that bind it to earthly reality."

"The heart and the feather are not shown here; just the scales and the sword."

"It depends which point of the First Judgment is selected for the painting. In this case, the archangel Michael is about to reveal that the accusations are false, to help Mary *pia advocata*, who advocates compassion in defence of the deceased, to save his soul."

"What's the purpose of it all?"

"It serves to preserve historical memory through the generations, until the time of the Second Judgment, the Universal One."

"I like the fresco on the altar," Arianna said, proceeding with the visit. "Mary is usually nursing Jesus on her left breast in domestic paintings, so he can feel the heartbeat of his mother. Here, though, the infant is sitting on Mary's lap, facing forwards."

"Holding a child on your lap, facing onlookers, means you accepts the child as your own, before God and the world," Enea explained, taking Arianna's hand. They came out of the small building and breathed in deeply, content that they could enjoy the beautiful sunny day together in the clear alpine landscape.

Around noon Amalia called them to lunch; the daughter of the livestock breeder who was putting them up. Amalia, who they called Mali, said her mother was in a hurry to close the kitchen because she wanted to work with the bees during the hottest part of the day. So that afternoon Enea and Arianna put on large hats with fine netting over them and went to the apiary with Mali and her mother, a dozen hives made of woven straw in a line at the bottom of the garden.

"Powerful people are like bees," said Arianna, watching some bees flying around.

"So powerful people must be good for something," commented her husband, lying down for a snooze in the grass.

"It depends," Arianna murmured, chewing a clover stem.

"When the bee lands on a flower," said Enea, leaning on one elbow to admire the regular profile of his wife "it's a good thing".

"But if it stings," the young woman replied, "it dies."

Over the next two weeks, Enea demonstrated his skills to Arianna by carefully restoring the fresco cycle in the chapel. The work was finished on 14th August, and the next day, Ascension Day, the couple from Piedmont joined the people from the farm for the a day's festivities. The merry band took a brisk walk to the top of the highest crag of the northern spur of Mount Pozza, and from that vantage point, known as Virgl, they looked out across the valley with the river Isarco running through it.

They ate bread and cheese and drank water that everyone had brought with them in gourds, and red wine from bottles given to them by herdsmen from Weinegg farm. When they returned they found the cavalier Johan Weineck waiting for them, who had come up from Bolzano to visit the chapel and pay his debts. Satisfied with the work done by the master from Como, Johan paid Enea with a bag of silver coins and two horses that he had raised: a stallion called Ielm and a mare called Puppe.

"*Master Enea*," said Johan in a fatherly tone," I trust that you will take Ielm and Puppe home at a sure, steady pace. If they have foals, I hope you will let me know. *Servus.*"

"*Servus,*" replied Enea, receiving the pair of chestnut horses with broad chests and long white manes.

The next morning Enea got Ielm ready and Mali helped Arianna to saddle Puppe, explaining this was the German word for doll. Arianna thanked her for the translation, but preferred to call the mare Pupa, retaining the sound that the animal was used to. Mounted on their docile horses, the young couple started out on the path that led downstream to the pass, side by side. "We'll go home via Trento and Bergamo," said Enea. "Cavalier Weineck informed me that some of his friends have been accused of heresy and are afraid they'll be sequestered and abused. Someone may take the opportunity of our passing through to entrust items or people to us for safekeeping."

Within the order founded by Francis of Assisi, a heated controversy was taking place on the poverty of Jesus and the disciples. After philosophical positions had been established with serious repercussions outside the Franciscan order, William of Ockham and Bonagrazia of Bergamo had been accused of heresy. Laymen sympathetic to the pauperist cause were accused alongside them, and their loved ones too; it was opportune to flee to Munich in Bavaria. The writings of the pauperists were philosophical and designed to separate imperial authority from papal authority, but it seemed all they achieved was torture, capital punishment and confiscation.

"Won't it be dangerous? We have no interest to defend; we are not partisan," Arianna objected; she was hoping to convince her husband to go via Lake Garda instead.

"As a master of Arts I *can* travel freely between construction sites," Enea explained. "As a faithful Catholic I *must* accept the condemnation of any heretical ideas by the ecclesial authorities. And as a man I *want* to help all human beings, without distinction."

They were welcomed cordially in Trento by the families of masters Adamo di Aragno and Egidio, with his son Giovanni di Campione. Giovanni was working on sculptures for the cathedral with some of his sons and grandsons, while his uncle Enrico and some other students and relatives were finishing the sculptures of Ghirlandina and the pulpit in the cathedral in Modena. Arianna made friends with the sculptors' wives and taught them to ride Pupa, doing exercises in the field behind the large construction site. Before leaving, Enea drew a wheel of fortune on a parchment that could already be seen in practice, in the rose window of the transept facing the piazza.

"Superimposed on the central ring," Enea explained to Arianna, holding up the drawing to the window on the building, to form an impression of the motif in the mind, "the personification of fortune is the central point around which the twelve months of the year revolve. On the outer ring there are twelve men who rise or fall according to what temporary position they are in."

"Who's the man sitting up high?" asked Arianna; she couldn't make out all the details.

"It's a man depicted with a crown on his head as a sign of governing power, and two cups in his hands to use in the exercise of virtue, called temperance. Before this became the episcopal cathedral, it was a cemetery church, so the theme of the provisional nature of human power is relevant; when the wheel turns, the crown will fall and the man who appears to be powerful will be like everyone else again," Enea explained, putting his arm around his wife's shoulders. They walked back slowly, and having made their decision to leave, Enea bought a few bottles of red wine at the *Al Volt* tavern, which he offered at dinner as thanks for the hospitality they'd received.

A month later, having encountered no armed gangs and with the season still favourably warm and dry, Enea and Arianna arrived in Bergamo, where they found Ugo da Campione at work in the Santa Maria Maggiore. This renowned master had been commissioned by the Longhi family of Montichiari degli Alessandrini to build the funeral monument for their poor dear Guglielmo, who was appointed as a cardinal in 1294 by Pope Celestino V and had died in 1319. Ugo had been asked to do the work following his success with the sculptures he'd completed eight years earlier in the Loggia degli Osii in Milan, in the Piazza dei Mercanti. Arianna was very much taken with the Longhi coat of arms, which was carved in high relief on the front of the sarcophagus: a lion rampant, with its tail held high, curving outwards like a tree. Ugo was happy to show her a miniature of the Liturgy of the Hours that he'd used as a model, with its *crest* painted *silver and a lion rampant in black.* Arianna remembered that the lions rampant of the Vallagarina coat of arms also faced left and seemed to be looking backwards, in contrast to the normal direction of reading. She asked why this was, but no one could offer a convincing reason. Before dinner, the masters discussed the iconographic themes to be developed in the basilica, and Arianna was fascinated to hear the description of an inlaid choir, designed as an enclosure around the main altar, the *sancta sanctorum* of the Eucharistic service. The inlays of various types of wood were to depict the initiatory journey required for liberation: from the *baptism of pharaoh* to the *liberation of the monotheistic people from polytheistic dominion.* From *social liberation from the masks of ecclesiastical, political and military powers* united in the symbol of a *dead serpent,* to *individual liberation from fear through ignorance*, represented by *a cage on the head of a virile soul riding* a *donkey, spurred on by twelve flames.*

Arianna recalled the motto of Casa Bellini: NUDO HOMINE VIRTUS CONTENTA EST, and ventured to intervene:

"Masters, how will you show that human beings can be male or female?"

The masters pretended not to hear, so not wishing to embarrass them, she fell silent and went on listening to the conversation. She later realised that her question had been irrelevant, since the choir stalls were for men only.

"Not to confuse the *vir* with the *homo*, what instructions shall we give the master of intarsia?" Ugo asked.

"The person without a mask will be naked and wearing a white cloak around his shoulders, like San Martino," replied the iconographer. "He will be a knight on guard, but will ride a humble donkey, like Our Lord Jesus when He entered Jerusalem. A cage will be hanging above his head, from which the rider's head will be emerging. There will be a helmet and a moretta mask hanging up behind him. In front of him, he will have to step over a cardinal's hat and a blind mask, painted with squinting eyes."

At this point Arianna thought that the masters of the art were going crazy; she asked to be excused, complaining of a slight headache, and left the banquet for the quiet of her room, where she waited patiently for her husband to return. To while away the time, she brushed her hair and unravelled the plait that she wore piled high on the back of her head, trying in vain to straighten out the waves that had formed in it. When Enea came in, he was tired and excited by the ideas that the discussions had thrown up.

"What are the masks you were talking about?" Arianna asked as she helped him undress.

"I asked about it after you left because I didn't know myself," he explained. "The Senate of the Res Publica of Venice issued an edict in 1296, proclaiming that as of that time, the day before Lent would be a holiday."

Lent starts on a Wednesday every year, so that would be a holiday Tuesday, would it? Arianna deduced, a little puzzled.

"Yes. A Tuesday that ends a period, which may start with the Epiphany, 6th January. Or it may start with Advent, in preparation for the mystery of Christmas. Or it may start at the end of October, when all the nameless dead and saints are celebrated."

What do the different possibilities depend on?

"On the *genius loci*, as far as I understand. It's the local communities that decide when the carnival starts."

"But what happens in the carnival that ends on the holiday Tuesday before Ash Wednesday, the beginning of Lent?"

"People can walk around the streets with masks on their faces too; a thing that's prohibited the rest of the year, for obvious security reasons."

"The master of iconography was describing two masks: what do they mean?"

"The one behind the knight wearing the white cloak swelled by the breeze is the moretta: a black mask that can only be held in front of the face by holding a flap sewn inside between your teeth."

"How inconvenient!" exclaimed Arianna, thinking what would happen if she were to go around wearing a mask like that. "So the person wearing it can watch, but can't make any intelligible comment!"

"Exactly," said Enea; "that's the distinctive trait of the moretta. On the other hand, anyone wearing other mask can't see; it has a pair of squinting eyes painted on it."

"So anyone who reads it should understand that a virile person is free from mental cages, muteness and blindness?" the woman reasoned. "And that he can ride, or in other words he's reached the age of maturity to live responsibly in society?"

"We didn't talk about that," replied Enea. "From what I studied in Como, any free man who's reached the age of thirty-three is considered an adult, and any free woman is considered an adult as long as she's married and mother to three children of either sex, born alive."

Arianna smiled a satisfied smile and took advantage of the revelation to embrace her now naked husband, whispering "I'd like to merit a white cloak myself, with your help."

AUTUMN

"For the theatre of the world" Enea began, "the writer of the story is not the main actor."

"... And he can't just be a spectator," Arianna continued.

"So who writes the story?" asked Verde. Balsamina wasn't listening to the conversation, she was too busy hoeing the earth in the *hortus conclusus* at Casa Speroni. But when grandfather Vittorio called the twins, they both ran towards him, wiping their hands on the aprons that were meant to save their clothes from getting dirty, if the girls hadn't got into the habit of sitting on the ground, or worse, on bales of hay for the stable. Ielm and Pupa were now their favourite horses, perhaps because of their broad, comfortable backs, their placid termperaments and the gentle look in their eyes. Margherita known as Verde loved the heavy stallion and Clemenza known as Balsamina considered Pupa her best friend. They each confided their innermost secrets to the horses, and showed no fear when riding in the saddle. The animals sensed the trust that was put in them, and carried them carefully, responding tamely to the voice of Vittorio in the sandy gallop between the walled garden and the moor. The breeder had clearly been attentive to their needs; although they were not as alert as sentinel horses, Ielm and Pupa were proving to be excellent for teaching the youngsters to ride. In the evening Arianna talked about the adventures she'd had on her honeymoon, which in the little girls' minds seemed to have taken place in wonderland.

One clear autumn Tuesday, William came knocking at the door of Casa Speroni. He had revived the bard again and arrived in the company of a lean and sinewy wanderer who said he came from Puglia.

Laura invited the travellers to wash and change their shirts, then asked them what news they had as she served them polenta and cheese with fresh water to drink.

"When I left Folgaria, Martino and Meb told me they were expecting the birth of their first child before they returned."

Laura was happy to hear that Meb was pregnant and deduced that the little family would be wintering with her maternal grandparents.

"Madonna Laura," continued William, "the knight who accompanies me is Robert of Brindisi."

"Good Lord, from Brindisi!" Laura exclaimed; "what induced to embark on such a long journey?"

"Famine, Madonna Laura," answered Robert humbly. "It had not rained for eight months when I set out to travel north."

"Did many people leave?"

"No, most people stayed to wait for better times. I encountered many soldiers on the way, on their way back to Milan to lend their support against Casa Visconti."

Laura poured fresh water into her guests' goblets whilst collecting her thoughts and deciding in which way to direct the conversation. She changed the subject.

"Where were you staying in Puglia, Monsignor Robert?"

"At the summer residence of the Bishop of Brindisi. To the north of the city where the chapel stood to guard the sacred image of Mary left by Saint Francis as an *ex voto* in thanksgiving for his safe return from the Holy Land."

"Is there a village near the chapel?"

"No. In 1300, King Carlo II donated the site to Archbishop Pandone, who decided to build the summer residence there so he could move the episcopal court out of the city, for the hottest period of the year at least. Filippo and Caterina D'Angiò wanted to erect a chapel dedicated to Santa Caterina d'Alessandria in the place, and I was called upon to supervise the building works."

"Who were the clients?" Laura asked.

"The Empress of Constantinople, Catherine II of Valois-Courtenay, and her husband Filippo I D'Angiò, Prince of Taranto. They wanted the building as an *ex voto*, in thanksgiving for the birth of their son Roberto, who came into the world in 1318."

"So you're a knight and a Master of the Art, Monsignor Robert?" asked William, to whom the traveller had introduced himself as Chevalier de Gascogne.

"Just as you are a bard and a philosopher, mon cher William," answered Robert with a smile.

"My lords, allow me to take this opportunity to ask your advice," Laura said, delighted to find herself in the company of such cultured people; "in a few weeks the little girls' parents will be coming to fetch them. We have taught them what we know; but with your assistance I'm sure the reputation of Casa Speroni would benefit enormously."

Before answering, the two guests tried some pears from the kitchen garden with hunks of mature cheese, and Robert offered dried figs stuffed with almonds, that he had brought from Puglia in his bag.

"We call them *pacciafichi* because they're the fruit of the Pica Pica tree," the traveller explained, pleased to see they were well received. "They stay soft even when they're left to dry, and when stuffed with almonds they make a nutritious meal."

William returned to the subject and promised to teach Verde and Balsamina some songs that they could sing without musical accompaniment. Robert asked how old the girls were and pledged to give them a few geometry demonstrations; he would draw some diagrams on the ground in the inner courtyard to help them understand shapes and their spatial relationships. So William and Robert sat among the children at dinner, who were excited to see the bard in the company of a friend.

"The sky has it. The earth has none at all," said Robert in play, posing them a simple riddle after the meal. "Sergio has it in front and Louis at the back. What is it?"

"... Grey? The sky's grey when it's cloudy, and there's no grey in the earth. Sergio can have grey eyes and Louis can have grey hair?" Balsamina guessed.

"Good try," said Robert, "but too fanciful, little lady."

After a few unsuccessful attempts, one of the stableman's sons shouted:

"the letter S!"

"Bravo!" the guest conceded, "What's your name?"

"Elio, sir. What's yours?"

"Robert."

"Robert, will you tell us a story?" Elio, Verde and Balsamina asked straight away in chorus.

"Certainly, Do you know the story of the Tetendoigt family?"

"Tetenduà?" Balsamina repeated; she'd never heard of such a name.

"Testa-sul-dito - 'head-on-a-finger' in the language they speak over the Alps, in Paris," William explained.

"We've never heard the story," Verde interrupted, to clarify the situation, "but tell us in Italian. Don't be like Meb, who talks to us in Greek and other peculiar languages."

Everyone laughed, thinking about their distant friends for a moment with a hint of nostalgia.

"There was once a house," Robert began, raising a clenched fist, "where there lived a father," he continued, raising his thumb, "a mother," he said, raising his forefinger.

"A grandfather," raising his middle finger.

"And a grandmother," raising his ring finger.

"The house was bordered by a forest, where the father went every day to hunt for wild animals to feed himself and the rest of the family," said Robert, bending his thumb down.

"The grandfather and the grandmother went out too," the narrator continued, folding his middle and ring fingers down, "they went to the vegetable garden or to the market, to sell vegetables and buy fruit."

With just his index finger raised, Robert picked up a goblet of water with his other hand and drank. Elio became impatient and asked where the son was. Robert put down the goblet and went on: "The mother stayed at home, cleaning, tidying up and getting dinner ready. Father returned after the hunt." He raised his thumb again.

"The grandfather and grandmother returned from the vegetable garden and the market," he continued, opening out his middle and ring fingers.

"The son is inside the mother, and when he's born," he exclaimed, raising his little finger too, "he'll be the smallest!"

Robert and William taught the children some geometric rules over the days that followed, as they had promised, using ropes knotted at regular intervals. Elio, Verde and Balsamina enjoyed learning how to mark a circle or a square on the ground, pretending they had to make an enclosure, which was an exercise they could do in the open air. In the afternoon Elio helped his father or went out riding with Vittorio, and the two scholars went for long walks, discussing philosophical topics.

"Master William," Robert asked, on one of their peripatetic discussions, "did you ever study the work of Aelredus Rievallensis?"

"The Cistercian Abbot of Rievaulx?"

"Yes, the son of a married presbyter who spent many years at the court of the King David I of Scotland," Robert confirmed. "Aelredus travelled around Scotland, England, the Ile de France, Burgundy and Provence."

"His principal mission was to convert the Picts, if I remember correctly," William mused.

"Not just that," Robert continued. "It's true that he converted Kirkcudbright, the head of the Picts of Galloway. But Aelredus is still a milestone through the writings he left us."

"At *Oxbridge* they're not considered specially important."

"The Catholic Church has canonised him and his name is remembered in religious services on 12th January," Robert continued, not allowing the conversation to stray away from the subject.

"Now I remember! In the first year of my studies," William suddenly exclaimed, "I studied the history of the first king of England, Edward the Confessor. Edward fought against Godwin, the Earl of Wessex, against the men of Lady Godiva and her husband Leofric, Earl of Mercia, and in the North against Siward, Earl of Northumbria."

"... And all this despite the fact that Edward had married Edith, Godwin's daughter," Robert went on. "The Saxon revolts against the Normans constrained Queen Edith to lock herself up in the convent of Wherwell and Edward to disarm the fourteen ships in the British fleet. He was thus able to lower taxes and regain the favour of the Anglo-Saxon people."

"Right!" William remembered something else: "Edward abolished the Danegeld - the tax for maintaining the army."

"He was able to do that by dint of his firm friendship with William, Duke of Normandy," Robert said, "and because the Vikings had desisted from attacking the English coast, engaged as they were in wars against the Danes and the Norwegians."

"Edward appointed William as his heir, but once the king died, his son-in-law Harold had himself crowned, ushering in a period of violence that culminated in the battle of Hastings on 14th October in the Year of the Lord 1066." William took up the story by summarising the history of the English monarchy: "After the victory, William had no other rivals and was able to subjugate the various Anglo-Saxon lords. On 25th December that year, the victor was crowned King of England under the name William I."

"Aelredus had up to six hundred monks under him, and wrote spiritual works as well as the history books you studied at University," Robert said solemnly, revealing a profound respect for Aelredus.

"Which work do you consider memorable, Robert?" William asked, amazed that an Angevin would honour an Anglo-Saxon author.

"In his *spechulum charitatis* he interprets the teachings of Bernardo di Clairvaux in a most personal and profound way," Robert explained. "In his *De spirituali amicitia* he tackles the theme of Greek love without false modesty, admitting that he himself was attracted to his fellow brothers as a novice. And *De Jesu puero duodenni* is also a highly original reflection on the three days Jesus spent with his teachers when he reached the age of majority - twelve."

"You really think that the *De spirituali amicitia* is anything other than a lament for death for a brother?!" William gasped.

"That's what my teachers taught," answered Robert, who was put on the defensive by the serious yet slightly ironic tone of his interlocutor.

"What is friendship?" asked William rhetorically, and went on, determined to take advantage of the obvious perplexity he'd provoked in the Cavalier de Gascogne: "Is friendship just a material manifestation or is it a spiritual gift? Is it only important when you're alive, or does it go beyond the boundary of bodily life?"

"I don't know, William," Robert conceded, ingratiatingly. "I studied the text as an example of respectfully-conducted Greek love."

"A superficial interpretation, in my opinion; remember we're talking about a Catholic saint," said William, and went on to explain how sentiments experienced remain inaccessible to the curiosity of posterity as they are restricted to the experience of the couple involved in the relationship.

"You're right," Robert agreed, wary of his interlocutor's peremptory tone. "In *De spirituali amicizia,* Aelredus reminds us how clandestine affairs among juvenile brothers had matured over the years into spiritual friendship, thus allowing them the saving action of Grace. Faith always opens up the sublime panorama that hope of eternal life has to offer!"

William was satisfied with Robert's ability to rise above it and changed the subject, inviting his friend back for dinner. The next morning Robert ate a hearty breakfast and departed, saying he wanted to get to Savoy before winter. Aldo said farewell to the traveller and closed the door behind him, then put his hand on his brother Elio's shoulder, pleased he'd had the opportunity to meet such a pleasant *fellow* and even more pleased to be able to return to looking after the horses now the dazzling distraction had gone beyond the Alps.

Enrico and Susanna Bellini returned to Casa Speroni in October too, and were happy to see how Verde and Balsamina had grown. Enrico wanted to stay for a week to select two mares and check how Pegaso's first foal was coming along. Susanna gave Laura two bottles of oil from her paternal grandparents' olive groves, and told her about the summer they'd spent in Liguria. Sadly, she also had to tell her friend that there had been a murder on the night between 10th and 11th August. Gabriella, a daughter of the House of Bisi di Angera had been killed whilst staying at a farm belonging to some acquaintances in San Lorenzo, along with other guests from Upper Piedmont. The woman had been recently widowed; she was still grieving and displaying some odd behaviour, frequently going off without warning. It was perhaps for this reason that her hosts waited until the afternoon of 11th August before going out to look for her. But it was only after a week searching that her body was discovered, by this time unrecognisable, in the woods above Zoagli, on the way to Chiavari. Her friends recognised the ragged black dress and the gold chain that the murderer had left round her neck, but all attempts to find the perpetrator were in vain, partly because of the taciturn nature of poor Gabriella, who didn't confide in other women. The body of the deceased woman was put in an olive wood coffin to give her a proper burial, and driven in a cart drawn by two black mares to the cemetery at Sesto Calende. Susanna went on, recalling that Enrico rode with the other armed knights, and she herself had travelled in a cart with the other women, their luggage and the bottles of olive oil. It had been a tiring journey hampered by frequent stops at border checkpoints between the different jurisdictions. The sentries trusted no one and had checked the contents of both carts on each occasion; fortunately the soldiers had been satisfied with money and had not requisitioned the olive oil. Laura was sorry for the sad fate of poor Gabriella; she'd known her cousin Gianmaria, who was an excellent riding instructor. To lighten the mood, the excellent hostess invited Susanna to join Giacomo, William and the children on a visit to the charcoal burners.

"I've heard of charcoal burners but I know nothing about them; what do they do?" Susanna asked Laura, as they walked toward the moor on the edge of the wood that had been cut down.

"Wood cutting is done in rotation, to allow the woods to get re-established," Laura explained. "The best of the cut logs are taken to the carpenters at the sawmill. Then the charcoal burners come along. They clear up the undergrowth and take the logs that are not suitable for seasoning to the moorland near the forest. They dig holes about seven feet deep in places that are sheltered from the prevailing winds, and fill them with twigs, staking them up around the walls to leave a deep hole in the middle. The stack has to protrude beyond the top of the hole to a height of about fourteen feet above the ground. Then the charcoal burners cover this fragile chimney with clods of turf."

"I'm curious to see this peculiar green dome!" exclaimed Susanna, trying to imagine what such a piece of work would look like, standing on the moor among the pheasants and partridges and hares hopping around.

"A hole has to be left in the top because, like I said, the grass-covered dome is just a chimney," continued the woman from Casa Speroni. "The charcoal burners set fire to the stack but the flames don't flare up, because there's not much air beneath the dome of earth and grass. The wood burns slowly inside it, and instead of turning to ash, it becomes charcoal."

"Now I think about it," Susanna recalled, "there were charcoal burners in the Ligurian Apennines too; they sold the charcoal to copper and iron prospectors working on the banks of the rivers."

"Metal prospectors are usually Lombards," remarked Laura; "lots of people prospect for copper, iron, gold, silver, lead, tin, sulphur, magnesium and rocks in the Ticino. It's tiring work but it's fascinating; those who do it talk of nothing else."

"Do the prospectors come to the breeding farm?"

"Yes. Usually, though, they take their mules or donkeys to the livestock market; when they change jobs they prefer to travel on horseback, to make a good impression. They come to us to buy old workhorses, and choose the most docile geldings. Prospectors are thespians; they exaggerate their misadventures like fishermen talking about pikes as big as whales and saying nothing about the carp they take to the fishmonger!"

It was time for refreshments. The company sat down to eat bread and cheese in a clearing, and William entertained his friends with a story he'd heard from some charcoal burners he once met further north.

"They say that Lombard Carlìn Scirisin," continued the traveller after eating and drinking, "was the first to look for specks of gold on the Piedmont side of Ticino, on the stretch of land between Casòn ad Muntlàm up to Raspagna."

"Oh!" Elio exclaimed, wide-eyed. "How big is a speck of gold?"

"Most of the time they're tiny specks but you sometimes find a round nugget, as thick as your little finger."

"How did Carlìn get the gold out of the river?" asked Balsamina, who was always interested to learn useful techniques.

"With the help of his sons and his son-in-law, Carlin carried sand from the river to the quarry, where he set up a water system called a *filarola* that allows it to drip through slowly and filter the different materials out of the sand."

"But how did they move the sand?" Balsamina insisted. She knew how laborious it was to move sand and rocks from the riverbank to the meadow.

"They used stretchers carried by two men, as if the sand were a wounded soldier being taken home after a battle."

"I like to think of prospectors as pious people," observed Susanna, "patiently selecting and recycling whatever the river gives them."

"Prospectors can fish too, whilst they're working," Laura added. They drop stones on the big rocks to drive out the fish hiding under them, then catch them with their bare hands."

"At the end of the working day," William agreed, "prospectors end up with fish, stones of various sizes and metals that are separated in turn with a sieve called a *trula*."

"Thank you, William," said Susanna, bringing the story-telling to an end; she was hoping to get back in time to bathe with her twins. "Who told you all this?"

"Cristiano Bolimperti, a descendant of Carlìn from the female line and an expert prospector in the Ticino territory between the bridge of Sesto Calende and the bridge of Oleggio."

After they'd eaten, the cheerful company set off again across the silent moorland, singing *The fox king and the bride*:

The Fox King went to war
The Fox King goes underground!

The Fox King draws his sword.
But when he's halfway there
he gets injured and returns
and has to go and see the pallbearer.

Tap, tap tap! He knocks at the door.

"Knock gently, my dear son."
Says his mother, telling him short:
"Your lady's growing a rare gift!"
"Open up, mother, I'm dying!"
"Be patient, son; she's getting dressed!"

"Oh my lady! Who's that singing?"
My daughter-in-law is a mother and the soldiers boast of it!"
"Oh my lady! What should I wear?"
"Wear red or wear black; but you must rejoice!"
"Oh my lady! Tell me why, if I am king,
your mouth tastes of roses and mine just of earth!"

And in the golden sunset, the refrain echoed at length:

"Oh my lady, can you tell me why, if I am king
your mouth tastes of roses and mine just of earth?!"

Susanna had to wait until the next day before she could prepare the bathtub to wash the children with soap made from soapwort leaves and rosemary, when Laura could attend to her needs and do the laundry at the same time. In the middle of the morning they poured boiling water in the bathtub and added cold water to cool it down, then Laura helped Susanna into the tub and handed Verde and Balsamina in with her. When they were all in the tub, Susanna soaped her daughters, reciting a nursery rhyme to amuse them:

Early, early in the morning
as soon as the sun is awake
like little goslings in the bath

Not in the water from the pond!
Fresh water from the spring
on your mouth and on your forehead
and a few drops here on your heart
and your tummy all covered in water,
like the stem of a lovely flower!

Into the pond go the little goslings
first they wash the their feet.
Then their faces, then their wings.
They all go "qua qua qua"
oh what fun they have!
And they teach us little girls
all mucky and moody
that we should never be afraid
of fresh clean water!

Mother and daughters then helped to hang out the linen that Laura and the stableman's wife had just washed. It was raining outside, so they opened the drying room in the barn, where the girls played among the bales of hay and immediately got their clothes dusty again. They were all feeling chilly by the time the work was done, so they went back to the kitchen to chat as they cooked, allowing Margherita to sit with the cat, Bastet, in front of the fireplace. Clemenza helped with the food preparation, trying to memorise what Laura was doing. Dinner that evening was a joyful, festive occasion, although overshadowed with sadness for their imminent departure. Verde sat under the table to eat, as usual.

Before kissing her parents goodnight, she steered the conversation to her own way of thinking with a rendition in her clear, sweet voice:

So the first cat
is a kitchen cat
in a tiny little voice
he start to mew

and miao miao miao
and miao miao miao
and miao miao FFF!

Susanna was delighted with the performance and her daughter advantage of her good humour to ask if she could take the cat back to Oleggio.

"Laura says I can take her with me if you don't mind," she told her mother in a soft, wheedling tone. "Please, Mamma! I promise I'll help more if Bastet is in the kitchen with me."

"How do you propose to keep her still for the journey?"

"Laura told me to put her in one of the cages she uses to take rabbits to the market," she answered without hesitation.

"... We've agreed that she'll come over and collect the cage next week, on market day," the child went on, not giving her mother chance to reply. "Then we can give her something nice to say thank you."

"You and Laura have thought of everything to make me to say yes, haven't you, darling?" said Susanna, giving her an affectionate hug. Clemenza pretended not to hear, she just cuddled her favourite pup quietly.

"Yes, Mamma. Thank you," she agreed candidly, which put an end to the discussion and settled that the big house would have its first kitchen cat, who became mother to some solitary males and many sociable housecats. The following morning the Bellinis returned to Oleggio and William set off on foot for Oxford. The bard philosopher started out hoping he wouldn't encounter the armed gang of Hugh De Spencer the younger, who had apparently curtailed his nautical pirating activities in the English Channel and managed to ingratiate himself into the favour of Edward II of England.

*

In late autumn the water froze in the ditches and a white frost released the travellers from the sight of mud caused by autumn rains, putting Martino in mind of the welcoming warmth of the farmhouse kitchen to which they were headed. The Visconti notary gave Bonaparte a drink, then unsaddled him and tied him up well into the stall so that he could eat the fodder in the manger. He went through the door from the stable into the kitchen and washed his hands and face in a basin beside the fireplace. Meb heard him moving about and came downstairs with little Giovan Battista in her arms arms, whom they called Giobatta. They exchanged a silent kiss, and whilst she sat sown to nurse the babay, the young father stirred the embers to make the flames burn higher in the fireplace and make the well-seasoned log crackle. The table was set, and two candles shone their light on the embroidered napkin laid over Saturday's bread, shaped in a plait. Martino thought it was a good thing to let the candles burn down to the bottom, *a gyertyàk csonkig égnek*, as grandmother Susanna would say in Hungarian. He sighed and Meb realised her husband was about to bring up a subject she was afraid she wouldn't like. When the baby had finished suckling and she'd burped him, she lay him on his side in the cradle, singing to him gently until he fell asleep. She calmly ladled bean and spelt soup into bowls from an earthenware pot that was keeping warm on a soapstone platter that Rebecca had given her. "When we get back to Oleggio, I must remember to take this stone with us; it's perfect for slow-cooked stews and soups," she said, to distract him.

"A stone for cooking?"

"Yes," she said, contentedly. "Emanuele buys them at the fair in Trento. The soapstone is extracted from a deep mine in Chiavenna; it's special because it's highly resistant to fire and keeps the temperature constant for a long time. Craftsmen work it with iron chisels and river water to make tiles out of it, like this one."

After the soup they had baked apples with honey, and when Meb had finished washing the dishes her husband finally told her what was on his mind.

"You nursed Giobatta like you wanted to when you were pregnant. Now we have to find a nurse and her child who can come and live with us." Martino blurted it all out in a single breath; he was afraid the young mother's reaction would be negative. She didn't answer; she just poured out a goblet of herbal liqueur for each of them and held her own up to propose a toast. He complied grudgingly and said he would talk to Rebecca and Clara the next day. Meb took the goblets to the sink, where she

317

lingered, holding back her tears. She could find no words to express the pain she felt at the thought of another woman nursing Giovan Battista. Taking a deep breath, she wiped her eyes on her apron to hide her distress.

"You decide," she said quickly. "I'll take Giobatta up, I'm too tired to argue."

Martino got up and hugged her, stroking her sides.

"We don't need to talk," he whispered in her ear; "Giobatta is sleeping soundly; the night has just begun and I love you so much."

That night Martino alleviated his anxieties and Meb waited patiently until it was time for Giobatta's dawn feed, when she would hold him closer than usual. They got up with the sun already high over the mountains, and as agreed, went to lunch with Clara for the first time since since she had given birth. Clara had prepared some savory pies and two jam tarts with Susanna's help. Meb went in carrying her son under the marten fur cloak but it was a struggle for her to put him in the arms of his grandmother; she was so jealous. Martino said without preamble that Giovan Battista needed a nurse and a milk brother, and that the two of them should be free of any family ties and come to live with them in Oleggio in the spring.

He then left the women and followed his father-in-law into Otto's room and got involved in a social game that Emanuele was fond of playing.

"... The cube advises us to set a stable point for each goal in life that we achieve," they heard their host saying as they entered his study. Aligerno had managed to teach Otto the Latin alphabet and Emanuele could finally open the beautiful pear wood box inlaid with squares and circles of different types of wood that he'd bought his son to play with, and which he now placed on the table by the window.

"I want to give you this game as a reward for learning the Latin alphabet; it's becoming popular all over Europe," said Emanuele with satisfaction. "Open the box, son!"

The boy lifted the lid: inside were three cubes and many handwritten parchments. He picked up the little cubes and saw that a different number of dots was carved on each side, up to six. "These cubes are called *lupercoli* because to play the game you have to make them jump like a hare - a lepro," explained his father. "The side of the cubes are called the *tessera* and each throw takes its name from number of dots engraved on it: *ace*, *deuce*, *trey*, *cater*, *cinque*, *sice*."

"I think I understand, Papa," said Otto, "but do I have to add the numbers together that come up on each side, or do I have to read them separately?"

"Bravo, that's a good question," beamed Emanuele, smiling complicity and explaining that you had to read each side in the order dictated by the Latin alphabet.

Aligerno and Martino kept quiet; they did not approve of these games of chance that had been in vogue among the military since ancient Roman times, and could not believe that a good man like their host would teach his son to play with dice.

"The soldiers in the Roman imperial army often played games of chance using dice similar to these," explained the Folgarian. "The most famous game was played three hundred years after the founding of Rome, when there was a law in force that forbade anyone, including the Roman army, to cross the boundary line of the Eternal City territory - the *limes* - bearing arms. The boundary

319

followed the course of the river Rubicone, in the area where it crosses the Via Consolare Emilia. On the evening of 10th January of DCCV Ab Urbe Condita, in the 705th year after the founding of Rome, historians revealed that the Roman general Julius Caesar was camped in Gallia Cisalpina, undecided as to whether he should cross the *limes* with weapons and start a civil war. With the intellect typical of the military, he left the decision to a throw of the dice; it was a *sice*. The river along which the army passed after crossing the boundary was renamed in memory of the event, and became known as the Val di Senio."

"If he marched against Rome, Julius Caesar was a traitor!" exclaimed Otto, scandalised.

"Cicero wrote that Giulio excelled in everything, except in the ability to find a good cause," commented Emanuele, "but after he'd won, Giulio claimed that he'd taken action because Rome was corrupt and he himself was incorruptible."

Aligerno and Martino said nothing, curious to see how this domestic exchange would evolve.

"Papa, Julius Caesar only needed to throw one die, but there are three here, and lots of manuscript sheets. What game is this?"

"Well spotted!" exclaimed Emanuele. He explained: "This game is not intended for you to try your luck; we don't consider there to be any point in that, and we avoid pointless actions at least as much as we avoid wasting time, energy and money."

Aligerno and Martino exchanged a knowing look and the tutor confirmed, "remember, Otto - a gentleman does not play at dice. It's not luck that acts on our behalf, it's grace."

The boy didn't answer, he just gave an imperceptible nod of the head and lowered his eyes as if to scrutinise the manuscripts. Martino saved him from embarrassment by saying: "Yes, Master Aligerno. I remember how hard it was, working out that baffling mystery."

"On my last trip to Zurich" said Emanuele, launching in to a tale, "I met some noble knights engaged in the annual tournament."

Otto listened in fascination, hanging on his father's words.

"They were representatives of the great northern houses," he continued, savouring the words and clearly admiring them. "The shields bore the lion rampant of Bohemia with its uptight tail in the form of a double spiral pointing towards the sky, and the eagle facing upwards and to the left. The House of Silesia was taking part with its eagle holding a white veil and horse blankets embroidered with the Gothic alphabet. When the Silesian champion won, the daughter of the richest merchant in Zurich presented him with a small coronet of roses, from which she had personally removed the thorns."

"What a charming thought," commented Martino drily.

"Girls from good families are educated too," Aligerno explained, addressing Otto and paying no attention to Martino. "Young men learn a profession and the ethics of chivalry, while young ladies prepare to become brides. Both men and women of the new patrician generation must learn the virtue of the *pietas*, to demonstrate their ability to be compassionate, towards themselves and towards their neighbours, when they are adults."

"Who else was there, Papa?" asked Otto, curious to learn about the customs of chivalry. "What were the shields and vestments like? What did the knights do?"

"As well as the knights engaging in the armed jousting tournament, fighting at first blood with spear and shield..." resumed Emanuele, and was immediately interrupted by his son, who asked what *at first blood* meant.

"It means that the first one to be injured is declared the loser, and his opponent the victor," replied his father. He went on: "There were also knight poets from the Houses of Neifen, Veldeke, Hohenburg, Botenlauben and Kirchberg."

"... Knight poets?" said the boy, puzzled.

"Yes. Mostly composers of minnesang: poems dedicated to courtly love, which I don't much care for," said Emanuele. "Iohan Heinrich was also there, grandson of the Marquis Ottone Ascanide of Brandenburg, God rest his soul."

"And what was this grandson doing, Papa?"

"I saw him playing with his orderly at a small table inlaid with a light and dark chequered pattern. Two sets of carved wooden figures formed two opposing teams: one light and one dark. Iohan told me he'd learned this game from the old marquis who had also left him some sheets similar to these in his will." So saying, he took the manuscripts out of the box and began to read them, under the watchful eye of those present. On one sheet there was a young man asking questions of a master, and other manuscripts reproduced the numerical tessere with the various possibilities for results and hints on how to proceed in the game; each of the remaining sheets bore a diagram with finely-drawn cartouches around it containing explanations. "The game of destinies," said Emanuele "allows us to interpret the apparent mystery of our destiny. I'll be the master, with your permission Aligerno."

"*Licet*" the tutor agreed, amused.

"Good, who wants to play with me?"

"Me!" said Aligerno, to the enormous relief of Otto and Martino, who were curious but had no inclination for puzzles.

"To work in idleness is laborious rest for us," Emanuele pronounced, auspiciously. "Aligerno, throw the dice."

The tutor obeyed.

"*Cater, cater, sice*," announced Emanuele, who had separated the sheets into different piles, and was holding in front of him a manuscript showing a wheel of fortune, from which hung a number of cartouches with instructions.

"Read the cartouches and decide if you'd rather answer questions on marriage, children, business or justice, happiness or life."

Aligern cast his eyes over them first, then chose one and read it out loud: "If you have a loss to recover, go to King Desiderio."

Emanuele looked through one of the piles of parchments and selected a sheet with a bust of a bearded man, armed with a long-bladed sword like the Lombards used. "King Desiderio seeks under the Sign of the Virgin," read master of the game Emanuele, and immediately carried out the instruction, looking through another pile. The maiden with the unicorn was in the middle of the table, with the various possible throws around it. The instruction to go to the Sphere of Jupiter on the banks of the river Caina corresponded to the sequence *cater-*

cater-sice. From the same pile of possible sequences, Emanuele drew out a sheet sheet with an old man in the centre, his mouth closed and his head covered; in his left hand was an oval shield depicting a face with a gaping mouth, and in his right an arrow pointing to the ground. He searched in the spokes pointing at the figure an read out loud: "Caina goes to the prophet Simeon, in verse XXVIII".

He looked through the other pile and read, "He who sins through malice deserves no grace: forget it and think about being just."

Aligerno clapped his hands, pleased with the advice, and complimented Emanuele for choosing such a clever social game. Next it was Martino's turn, and finally Otto.

While the men were amusing themselves thus, Clara and Rebecca left the new mother with her baby and went to talk to Elsa, the laundress.

On the following Wednesday at around noon, Meb was hoeing the soil in the kitchen garden behind the house. Giobatta was sleeping in his cradle nearby, wrapped in the marten cloak. Rebecca approached her, followed by a young girl who was holding a child in her arms; the child had snow-white hair and cheeks as rosy as wild apples.

"But he's naked!" Meb exclaimed, taking off her shawl to cover the baby. "Mamma, have you gone crazy?" she asked without waiting for an answer. Taking the child, she wrapped him in the shawl, saying in a soft voice "little darling, who would bring you out in the cold and frost like that!"

Rebecca held the girl back and introduced the brother and sister to her daughter as Angiolo and Marta, orphans with no grandparents or other relatives within reach. Their father had died in an avalanche towards the end of winter, and their mother had died of starvation a week ago.

"God willing, you have milk for your son," Rebecca went on. "Marta is used to caring for Angiolo, who is six months older than Giobatta and could become a brother to him, although not a milk brother."

Meb looked at the girl more closely. Reassured by the words of the wise grandmother, she lowered her defences and gave the girl a smile.

"I'm pleased to meet you, Marta. Could you finish the hoeing here, where I've pulled the weeds up around the cabbages?"

"Yes," Marta agreed willingly, setting to work diligently.

Martino was tired when he returned; he lingered in the stable longer than usual taking care of Bonaparte, to relax. When he entered the kitchen he found Rebecca chopping meat up and hoped it would be goulash at dinner. Then he noticed Meb was nursing, and beside her sat a girl, holding a baby on her lap that could already sit up and support his own head. He looked more closely; this couldn't be the nurse, she was still a child. His wife greeted him spiritedly, and he asked her if there was any news.

"This girl is called Marta and the baby is her brother, Angiolo," Meb explained. "Their father died in an avalanche in the Alps at the end of the winter; their mother managed to wean the baby but died of starvation last week, poor dear. They're alone and they have nothing. Their parents came from distant Nordic lands where they speak in languages that Marta remembers only vaguely."

Martino greeted Marta but asked no questions. He was beginning to understand what the women wanted, but pretended he knew nothing of it and just asked Rebecca what she was cooking for dinner.

"Goulash," replied his mother-in-law, which told him the women had already made their decision and his mother-in-law was preparing his favourite dish to obtain his consent without further discussion.

"Marta's been helping me a lot in the garden today," said Meb. "She's changed Giobatta's nappy too; then she wanted to wash him, like she does Angiolo."

Excellent arguments in her favour, thought Martino as he drank a goblet of the hop beer that Emanuele had given him.

"Elsa, the washerwoman, was a friend of Marta's mother," Rebecca added, considering this to be an important reference.

"Marta," said the notary Visconti, taking a direct approach, "are you willing to take Angiolo away with us, when we return to Oleggio?"

"Yessir," replied the girl, without hesitation.

"Is there anyone else who can take care of you, apart from me?" he persisted, looking her in the eye.

"No sir," said Marta, meeting his gaze and showing no diffidence.

"Well then, Meb," Martino went on, and turning calmly to his wife, asked, "where will Marta and Angiolo sleep?"

"There. See what Clara and Otto brought us this afternoon!"

"I see," the man noted, going towards the dimly-lit space under the stairs, where he found a bed and a baby's crib. He wasn't sure he should rejoice in the situation; this was not the normal custom of entrusting a new baby into the care of a nurse to feed and wean it, relieving the parents of the task. His intention was to revive the intimacy he shared with his wife, and he didn't know how to make her understand this without going into too many details. He sighed, then an idea came to him and he asked how old Angiolo was.

"Seven months," replied Marta.

"When was he weaned?" he continued, under the inquiring gaze of his wife and mother-in-law.

"Mamma was sad when Papa died so suddenly," the girl recalled. "In September her milk failed; Angiolo was five months old and we started soaking a piece of cloth in goat's milk for him to suck." She went on, her voice breaking at the memory: "Then mamma got thinner and wearier, until last Friday, when she died. I'm weaning my little brother now, giving him new things to try every week; I chew it up for him first because he doesn't have any teeth yet."

"Very good," the young father commented as he washed his hands and dried them. Whilst they were eating their hearty meal, Rebecca told anecdotes about local customs.

"Here in the mountains they use wood to solve all their problems. They even stuff pillows with pine wood shavings instead of goose feathers or sheep's wool!" she said, amused at the idea that they would rather have the scent of wood than the softness of traditional types of padding. After dinner, Martino walked back with Rebecca to Aligerno, describing the mill he'd visited for work the day before. Afterwards he stopped at Giorgio's inn for a beer, and asked where he could buy a pregnant goat. At the end of the evening he went upstairs without disturbing Angiolo and Marta, who were both sleeping the sleep of the innocent, as they say. The stairs creaked but Giovan Battista too slept on, in his crib beside their double bed, so Martino undressed quickly and joined his wide under the covers. Meb caressed him, welcoming him into her strong, warm arms that smelled so good. There was no need for talking; they fell into the harmony that people in love know so well, and afterwards exchanged some languid kisses and lay back to back, protecting each other. Martino was tired, but satisfied with his day's work. Before he fell asleep, he thought about the document he'd endorsed confirming ownership of a mill to the miller's wife after he died. In drawing up the widow's own will, he'd advised her ihis experiece as a notary to speak to the apothecary about it; a highly-respected man in the village. The representatives of the Magnificent Community had also instructed her to do this, hoping the intervention of the man they regarded so highly would persuade the old woman to nominate Silvio Pistori as her heir, the man who had been the old miller's trusted helper and could still grind barley and rye.

"Are you thinking about the news?" Meb murmured, half asleep.

"No, my love. I was thinking of the vague dreams that you have in your youth, and the more concrete expectations that adulthood brings."

THE END

EPILOGUE

Seven years later, Marta married the great-grandson of Nella the farmer in Oleggio, and lived a long life in the biggest farmhouse in Mezzomerico, surrounded by her eight daughters and a score of grandchildren. Her brother Angiolo became Verde's cook when her husband Carlo Cattaneo took her to the island of Camogli, from where Margherita wrote many pleas to Genoan galley ship owners, and the renowned and universally-acknowledged warning: "*En voler guerra comenzar guàrdense de trabucar e ponnan mente a li Pissan chi, cubitando esser sovram e sobranzar li Genoeixi, son quasi tutti morti e preis; e vegnui soto lor pè per gran zuixo de De*". As an adult, Angiolo was taken as steward on board a galley ship owned by Samuele Spinola, and after disembarking on the island of Malta, he married the enchanting Isabella and started a happy dynasty of fishermen and cooks on the nearby island of Gozo.

Many the values that inspired the lives of the characters in this story continue to illuminate the thoughts, words, omissions and deeds of those who love.

Printed in March 2018
by Youcanprint *Self-Publishing*

www.ingramcontent.com/pod-product-compliance
Lightning Source LLC
Chambersburg PA
CBHW050922030726
47503CB00007BB/2419